AMANDA RADLEY

SIGN UP TO WIN

Firstly, thank you for purchasing *Lost at Sea* I really appreciate your support and hope you enjoy the book!

Head over to my website and sign up to my mailing list to be kept up to date with all my latest releases, promotions, and giveaways.

www.amandaradley.com

LOST AT SEA

RUNNING FROM DIEGO

Annie Peck hurried as much as possible without looking as if she was running for her life.

Which she was.

Her eyes darted around the wide and empty backstreets of Barcelona, searching for anyone who looked out of place. In particular, she was looking for anyone who might have followed her.

She knew she had to do her best to look casual and relaxed, to appear like a tourist strolling about the city, even if her heart was threatening to beat out of her chest and her breath came in short, sharp pants.

Getting out of the city was her number-one priority, even if she currently had no idea how she would manage that seemingly impossible feat. She imagined that Diego's people were spread across Barcelona looking for her.

The grotty hotel she'd been staying in had accepting cash and asked no questions, but remaining there for much longer would just make her escape all the more difficult.

People talked, and she knew word of an English woman who never left the hotel would soon filter through to the ears of someone in the Ortega clan. And soon after that, she'd be dead.

A shiver run up her spine, and she tried to convince herself it was the chilly breeze in the morning air.

She stopped walking and sucked in a deep breath, marvelling at how shaky it sounded. She turned to look around, just in case.

An elderly woman was crossing the road in the distance, a mother was walking with her toddler, and a man walked his dog. Everything seemed normal and safe, but Annie knew from bitter experience that could all vanish in a second if Diego's men found her.

She needed a plan. Her cash supply was running dangerously low, and she couldn't trust anyone.

Her life had completely turned around in the space of just forty-eight hours. Being in the wrong place at the wrong time had ended her carefree lifestyle and would probably lead to her death.

She'd turned thirty-one a few days earlier, and now she doubted she'd see the end of the week.

"Excuse me, do you speak English?"

The young woman had appeared from nowhere and caused Annie to jump.

"Oh, I'm sorry, I didn't mean to scare you! I just need directions," the woman said, apologetically.

Annie took a couple of deep breaths and looked at the young backpacker in front of her. She seemed legitimate enough.

"Where are you heading?" Annie asked.

"Oh, you're English," the girl sounded surprised, no doubt assuming that Annie's olive-skinned appearance meant she was from the region.

She would surely be shocked to learn that Annie was from North Yorkshire and, after five whole years living in Spain, had only learnt how to order a beer. And to say *I love you*.

She shuddered at the thought of all the times she'd said those words, to a man like Diego. Especially when she'd known that it hadn't been love.

"I'm looking for this art gallery." The girl pointed to a spot on the paper map she clutched, a map she obviously couldn't read if she was asking for directions.

Annie gestured behind her. "Down there, turn left when you get to the main street. Walk for about ten minutes, and you'll start seeing signs. It's on the right."

"Thanks, you're a life-saver."

Annie quickly continued walking, knowing that the girl was about to attempt to strike up a conversation. It's what young travellers often did: find people from their own country and chat about tourist tips.

It's what Annie had done. It's what led to Annie staying in Spain when she should have just gone home. Not that she felt she had a home any longer. She felt nomadic and lost, feelings that she knew had always been there but had been lurking behind a seemingly perfect life in Spain.

It was only when everything had gone wrong two short days ago that she had been forced to face up to things and realise that her life was a façade. She'd lived in a semi-daze for five years, not having the courage or the strength to acknowledge what had happened.

A couple of stray tears fell down her cheeks, and she hastily brushed them away. She didn't have time to think about her parents now.

She tried to tell herself that, in some ways, what had happened was a good thing. At least now they were safe from Diego.

She'd been twenty-six back then, young and naïve but thinking she knew everything. Now, at thirty-one, she would give anything to be able to go back in time and shake some sense into herself.

Not that she would have listened. Diego was charming, rich, powerful, and so handsome it made her knees buckle. And she was a mess. She needed saving, and he was there to save her.

She shook her head. She needed to focus, not think of the mistakes of the past. There were plenty of them, and she didn't have the time to dwell on each one.

Getting out of Barcelona needed to be her one and only focus.

She knew that they'd expect her to go to the airport, but she also knew that the Ortega family had people working there. She'd be seen in minutes if she tried to fly out of Barcelona.

That left driving or getting the train. The train seemed like the better option of the two. Safety in numbers… maybe they wouldn't kill her if she was found in a packed train carriage.

Maybe.

"Get a hold of yourself, Annie," she muttered. Falling apart now was not an option. She needed to keep everything together if she was going to get herself out of the city, and, hopefully, the situation she'd found herself in.

She adjusted her dark glasses and pulled her Hermès scarf up a little higher to obscure her face without looking too suspicious. Unfortunately, there was no way to get from her location to the train station without crossing some of the busiest roads in Barcelona.

She sucked in a deep breath and turned onto the main road at as fast a pace as she dared.

The ten-minute walk felt like it took half an hour. Across the short distance, Annie had been close to having a panic attack. Barcelona had been her hometown for five years. It was a city, but it wasn't that populated. Even with the tourist season kicking off, it still felt like getting lost in a crowd was an impossible task.

Thankfully, the railway station had multiple entrances, and Annie knew to find a rarely used one. She walked through the wide-open space of Barcelona's central rail hub. Her heels clicked on the marble floor, and she caught a glimpse of her reflection in the glass windows of the many shops she passed. She wondered if she stuck out as much as she thought or if it was just paranoia that was racing through her veins.

She found a departure board and stared at the names of stations.

Madrid, Paris, Lyon.

She didn't know which was best. She'd gotten as far as

deciding she needed to get out of Barcelona. Where she was actually heading was a completely different matter.

Wherever it was, it needed to be completely unpredictable, somewhere they'd never think to look. Somewhere she could lie low and, hopefully, reinvent herself.

CHANGEOVER DAY

Captain Caroline West mingled with departing guests in the main promenade of the *Fortuna Dream*. She knew her cheeks would hurt by the end of the day with the permanent smile she had plastered on her face.

Guests of the Dream Cruise Company expected a certain level of service. They wanted their cruise to be luxurious, relaxing, and something to brag about when they got back to shore. Nothing said status like saying you'd met the captain. Or spoken with her, dined with her, danced with her. She was a highly sought-after commodity.

Essentially, there were times when Caroline knew that her years of training and experience were pushed to one side to ensure that Mr and Mrs Carlisle from Cornwall could say they'd had a one-on-one chat with the captain about the cost of octopus.

It hadn't been the career she'd set out to achieve. Not that being the captain of one of the largest ships for the Dream Cruise Company was to be sniffed at. The pay was good, she was in charge of an impressive ship, and she enjoyed her job.

For the most part.

"Thank you so much for joining us," she said to the couple from Luton who had studiously attempted to bump into her at every given opportunity. She shook their hands and ensured she made eye contact and maintained her smile. "It was so lovely seeing you."

The couple beamed with excitement and assured her that they would be back next year.

The personal touch was something that had been drilled into her by Dream. She may be the captain of the *Fortuna*, but that didn't mean she simply managed the day-to-day running of the ship. It was an essential part of her role to socialise, to give speeches, to dine and dance with the guests, to always be ready with a smile.

Most of her schedule was packed with opportunities to meet with guests or feature heavily on the ship's dedicated television channel, where she spoke about weather, safety, and excursions.

She didn't enjoy that part of her job as much. She felt as if she were trapped in a goldfish bowl, with guests able to tap the glass at any time. Walking from one end of the ship to the other should take a normal, healthy adult around four minutes. Caroline knew she'd never manage it in under thirty.

"Captain West!"

Caroline turned to see Archie McFarlane making his way past the coffee shop on the promenade. He leaned heavily on his walking stick as he hurriedly tottered towards her.

"My dear," he said. "It's been a sensational trip. Sensational. Hasn't it, Agnes?"

Agnes McFarlane opened her mouth to speak but didn't get a chance to produce any actual words before Archie and his motormouth were off again.

"If I didn't know any better, I'd say you even controlled the weather for us," he enthused. "Beautiful. Not too hot, though. I can't stand it when it's too hot. Neither can Agnes. Can you, dear?"

Agnes tried again but was too slow.

"We'll be back later in the season, so we'll see you again soon. I didn't finish telling you the story of my boy and his bike being stolen in Cambridge," Archie continued.

Caroline leaned closer to him, knowing that he was very hard of hearing. "I look forward to it, Mr McFarlane. It's been wonderful having you on board, and I look forward to seeing you in a few short months."

Archie tapped Caroline's hand politely and nodded before turning to leave.

Agnes opened her mouth to say her own farewell but stopped when Archie called out to her to hurry up. She offered Caroline a tight smile before rushing off.

"One day, we may get to hear Agnes McFarlane actually speak," Thomas Barridge spoke softly in her ear.

"I doubt that very much," she whispered to her staff captain. "Not if Archie McFarlane has anything to say about it."

He chuckled. "True, true." He stood up straight and gazed around the emptying promenade. "Do you want to head off for a while? I think that's most of the rush dealt with."

Caroline lifted up the sleeve of her formal jacket and looked at her watch. It was changeover day which meant all of the passengers who had been on board for the week-long tour of the western Mediterranean were disembarking. A new batch of guests would be boarding within a couple of hours.

For a few short hours, *Fortuna* would be a hive of activity as the two thousand crew and staff prepared for the next intake. Over the course of the afternoon, more than five thousand new passengers would board, and during that time the captain would be expected to be present during at least the busiest periods to welcome people aboard, especially the Dreams Plus passengers, frequent cruisers who required a little more special attention.

Changeover day was the most stressful day for everyone on board. Personally, Caroline felt pulled in a hundred different directions. As ship's master, she was responsible for the vessel's mechanical, technical, safety, and navigational details. On top of those responsibilities, she also needed to liaise with the rest of her team, including the engineers, her deck officers, and, most importantly, the hotel director, whom she had a meeting with in just under five minutes.

"Yes," she agreed. "I have to see Dominic; I have my radio with me if you need me."

"Oh, you remembered it this time?" Thomas teased.

"I always remember it," she replied. "Sometimes I just ignore you."

She winked and discreetly made her way up a small spiral staircase to the upper level of the promenade so that she could sneak into the crew-only area of the ship.

As usual, she was running late. Not being able to walk the ship without being stopped by someone wanting to talk to her was utterly exhausting. There wasn't a single member of her crew who ever expected her to be on time for anything, but she still felt guilty for being late. Caroline was used to a military life and being on time, even after years of working for Dream.

Not that working on a cruise line was that different from the Royal Navy in some respects. There was still a very strict hierarchy, rules and procedures, uniforms and titles.

It was just all tied up with a twenty-four-hour party mentality, thousands of guests, and spending six months of the year in the Caribbean and six months in the Mediterranean.

Almost identical, she joked to herself.

MIRROR IMAGE

Annie rushed into the ladies' bathroom, away from the bustling crowd of Barcelona's central railway station. She'd done it. A one-way ticket to Paris was now clutched in her hand, and she was ready to depart in just under two hours.

She walked over to the sinks and stared at her reflection. Her long, brown hair was swept up into a ponytail and hidden under a hat. She hadn't washed it in a couple of days and dreaded to think what it would look like down. Bags were obvious under her light brown eyes.

All she wanted to do was get out of the city.

But she had to wait, which was increasingly difficult as Annie was convinced she'd been followed, or at least spotted. Nightmare scenarios played over and over in her head, and she was surprised that she hadn't suffered a complete breakdown yet.

The door to the bathrooms opened, and she held her breath. She glanced in the mirror to see who was coming into the space.

Her breath caught in her chest, and her eyes widened.

She'd finally cracked. It was the only explanation for what she was seeing. The stress had obviously gotten to her, and she was hallucinating. That was the only way to explain why she was looking at her body double in the mirror.

Annie slowly turned around, aware that her mouth hung open and her eyes were as wide as saucers. Her doppelgänger stared back with identical astonishment. A few moments of silence passed between them in the empty bathroom before the other woman started to speak in excited Spanish.

Annie held up her hand. "I'm sorry, I... I don't speak Spanish."

"Oh, you're English?" The woman looked confused. Her English was impeccable, with just the slightest accent.

"Yeah, my mum's Italian," she said to explain her slightly Latin looks. "My name's Annie."

"I'm Serena, and you look..." Serena was looking Annie up and down in fascination. "We are twins!"

Annie nodded slowly. "We are. What are the odds?" It was only then that Annie noticed that Serena's eyes were red, and she clutched a used tissue in her hand. "Are you okay?"

"No," Serena said simply. "But you will think me ridiculous."

She pulled the case she'd been dragging behind her farther into the bathroom and parked it out of the way against a wall. She walked over to the mirror and started to fluff her mid-length brown hair.

Annie couldn't help but stare at her. Serena was a

couple of inches taller than she was. Her hair was a little shorter, her nose a little thinner. Side by side, they were certainly not identical, but the likeness was astonishing.

"I should ask you if *you* are okay. You look terrible, too," Serena said. She opened her handbag and fished out a makeup bag. "No offence."

"None taken," Annie replied. "I look a mess."

Serena unzipped her makeup kit and placed it on the counter between the two sinks. She gestured to the contents. "Please, help yourself."

Annie hesitantly stepped forward. The makeup selection was enormous for such a small bag. She picked up some concealer and started to apply it to the bags under her eyes. It wouldn't erase them, but it would help.

"So, what is your story?" Serena asked. "You are hiding out in here like me, *sí?*"

Annie didn't know how to answer that question. Telling a complete stranger that she'd witnessed something she shouldn't and that now the mob was after her wasn't exactly a good idea.

"I'm... trying to leave town," Annie explained. "I've left a bad relationship. I need to get away from here."

Serena made eye contact with her reflection. "I'm sorry to hear that."

Annie shrugged. "I'll be okay. Just... need to get out of here. What's your story?"

Serena put the cap back on her lipstick and let out a soft sigh. "It is silly."

"It's upset you," Annie pointed out. "Can't be all that silly."

Serena frowned. "You don't recognise me?"

Annie's eyebrows lifted. "Should I?"

Serena shrugged. "You like music?"

"Some."

Serena put the lipstick back in the makeup bag and walked over to her suitcase. She opened the front zip and pulled out a CD case and handed it to Annie.

She looked at it for a moment before realising the figure in the black-and-white photo on the cover was Serena. She wore a floor-length ballgown and was looking up at the sky.

"You're a singer?" Annie asked.

She turned the CD over and looked at the playlist on the back.

"Yes, I sing opera."

"Oh." Annie looked at the front cover again. *An Evening with Serena Rubio*. Cool. But this doesn't explain why you were crying."

Serena folded her arms and leaned back against the tiled wall. "My voice, it needs to be rested, but I have a tour coming up. If word gets out that my voice is not strong, then ticket sales could fall. Venues may cancel."

Annie nodded. "Oh, I see. That's awful."

Serena quickly shook her head. "That is not why I am sad. It has happened before. It is common for singers; our voices are more fragile than people expect. No, the problem is that my manager booked me to go on holiday." Serena gestured to the suitcase with irritation. "A cruise. I hate cruises. I cannot swim, and I hate being out of communication with the world. It's for seven days. He hopes that I will rest my voice and be well when I get back."

Annie smiled. "Okay, yeah, crying because you're forced to go on a cruise is a bit weird."

"No, you don't understand." Serena pushed herself away from the wall and started to pace. "My manager forced me to split up with my boyfriend. He said that he was a bad influence on me. But I love him. So, I lied and said that we broke up. But we didn't. My boyfriend is in Australia, and I desperately want to see him. He was supposed to visit here, but then my manager sent me on this cruise to rest my voice. So now he lands tomorrow, and I will be gone. And now I won't see him, and I don't know when I will see him. And I hate cruises."

Annie blew out a breath. "Wow, yeah, that..." She let the sentence trail away, not knowing what she could say to make all of that better. Serena seemed to be in a heart-breaking situation, forced to be apart from someone she loved.

"Can't you just... not go on the cruise?" Annie asked.

Serena shook her head. "No, my manager will hear that I didn't go and will be very angry with me. He thinks that it is essential that I get away from everything, away from my friends, my family, social media, fans. He wants me to float around the sea without saying a word for seven days. Come back refreshed." Serena snorted a laugh before launching into a stream of Spanish which didn't sound complimentary.

"I'm sorry," she said, looking suddenly sheepish. "I just... I want to see my boyfriend. You know when you love someone, when you feel this *need* to be with them. When you know they will fix everything and make you feel safe and happy?"

"I know what you mean," Annie said.

It was a lie. Annie had no idea what Serena meant. She'd yet to find someone who made her feel like that. There had never been a romantic partner in her life who made her feel safe, no one who fixed everything. She'd thought she'd experienced love, but now she honestly wasn't sure. Had she ever loved Diego? Probably not.

She'd been so lost in her thoughts that she hadn't noticed Serena staring at her.

"What is it?" Annie turned to look in the mirror, wondering if she'd gone too far with the concealer.

Serena spun around and opened her suitcase. She pulled out a floppy straw hat and a pair of large, dark sunglasses. She grabbed Annie's arm and turned her to face her, taking off Annie's hat and placing the straw one on her head as she did.

"What are you doing?" Annie asked as a pair of sunglasses were shoved onto her face.

"You look just like me," Serena said. "It must be fate. God has sent you to me."

Annie wanted to argue that if God had sent Annie to Serena, then God was willing to put Serena into potential mortal danger.

The last thing anyone in Barcelona wanted right now was to look like Annie Peck. If Annie had to look at Serena twice to check that she wasn't losing her mind, then the Ortega family wouldn't hesitate to snatch Serena off the streets. Would they believe Serena when she said she wasn't Annie? Even if they did, it would be too late by then.

"You will be me," Serena announced.

Annie yanked the sunglasses from her face. "What?!"

"You want to leave town; you can be me." Serena was grinning from ear to ear, her mind clearly made up.

"Wait, no… no. I can't do that!"

"You can, you look like me."

"But I'm not you. I… I don't speak Spanish, I can't sing!" Annie pulled off the hat and held it out to Serena, who refused to take it.

"It is an English cruise company, and I spend a lot of my time speaking English. And you're supposed to be resting your voice," Serena said.

"No, *you* are supposed to be resting *your* voice. Not me."

"No one will know who you are, or who I am. You proved that; you didn't know who I was. You will be just another passenger. Someone who keeps to themselves. You can eat and drink, sunbathe." Serena got her phone out of her bag and started typing.

"Wait, what are you doing?" Annie reached for the phone.

Serena held it out of reach. "Telling Michael that I will see him at the airport."

"No, wait! I haven't agreed to anything."

"I will pay you." Serena lowered the phone and looked at her earnestly. "I will pay you five hundred euros per day you spend on this cruise. Seven days. Three and a half thousand euros. Up front."

Annie licked her lips and blinked rapidly. She had money in the bank, but she didn't know how far Diego's reach spread.

In her paranoia she had convinced herself that a

hacker could easily track her bank account, locating the cash machine or branch she used and putting her at risk. She needed money to get away from Diego, and cash was preferable. Three and a half thousand euros in cash would go a long way to helping with that. And it would be untraceable.

"And you will get out of town, away from your boyfriend, girlfriend, whoever," Serena continued. "You can board the ship in one hour. Set sail and see France and Italy. Free food, drink, entertainment. There are many pools, a casino."

"You were just telling me how much you hate cruising," Annie pointed out.

"Yes, but you will love it," Serena assured her. "Please."

"It's identity fraud," Annie said.

"Who will ever know? I will give you my passport, my credit cards. You will be me. I will meet you when you get off the ship next week and you can give me everything back," Serena said.

"You're placing a lot of trust in a complete stranger."

"I believe this is fate," Serena repeated. "I think God has put us together to help us both."

Annie let out a breath and turned away from Serena to get some space to think. A week on a cruise ship sounded like heaven compared to how her life had been over the last two days. But it was still fraud, and she was in enough trouble as it was.

She knew exactly what the Ortega clan would do to her if they found her. Or anyone who looked like her.

She swallowed hard.

Serena was in real danger, but Annie couldn't explain

to her why. She either needed to convince her to get on the ship or out of Barcelona. She couldn't stand the idea of Serena's blood being on her hands. Even if she didn't hurt her personally, she'd still feel entirely to blame.

Three and a half thousand euros in cash didn't sour the deal, though. She reasoned she could always pay Serena back later when she had gotten away from Diego and was safe.

Annie tightly shut her eyes. She didn't know what to do. She tried to centre herself and remember her plan. Get out of the city. Don't be traceable.

Going on a cruise ship under the name of an opera singer would certainly cover both of those bases. But it was against the law. Could it even work? Would anyone believe she was Serena? It was possible. Especially if she had Serena's ID and all her belongings.

She spun around. "Okay, but on one condition."

Serena looked happy enough to burst. "Name it."

"You have to get out of Barcelona. As you say, we look the same, and one of my friends might recognise me." Annie didn't want to mention that those friends could rat her out to the mob and have her killed; she just had to hope Serena would keep to her word.

"Absolutely. I will pick Michael up from the airport tomorrow morning, and we will hire a car and drive into the country. Find a hotel for the week."

Annie couldn't believe she was considering this. She thought about her train ticket to Paris, a ticket which assured she'd get out of the city, but a ticket which could easily be traced by the Ortega family and their connections.

A week aboard a cruise ship would give her the time and space to come up with a real plan. She could even use the cruise to vanish into France or Italy, sending Serena's belongings back via the mail service. No one would ever know where she was.

"If you worry about pretending to be me, you can stay in your suite all day. They have room service," Serena said, trying to sweeten the deal.

Annie worried her lip between her teeth. It was a risk, but everything she'd done lately or would do in the near future would be a risk. If she could get away with it, she'd be safer aboard the cruise ship with three and a half thousand euros in her pocket. It meant options, untraceable paths to a new life.

"Okay, I'll do it," she agreed.

Serena squealed with excitement. "Thank you!"

Annie found herself wrapped in a hug for a moment before Serena stepped back and started rummaging through her handbag.

"We don't have much time. You need to board in about an hour. Let's get you ready! I will tell you everything you need to know."

STATUS REPORT

CAROLINE WALKED BRISKLY through deck ten. She was never off duty, which meant she was hardly ever out of uniform, and that made her easy to spot on the crowded upper decks. Even when she was out of uniform, there were still plenty of people who recognised her.

Such was the difficulty of being one of the few female cruise ship captains in the world. Management for Dream Cruise Company were always asking her to conduct interviews with newspapers and magazines, and her photo was all over the Internet.

So, she used the mid-decks if she needed to get anywhere fast. Deck ten was a favourite because it mainly consisted of larger guest staterooms and suites, which meant there were fewer than the lower decks, where more rooms were crammed onto each floor.

Travelling through deck one in the bowels of the ship was almost impossible. The crew-only area was as hectic as the busy upper decks, and she couldn't walk a few steps without someone stopping her to ask a question, offer up a suggestion, or complain about something which should be funnelled through Dominic.

Staff were split into three categories: crew, officers, and staff. Caroline had responsibility for crew and officers, but staff were out of her remit and managed by Dominic Yang, the hotel director of *Fortuna*.

"Eagle One?" Her radio cracked to life.

She unclipped it from her belt and pressed down the button. "On my way, Dom."

"Roger that."

She put the radio back on her belt and picked up the pace a little as she approached the forward-section stairwell. She jogged up the stairs, passing three decks with ease. Her colleagues from the Royal Navy had suggested that her level of fitness would fade once she started working on the cruise lines. Never-ending buffets and lounging around was what they had assumed.

The truth had been quite the opposite. Caroline was in the best shape of her life with all the running around she had to do. *Fortuna* was bigger than the largest aircraft carrier built to date and three-quarters of the height of the Statue of Liberty.

She walked down a couple of corridors before entering the ship's library. The room was opulent and well-furnished with beautiful hardwood floors, tall, backlit bookshelves, and plenty of luxurious seating.

The room was often bustling with passengers, but on changeover day it was closed to the public. Dominic and Caroline used the opportunity to meet somewhere brighter and more spacious than either of their offices.

"Sorry I'm late," she apologised immediately.

Dominic was sat in a high-back leather seat, a large stack of paperwork in his lap.

"No problem," he replied, clearly used to her delayed arrivals.

She took the seat opposite him and let out a relieved sigh. It wasn't sitting down that prompted the sound, it was being alone. Or at least being out of the reach of passengers for a few moments.

"Shall I begin?" he asked, gesturing to a sheet of paper which presumably contained his status report.

"Please do."

"Successful trip, we conducted three weddings, as you know, and everyone was happy with that. We had five drunk-and-disorderly arrests, but they were nothing to write home about. Maintenance is getting to the room complaints; again, there's nothing major. Housekeeping are short-staffed but managing; I'm hoping for replacements to join us at Marseille. The whirlpool on the aft deck is being serviced. There was a problem with a filter, so we're hoping we can get that fixed before all aboard."

Caroline nodded. She picked up the report that was on the coffee table in front of her. While the hotel side of the cruise wasn't strictly anything to do with her, she still liked to be kept informed.

"Ninety-two-percent capacity for this sailing," Dominic continued. "One wedding, and we'll have two passengers celebrating their hundredth birthday, if you can believe that."

She couldn't. At fifty-five, she assumed she had another twenty-five years left if she was lucky and nothing untoward happened. The thought of having forty-five more years to live was hard to imagine.

"Will they be at my table?" she asked.

"No, one has special dietary requirements and won't be attending the main dining room at all. The other eats at five every day so can't wait for your table to dine later."

"I understand. I'll make a note to seek them out and congratulate them."

"Speaking of congratulations..." Dominic grinned and looked over the report at Caroline.

"No." She broke eye contact and fixed her gaze on the paper in her hands.

"Come on, Caroline," he pleaded.

"No, I won't be made to celebrate something I don't see any point in celebrating."

"Five years as ship's master is a big achievement. First woman for Dreams, captaining the best ship in the fleet. The crew want to celebrate," Dominic said.

"Then let them, I just don't feel the need to be a part of it. You know I'm not a party person." She shifted in her seat, the soft leather at odds with the discomfort she was feeling with the direction of the conversation.

It wasn't the first time the point had been brought up. In fact, Dominic brought it up almost every week. And every week, Caroline batted it away. However, she knew she'd have to cave in, or at least compromise, eventually.

"We'll talk about this later. I have the whole summer to convince you."

"And I have the whole summer to tell you no," she replied, a grin curling at her lips.

Working side by side with a party-loving civilian would never have been something she thought she'd enjoy doing. She'd never been accused of being fun. Life in the Royal Navy had always been serious, and she'd been so focussed on her career that she'd never bothered with the social aspect of ship life.

Now she worked in a place where having fun was literally a part of the job description. Dominic's entire role as hotel director was to ensure that every single guest was having the best time possible. Yes, he was dedicated and well-organised, but he was also the life and soul of every single event.

Caroline and Dominic were like chalk and cheese, one strait-laced and bureaucratic, the other a full-of-life party machine. And yet their roles on board brought them together to work hand in hand.

On their first day working together, Dominic had told Caroline, "You're driving the party bus, and I'm doing the karaoke. As long as we both focus on that, we'll be just fine."

Of course, both of their jobs were a lot more complicated than that, but the analogy was accurate. Caroline didn't interfere in any of the events planning, and Dominic didn't complain when bad weather prevented them from docking on time.

Over the years they had bonded and become a strong team. Part of the success of *Fortuna* lay with their relationship which ensured the ship ran like clockwork.

"Fine," Dominic conceded, at least for now. "Let's tick off the schedule. I notice there was a change for Napoli?"

The meeting with Dominic took less than hour, but that still meant that Caroline was late for her next meeting with Doctor Mara Perry, the chief medical officer on board *Fortuna*. Mara had been on board for two years, and Caroline had quickly become friends with her. It had been fantastic to finally have another woman in a senior position.

Caroline entered the ship's hospital and nodded to the nurse on duty at the reception window. She passed through the main ward and the consulting rooms and entered Mara's office at the end of the corridor.

"Sorry I'm late." She leaned on the doorframe. "And I only have ten minutes before I have a telephone call with head office."

Mara put her hand to her chest in fake shock. "I have a whole *ten* minutes?"

"No, you have five. I have to get up to my quarters." Caroline stepped into the room and took a chair.

"Well, I only need two minutes anyway," Mara said. "Housekeeping seem to be getting a little lax with disinfecting. I know we've discussed this before, but my team did some random swabbing over the last week and the results are steadily getting worse."

"I'm aware, and I did bring it up with Dominic and with the head of housekeeping directly. They're understaffed, but they have some temps on board at the moment and they are getting new people at Marseille. Obviously, I've emphasised the importance of this, and they are ramping up their efforts."

"Good, no one wants to float around in a filthy Petri dish," Mara said.

Caroline winced. "Thank you for the mental image."

"You're welcome. You've not had a large-scale contagious event on board *Fortuna*. Trust me… it's not pretty."

Caroline was proud and thankful that *Fortuna* hadn't suffered from that kind of medical incident during her tenure. The media always swept in and gleefully reported when a ship came down with multiple cases of stomach flu, or worse. The reputation of a cruise company could be lost with one thirty-second news video on social media.

"Continue your swabbing and let me know if it gets any worse, but I'm convinced that the necessary parties are taking things seriously and that it will be resolved as quickly as possible."

"Wonderful, one more thing." Mara removed her glasses and gazed keenly at Caroline. It was a move she often made when she intended to ask Caroline something personal. Caroline held a breath and attempted to look as normal as possible.

"Yes?"

"How are you sleeping? Any better?" Mara asked.

Caroline nodded. "A little."

After a prolonged period of insomnia, she'd had to approach the hospital wing for sleeping pills. Her desire to not call attention to her sleeplessness had been beaten by her still-greater desire to not make a mistake at her post. She'd deliberately waited for Mara to be off-duty to visit one of the other attending doctors. Sadly, Mara was detail-orientated and saw the paperwork and dragged Caroline in for a consultation.

She liked and trusted Mara, but she also knew that Mara was legally obligated to tell on her to the higher-ups if she felt anything was wrong.

Caroline still wasn't sleeping as well as she'd like, but she was managing.

Mara's eyes narrowed thoughtfully. "Of course, you'd tell me if anything was wrong."

"Of course, it's in my contract," Carolina said with a grin.

Mara rolled her eyes. "I mean as a friend."

"Of course, I tell you everything," Caroline lied. Not that it felt like much of a lie. She was private and hardly told anyone anything, so the fact that Mara was as close as she'd gotten was progress in Caroline's mind. Even so, she wasn't about to tell Mara about her problems sleeping. Not yet, anyway.

"Oh, of course you do," Mara said with a chuckle. She put her glasses back on. "How will we fill the other two and a half minutes you have kindly assigned me?"

"I could beg you to convince Dominic to drop the idea of a celebration for my five-year anniversary on board?" Caroline hoped.

"Not happening." Mara shook her head. "You should celebrate. It's a big deal."

Caroline slumped back in her chair and let out a long breath. "You know I don't want to celebrate this. I mean, I love you all and the job is wonderful… but celebrating five years here is just a reminder of what I lost."

Mara leaned forward and put a comforting hand on Caroline's knee. "It was a long time ago; you need to move on."

"I don't know if I can. I spent all my working life in the Royal Navy up until that point. As a little girl, I never dreamed of being a cruise ship captain. While this is a big deal for many, and I completely understand why it is, for me it's just a reminder that I've been doing something I never wanted to do for five whole years. That my life crumbled apart, and I had to rebuild it and *fell* into this." Caroline gestured to her surroundings.

"Then do it for the crew. They love you, and they want to celebrate for you. Dominic will organise everything. You just show up and have a glass of cheap fizz and make a toast. Say hello to people for half an hour and then you can disappear. Job done."

Caroline contemplated it for a moment. "I don't really have much of a choice, do I?"

"Not really. It's like you always say, as ship's master you have all of the power over everyone on board, but absolutely no power over yourself." Mara shrugged. "It is what it is."

Caroline liked Mara's pragmatic outlook, except when it was directed squarely at her.

"Fine. I'll push back for a few more weeks, just to make a statement," Caroline decided.

"Good idea, it will probably encourage Dominic to scale back his plans."

Caroline raised an eyebrow. "You know his plans?"

Mara's eyes flew open. She looked at her watch. "My, is that the time? You better get going if you're going to make that call."

Caroline chuckled. "Fine, I'm going, but I won't forget that!"

"Don't know what you mean!" Mara called after her as she left.

ALL ABOARD

ANNIE'S HEART slammed into her ribs with such a ferocity that she wondered if she might pass out. She was well beyond the point of no return. She'd checked in at the desk in the port building with Serena's documents, and somehow it had miraculously all gone to plan.

The agent hadn't given her a second look while they processed her paperwork, swiped Serena's credit card, and issued Annie with a plastic card which acted as her room key, ID, and payment method aboard the ship.

Annie had thanked the agent and was now tightly holding the handrail of a long escalator that would take her from the port terminal to the ship. There was no way she could turn back now.

She was grateful for the large, dark sunglasses Serena had loaned her. The glasses and a change of hairstyle meant that most of her face was now covered. All she needed to do was to get on board, get to her room, and finally relax.

Or at least attempt to relax. Unwinding seemed

impossible at the moment. She'd gone from running away from a well-known mob boss to committing identity fraud. In fact, she'd probably done more than just that, but she still hadn't had time to properly examine the illegality of what she was doing.

Serena Rubio had been very persuasive. Annie had gone back and forth on whether or not the plan was a good one, but Serena had been adamant: Annie had been sent by God to ensure that Serena could stay in Spain and spend time with her Australian boyfriend.

Annie thought it was a ridiculous thing to believe, but she had to admit that the chain of events had been strangely fortuitous for her. She wanted to leave Barcelona without being seen, and a famous opera singer handing over fistfuls of cash, her passport, and a ticket on an all-expenses-paid cruise was a great way to do it.

Except that now, Annie was petrified. She was convinced that she would be discovered, arrested, and then bailed out by her ex-boyfriend Diego.

And then she'd be killed, of that she had no doubt.

She got to the top of the escalator and walked through an automatic door to an outside gangway. The ship was right in front of her, moored up and imposing on the dock. It stretched so far in either direction that she couldn't see the front or the back of it from her vantage point. She could only just about see the top deck, and the people walking up there looked tiny. It wasn't a ship so much as a city.

One which she had to board before she started to draw too much attention to herself. She walked along the gangway and towards a bridge that would take her into the ship.

She checked her ticket.

Fortuna. *Let's hope it brings me some luck,* she thought.

A smartly dressed member of the crew met her at the entrance to the ship with a scanner in their hand.

"Good afternoon, may I see your pass?"

Annie held up the plastic card she'd just been issued.

"Have you been on a Dream cruise before?" the crew member asked as they scanned the card. They were about to hand it back when they paused, staring at the card.

Annie swallowed. She'd been discovered. She wondered if she'd get very far if she ran. Much like an airport terminal, the port building was full of security guards and some of them were armed.

"Oh, wow, Miss Rubio! I'm such a big fan!"

Annie felt her eyes widen and was again relieved for the dark glasses that hid her expression.

"Thank you, Jenn," Annie said as she read the name badge on the crisp, white, short-sleeved shirt of the crew uniform. Luckily Serena spoke with only a slight accent, which Annie found easy to reproduce. But this was the first real test. This was a fan, someone who may have intimate knowledge of Serena Rubio, details which Annie hadn't had a chance to fully research yet.

Jenn blushed and handed back the ID card. "I loved your latest album. My boyfriend took me to see you in Madrid last year, and you were amazing!"

Annie smiled. She realised that Jenn's gushing behaviour was starting to attract attention from other passengers. The reality of pretending to be someone else was now setting in. She needed to research Serena properly, and she needed to do it fast.

Annie had dumped her mobile phone immediately after she had run from Diego, and Serena had kept her phone, which meant that Annie was now without her usual trusty method of research.

Since she'd first been given a hand-me-down phone from her father, Annie had been glued to the screen. She quickly realised the world was at her fingertips, and she could instantly learn about anything she liked. Being without her phone made her feel even more lost.

"I'm sorry, you are probably tired, and here I am going on and on!" Jenn apologised. "Your stateroom is on deck fourteen, you can take the elevators behind me. Your room is ready, and your luggage will be delivered within the hour. If you need anything at all, just ask a member of the crew."

Annie nodded and smiled, hoping it looked realistic. She was shaking and desperately trying to look composed while attempting to not pass out or throw up. She passed the security podium and was immediately greeted by another member of staff, this one holding a tray of Champagne flutes.

"Madam?" He lowered the tray for Annie to take a glass, which she did.

"Thank you," she said, belatedly realising that she'd forgotten the accent. Luckily, he didn't seem to notice.

Annie stepped farther into the ship. Not that it felt like she was on a ship. Suddenly she was on a street, a long street which was filled with coffee shops, restaurants, shops, guest services, and more.

People were milling about, eating, drinking Champagne, and exploring.

"Good afternoon, welcome to *Fortuna* and welcome to the promenade. Do you need any directions?"

Annie shook her head, smiling at the helpful crew member but quickly backing away from them, too. She needed to get out of the crowded space and to her room where it would be safe.

She walked down the promenade, peeking into the shops and bars as she went. As she walked, she realised she was being followed. It wasn't paranoia. She could feel someone right behind her no matter how much she zigzagged her way down the fake street.

When she reached the bank of elevators, the signage told her she was on deck five. She pressed the up button and turned to see who was following her.

The couple in their sixties smiled warmly and stood beside her, also waiting for the elevator. When it arrived, they all got into the car.

Annie pressed the button for deck fourteen and was relieved when the couple selected deck thirteen. She tried to break eye contact by looking at the floor.

A smile curled at her lips as she noticed the floor of the elevator cart had an ornate sign signalling the day of the week, *Sunday*. She'd never seen an elevator with the weekday embedded into the floor before.

"People get confused on a cruise," the man explained at Annie's expression.

"Are you cruising alone, dear?" the woman asked.

"I am," Annie admitted.

"Well, plenty of people cruise alone, but they aren't

alone for very long! We're a very friendly bunch on board, aren't we, Graham?"

"Absolutely! No one is lonely aboard a Dream cruise," Graham agreed with gusto. "Have you cruised before?"

Annie assumed that Serena hadn't, so she shook her head.

"Oh, you're going to have the best time, isn't she, Graham?" The woman put her hand out. "I'm Louise."

Annie shook her hand. "Nice to meet you," she said before shaking Graham's hand, too.

"You must join us for dinner," Graham offered.

Annie had no desire to be rude, or to potentially damage Serena's name, so she nodded in silent agreement.

She fully intended to lock herself away in her room for the entire trip, so it didn't matter what she said. They were going to another floor and would never see her again.

"Wonderful, we'll see you at dinner time," Louise said. "If not before!"

The doors opened, and the couple left, saying goodbye and promising to show her all the fun of *Fortuna* that evening. Annie kept smiling and nodding right up until the doors thankfully closed.

Then she slumped against the back wall of the elevator car and let out a shaky breath.

"Cruising will be the death of me," she muttered to herself.

ELVIN

AFTER A SHORT WALK down a corridor filled with stateroom doors, Annie found her home for the week. She swiped her pass card, waited for a green light to illuminate, and then stepped into the room. She dropped her bag on the sofa and looked around the room with an open mouth.

She'd always thought cabins on board cruise ships were pokey little spaces with hardly enough room to get into bed each night. That certainly wasn't true of this particular stateroom. It wasn't enormous, but it wasn't cramped either. There was a king-size bed, two small bedside cabinets, a two-seater sofa, a small wardrobe, a desk with chair, and a television. It was everything she could need for a week-long stay without feeling too confined, especially considering she was intending to spend as much time in her room as possible.

She walked over to the balcony and opened the heavy sliding door. She stepped outside and looked at the bustling port area below her. People were still arriving, walking along the terminal building's gangway to gain access to the ship. Beyond that there was a large taxi area, a number of black cars dropping people off and speeding away to pick up more fares.

She wondered how many people the ship could hold at any one time. It was enormous, both in length and in height.

There was a knock on the door, interrupting her thoughts.

She spun around, her blood running cold. Not only was she terrified about the Ortegas finding her, she was now also worried that her identity would be discovered, and she'd be kicked off the ship.

Or worse, arrested.

"Housekeeping!" A male voice called out.

Annie grimaced. She couldn't pretend she wasn't in; there was a chance that he'd enter the room if he thought it was unoccupied. She hadn't thought to slap the 'do not disturb' magnet on the outside of the door.

She quickly crossed the room and opened the door, just a crack.

A young man smiled at her. "Hello, Miss Serena. I am Elvin."

"Hi."

"I am here to introduce you to your stateroom. I can come back later?"

His smile never wavered. Annie realised it would be better to get it over and done with, rather than to have the poor man come back at a later time.

She took a step back and pulled the heavy door open.

Elvin entered the room. "Welcome to *Fortuna*."

Annie closed the door. "Thank you."

"I am your stateroom attendant; my name is Elvin. If you need anything then you can call me on your phone." He gestured to the telephone beside the bed, pointing to a specific button. "You can order food or drinks. I can come and clean your room, replace your towels. Whatever you need."

"That's great, thank you."

"I will come and clean the room twice a day."

"Twice?" Annie had stayed in hotels before but never received housekeeping twice in a single day.

"Yes, ma'am. Once between nine and two in the afternoon, and again in the evening between five and nine."

"Wow. Do you ever sleep?" Annie asked.

"Yes, ma'am. Every member of staff gets ten hours of mandatory rest every day." Elvin's smile seemed to be a permanent feature. It never waned, and it seemed genuine. "Unfortunately, there has been a problem with some of our scanners and luggage delivery has been delayed. I know this is a terrible inconvenience, and I would like to apologise on behalf—"

Annie raised her hand, cutting off the prepared speech that Elvin had obviously been asked to repeat to everyone he met.

"It's fine, I won't need my case for a while anyway. As long as I have it before bed," she said with a chuckle.

"We will get it to you as soon as we can," he promised. He turned and walked over to the balcony. "If you need more chairs for the balcony, I can get them for you, if you want to invite anyone you are travelling with to your stateroom."

"Oh, I'll be on my own all of the time," Annie said.

Elvin's cheery disposition faltered for a nanosecond before springing back to life. "I'm sure you will meet lots of people on board. We have many solo travellers; they leave with many new friends."

Annie got the distinct impression that wanting to have a quiet cruise, alone in her room, was going to thoroughly confuse poor Elvin. She offered him a tight grin and nodded.

He pointed to the television. "You can do lots of things on your television. You can order room service, and then I will deliver it to you. Or you can call me. But if you prefer to use the television, then you can. You can book dining reservations at any of our restaurants. You can have a look at the activities on board." He held out the remote control and gestured to a button. "You can also watch our on-board TV shows. Our hotel director, Dominic, will speak to you every day about our activities on board and our shore excursions. And you can watch the weather with Captain West."

Annie tried to look enthused, but she didn't intend to participate in any activities or go on any shore excursions, and she really didn't care about the weather.

Elvin seemed to sense her despondency. "There are other channels." He put the remote down. "Do you have any questions?"

"No, I think I'll be fine," Annie said. "To be honest, Elvin, I'm planning to have a nice, quiet holiday. Lots of rest. I'll probably be in my room, or on my balcony, most of the time."

"We have many swimming pools and whirlpools you can rest by," Elvin explained.

"I like things quiet," Annie said.

"We have an adults-only solarium. Very quiet. And bar service directly to your sunbed."

It sounded very appealing, but Annie had to remind herself that she was supposed to be keeping a low profile.

Elvin must have noticed her lack of enthusiasm. "We also have a casino, many restaurants, bars. Lots to do. You can ask me anything. Or look at your TV."

"Thank you. I will." Annie realised that she sounded miserable and that Elvin was doing his upmost to provide her with the best customer service he could. She felt guilty for sounding so down. "I'm very tired, I've travelled a long way. I'll feel better when I have rested and eaten."

"Would you like me to get you some room service?" Elvin perked up at the news that he could help Annie to feel better. He grabbed the food menu from a magazine rack on the wall. "It's all very, very good."

Annie chuckled. "No, I'm okay at the moment, but thank you so much, Elvin. I appreciate you being so helpful. I just need a while to get used to my new surroundings and have a break. Probably on the balcony."

He nodded. "Very well, Miss Serena. I will come by to clean your room later tonight. If you need anything—"

"I'll call you." Annie smiled. "Thanks, Elvin."

Elvin hurried from the room, leaving Annie to wonder just what he would be cleaning when he came by in a few short hours. Life aboard a cruise ship was a completely new experience. She could tell already that Elvin was going to find her a mystery, the strange woman on deck fourteen who never wanted to leave her room.

Annie considered the point for a while. She needed to keep a low profile but not so much that she looked suspicious. Maybe checking out the pool would be a good idea, just once or twice so as not to look odd.

Her heart was still beating hard and fast. She sat on the sofa and stared at her shaking hands. She wondered when she'd start to feel more like herself. Or if she ever would again.

MUSTER DRILL

CAROLINE WALKED onto the bridge and approached Natalie Rodriguez, the shift navigational officer.

"Anything more regarding the low pressure coming from the east?" she asked.

Natalie shook her head. "No, it's still travelling at the same speed. I think it will hit us on the way to Marseille."

"Still around midnight?"

"Yes." Natalie pulled some papers from the tray on the navigation station and handed them over.

Caroline read them. Nothing had changed since the last weather update, but she needed to be certain. *Fortuna* was a luxury cruise liner, and they needed to do everything they possibly could to make the journey as smooth as possible.

Weather was the unknown element when it came to cruising, but forward planning could eliminate almost all related issues. Keeping up to date was essential.

"Okay," she said. "Stick with the current plan, we'll come out of Palma and move as quickly as we can up until the winds begin. Then we'll ease off for the sake of comfort until the winds die down again. Anything more about the conditions in La Spezia?"

"Yes, I've plotted a new route to get around the tanker there. They say their engines should be up and running before we get there, but judging from what they'd been saying before…"

Caroline rolled her eyes. "Indeed. Keep to your new route. Conditions are going to be clear enough that we can add a little time to ensure we're out of their way."

Natalie nodded her understanding and returned her attention to the navigational maps.

Caroline crossed towards one of the bridge wings, a part of the room that jutted out from the ship to allow a good view of the side of the vessel for navigating the ship in and out of ports. Thomas stood there, looking down at the port.

"Everything in hand?" she asked.

"Yes, we're getting the last people aboard now. Nothing to report."

"Excellent, I want you to join me at the cocktail party after dinner tonight. Practise for that promotion."

"I haven't been promoted yet," he reminded her.

"Yet," she repeated. "It's bound to be coming this term. It will be good for you to shadow me a little more for the entertainment side of things."

Thomas let out a tiny sigh.

"You certainly can't do that once you're promoted," she chided him.

"I wouldn't in front of the guests."

"At all." She gestured to the people walking aboard the

ship down below them. "You have to be on twenty-four seven. They can't ever see you as anything other than deliriously happy to see them. I know you started this career to be a bridge officer and to focus on the technical side of things, but sadly you're good at your job and that means progression to the showbiz side of this business. You can't pass up another promotion."

Thomas smiled a big, wide, and extremely fake grin.

"Beautiful," Caroline said. "Just keep that up for the next five months."

"Sure thing." He picked up a pair of binoculars from the wing console and kept watch of the deliveries being taken aboard the ship.

Caroline turned and walked into the SCC, the Security Command Centre, located behind the main bridge controls. She looked over the shoulders of the various bridge crew members at their screens. She trusted her crew; most of them had been handpicked by her. With a rotational schedule of between ten and sixteen weeks, it was easy to reassign anyone she didn't feel was doing the job to the best of their ability.

An alarm sounded; someone was opening a secure door down on deck one. Within a couple of seconds, a bridge officer had located the area on the expansive CCTV network, called security, and was in the process of calling the nearest telephone to the location.

On such a vast ship it was common for people to take the wrong door and try to enter locations where they weren't supposed to be. Most of the time it was a mistake, human error, but that didn't mean that protocol wasn't followed to the letter each time.

She peered at the screen. It appeared to be a member of the cleaning staff who had presumably gotten turned around and was accessing the wrong door. She waited, listening as the bridge crew member spoke to the cleaner, had them close and seal the door, and then instructed them on where to go. A few moments later, a security officer arrived and checked the door was sealed.

Caroline put her hand on the officer's shoulder and squeezed it in a silent indication of a job well done. She needed every single member of her team to be operating at the top of their abilities every moment they were on duty. Between them, they were responsible for the safety of thousands of people, both passengers and fellow crew members.

As master of *Fortuna*, she never allowed herself to forget that safety was her number-one priority. Nothing could slip past her. If something did, the results could be catastrophic.

She looked at her watch. It was coming up to quarter past four, which meant it was time for the bridge and all operational areas of the ship to become a hive of activity.

It was time for the muster drill.

MUSTARD DRILL

ANNIE ALLOWED her eyes to flutter closed and softly blew out a slow breath. The adrenaline was finally dissipating, and exhaustion was taking over. The stateroom bed was surprisingly comfortable, and she felt like she could just sleep through until the next day. Waking up in the middle of the ocean, far away from Diego, seemed perfect.

If she was lucky, no one would know where Annie Peck had disappeared to. Hopefully Serena had kept her word and had also gotten out of Barcelona.

Maybe she could get away with it.

A loud beep sounded from the ceiling. Annie's eyes flew open in shock.

"Good afternoon, ladies and gentlemen, welcome to *Fortuna*," a male voice said through the speaker in the room. "In just half an hour we will be performing our mandatory muster drill, as required by the International Convention for the Safety of Life at Sea. At this time, we will ask that all guests report immediately to their assembly point, which is displayed on your pass key. In fifteen minutes, all ship services will be suspended for the duration of the drill. We thank you for your participation. Please listen out for further announcements."

Annie sat up in bed and rubbed tiredly at her eyes. "What the hell is a 'mustard drill'?"

She reached for the phone and picked up the handset, pressing the button marked 'stateroom attendant.'

It rang three times before Elvin answered, "Yes, Miss Serena?"

"Elvin, what's a mustard drill?"

"Muster drill, Miss Serena."

"Okay, what's a muster drill?"

"I will come to your room."

Elvin hung up the phone, and Annie sat up. She stretched her arms up, satisfied with the tiny pops she heard down her spine. Exhaustion had come over her so quickly that she hadn't gotten undressed, which now seemed fortuitous.

A few moments passed before she heard a knock on the door. She crossed the room and opened the door, gesturing for Elvin to come inside.

"Thank you, miss." He looked at the desk and picked up Annie's pass key. He held it up and pointed to it. "This is your drill station for the muster drill. B02, that is by guest services on the promenade. Everyone must go."

"Everyone?" Annie asked.

"Everyone. All passengers and all crew."

"Okay. So, I have to go to guest services?"

"Yes."

"For how long?"

"Until Captain West dismisses us."

Great, just what I need, another man ordering me around, Annie thought.

"It's for safety," Elvin explained. "So you know where to go in case something happens."

Annie pinched the bridge of her nose. All she wanted to do was sleep. "Okay, fine, do I need to take anything with me?"

"Just your pass key. You will use your pass for everything; you should always have it with you. You can go now if you like, then you can get a seat. It will get busy."

"Sounds like a good idea. Thanks for your help, Elvin."

Elvin handed her the pass card and rushed around her to open the door. He really was the sweetest thing, and Annie felt bad that she had encountered him at a time when her life was in such disarray. Usually she'd be nicer and more engaged, but all she wanted to do now was get the drill over with and get some sleep.

She walked out into the corridor and stopped to look in both directions. Elvin appeared beside her and pointed to the right. "That is your closest stairwell. There will be people there guiding you."

"Okay. I'll guess I'll see you later," Annie said. "Have a nice… muster!"

She walked down the corridor until she found a door that led to a stairwell. Two members of staff were stood there, guiding people.

Annie held up her pass card to one of them.

"Guest services, you need to go down to deck five."

"Thank you," Annie said. She joined a small stream of people making their way down the stairs.

Fortuna was a beautiful ship. Luscious, thick carpet, light wood, and glass. It wasn't anything like Annie had expected of a cruise ship. Not that she had spent that much time considering it.

She'd never thought she'd be on one. Life certainly had fun surprising her.

She reached the fifth deck and saw more members of the crew guiding people. She held up her card again and was politely pointed in the right direction. The promenade was bustling with people, and she could see that it had been split into various areas for people to gather for the drill.

There were people milling about by the spa registration, people by the café, people by the Champagne bar. And then there were people filing into the guest services area, all having their passes scanned as they did.

Annie held out her pass to allow it to be scanned.

"Thank you, Miss Rubio. If you want to head inside, we'll let you know when the drill is complete."

"Thank you." Annie stepped inside and looked around the large space. There were only a couple of tables and chairs which had been placed there specifically for the drill. Her gaze fell on the couple from the elevator who were eagerly waving to her.

Great, she thought. *These two again.*

She walked over to them, and the man stood up and pulled out a chair for her. She wished she'd paid a little more attention to them and could remember their names.

"Funny seeing you again, isn't it, Graham?" the woman said.

"Yes, we have the same muster station. It must be fate," Graham replied.

Annie offered a quick, tight smile.

"How are you finding the ship?" the woman asked.

"I've not really explored much," Annie admitted. "I'm intending to have a quiet holiday, just resting and relaxing. On my own."

Graham let out a laugh. "You'll be bored in no time and missing all the amazing facilities on the ship. We can show you around."

"Really, that's not necessary," Annie argued.

"But I insist—"

"Graham, leave the poor girl alone," the woman replied.

"But, Louise—"

"No, she said she wants to be alone, so just accept it. Not everyone wants to examine every square inch of the ship like you do. Some people just want to order room service and relax on their balcony." Louise paused her chastisement of Graham and turned to Annie. "Do you have a balcony?"

"I do," Annie confirmed.

"Sea view?" Graham quizzed.

"Yes," Annie said.

"Well, there you go. That's a perfectly fine way of spending a holiday," Louise said. "Some quiet time in your room. We'll join you for dinner tonight in the main dining room, and then you can ask us any questions you might have, what with you being new to cruising and the ship."

Annie nodded her agreement. She had no intention of

dining with them that evening, but she didn't want to tell them that now and create a bad atmosphere. They had no idea where she was on a ship of thousands. Once the drill was over, it would be easy to lose them.

"I don't think we got your name?" Graham said.

"Serena Rubio," Annie said, hoping her cheeks weren't as red as she felt they might be.

"Pleasure to meet you," Graham said. "Sorry if I'm a bit pushy. I just love these ships, and I know some people miss some of the wonderful things on board."

"But if she wants to know about them, she'll ask," Louise said, effectively stopping another attack from Graham.

Silence loomed over the table, and Annie wasn't in the mood to break the deadlock. Instead, she observed her fellow passengers making their way to various assembly points. She was pleasantly surprised by the sheer diversity of people on board.

She'd always assumed that cruises were for the rich and that a cruise consisted of mainly wealthy white couples, but that didn't seem to be the case aboard *Fortuna*. There were people from various ethnicities, a wide age range, families, solo travellers, and she could even see a few same-sex couples.

She people-watched for a while, soaking up the atmosphere. While no one wanted to assemble for an emergency drill, everyone still seemed excited with the prospect of being on the ship. She heard snippets of conversations talking about the pools, the shows, the food, and the excursions.

Deep down, she started to feel a little tingle of excitement herself.

She'd gotten away with it. She was on a ship where, surely, she was safe? Who could possibly know she was on board? The gangway had been raised, so everyone was aboard. There was a good chance that she had seven days of respite from the nightmare that was her life now. A whole week of not looking over her shoulder. Time to make plans and implement them. Time to rest.

Once the drill was over and they could finally be dismissed.

She turned back to Louise. "How long does this usually take?"

"Not long," Louise reassured her. "They have to make sure everyone has attended. Then they do some things on the bridge, totalling numbers, I suppose. Then we watch a video, and then the captain will speak to us."

It sounded longer than Annie would like, but she knew there was little she could do but wait. She carried on looking around the promenade, wondering if she might pop out of her room now and then and sample one of the cafés.

It seemed entirely likely that once she was at sea, she would be safe from the Ortegas. From there on, her only issue would be pretending to be Serena Rubio and ensuring that no one realised she wasn't who she said she was. Keeping to herself would solve that issue—weren't celebrities meant to be standoffish anyway?

After a few minutes, screens around the guest services area sprang to life. Annie turned in her chair and looked at one of the screens behind a guest services desk. The chatter from the crowd died down, and a safety video began to play. It was a cartoon, taking the edge off of the fact it was discussing fire, crashes, evacuations, and life vests. Annie half-listened, assuming that in the event of a disaster, she'd probably just follow Elvin as he seemed capable enough.

The video went on for a few minutes. At the end they explained that the ship's emergency signal was seven short blasts on the ship's whistle followed by one long blast, as well as an internal alarm system.

A few seconds went by before the ship's whistle started to sound, and an internal alarm blared through the promenade.

Well, I won't miss that, Annie thought.

Finally, the alarms ended, and the screens changed to advise passengers to wait for a message from the captain.

Annie looked at her watch. She'd been there for twenty minutes.

"Not long now," Graham reassured her. "And then we can go and get ready for dinner. We're dining at eight, same as you." He gestured to the pass key that Annie had tossed onto the table when she sat down.

She looked at the card, noting that her dining time was listed as well as the deck number where her dining room was located. She snatched up the card, thankful that her room number was on the back and out of view.

She was about to reply when the screens flickered. Annie turned to see the screen. A lump formed in her throat at the sight of a gorgeous older woman dressed in a crisp, white shirt, black tie, and a navy-blue blazer with sparkling brass buttons.

"Good afternoon, ladies and gentlemen," the woman

said. "I'm Captain Caroline West, and I'd like to personally welcome you aboard *Fortuna*, one of the largest cruise ships in the world. Thank you for attending the muster drill, your safety is important to us. In fact, safety is my number-one priority."

Annie couldn't help but stare.

Caroline West was confident, welcoming, authoritative, and attractive. She wasn't at all what Annie had been expecting. In her mind, Captain West had been a man, definitely white, probably old. She guessed Caroline was in her early fifties, old enough to command respect but still in her prime.

"She's been in charge of *Fortuna* for five years now," Graham explained. "Great captain."

Annie looked around and noticed people were glued to the televisions in a way they weren't with the safety video. People were enraptured, taking in every word.

She's a celebrity, Annie realised. Through the murmuring chatter, she could hear snippets of conversations of people saying they'd seen her, spoken to her, shared an anecdote with her.

Annie realised that she'd completely tuned out of whatever Captain West was saying and turned her attention back to the screen.

"So, with that, I again welcome you aboard, and I hope to see many of you throughout this week-long cruise to some of the most wonderful destinations in the western Mediterranean. Thank you, crew dismissed."

Immediately, the staff around them started to move from where they were politely barricading people into their muster assembly points, and large swathes of people started to move.

"I'll see you later," Annie said, hurrying to get up and get lost in the crowd before Graham or Louise could realise they hadn't set up a meeting time or place, and had no idea where her room was.

"See you later," Louise called back.

THE SHELBYS

ANNIE TURNED onto her back in the soft bed and stretched her arms out wide. She must have fallen asleep the moment her head hit the pillow because she didn't remember much after returning to the room following the drill.

She picked up her watch from the bedside cabinet and squinted at the display. It was seven; she'd been asleep for more than two hours. A bit longer than the quick catnap she had planned, but obviously she needed the rest.

She reached for the remote control and turned on the television. She hated the silence and needed some background noise, anything to feel like she wasn't completely alone. Channel-hopping for a while, she stopped when she saw Caroline West.

Her thumb hovered over the channel button, debating whether she would move on or stay and listen to the captain talk about weather fronts.

"Suppose it's good to know what the weather will be

like tomorrow," she mumbled to herself, tossing the remote control on the bed.

A loud rap sounded at her stateroom door, and she jumped in surprise. She got up, glad that she had, again, fallen asleep fully dressed, and rushed over to look through the peephole.

Elvin stood in the corridor, his hand resting on the handle of her suitcase. Serena's case.

She took a deep breath and reminded herself to maintain her slight Spanish accent, aware that she was already forgetting it on occasions. She opened the door wide for him to enter the room.

"Hello, Miss Serena. Here is your luggage."

She'd forgotten all about the luggage issue. Being tired and drained from recent events had definitely left her muddled.

"Thank you, Elvin."

He entered the room and pulled a luggage rack from the wardrobe and lifted the heavy case onto it. "Can I get you anything else?"

"Yes, I think I might order room service," Annie said, plucking up the room service menu from the magazine rack.

"But you are dining in the dining room?"

Annie looked over the top of the menu. "No, I'm not."

"Mr Shelby asked me where your room was. He said you were dining together tonight," Elvin explained, looking a little confused.

"Shelby? Graham Shelby?" Annie asked.

Elvin smiled in relief. "Yes, Mr Graham."

Annie let out a groan. "Oh, Elvin, I wanted to hide from them. I wanted to have a quiet dinner alone."

All traces of happiness vanished from Elvin's face in a flash. "I'm so sorry, Miss Serena. He said that you had spoken but had forgotten to give him your room number. He will be here to pick you up at five to eight."

Elvin looked heartbroken that he had done something wrong.

"Okay. It's not a problem," Annie said, wanting to reassure Elvin that he hadn't committed some hideous crime. "I was just feeling a bit tired, but I have my case now, so I suppose I can get ready quickly and have one dinner with them."

"I could tell him you are unwell?" Elvin suggested.

Annie scrunched up her nose and shook her head. "I think then he would just insist that I go tomorrow. Might as well get it done."

She smothered a yawn with her hand.

"You are tired. Should I get you some tea? Coffee?" Elvin asked, almost bouncing with the thrill of having a way to put things right.

Annie realised she could probably do with a kick of caffeine if she was going to sit through a three-course meal with the Shelbys.

"You know what, Elvin, that's a great idea. I'd love some coffee."

Elvin was already moving when Annie realised something.

"Oh, Elvin, what's the dress code for dinner?"

"It is not a formal night tonight. So, casual." Elvin looked like he wasn't saying something.

"But… you'd recommend I dress a little formally?" she guessed.

"The Shelbys are on the big table, so it might be a good idea?"

"Formal, it is." She nodded.

"I will get you that coffee."

"Brilliant, I'll need to speed up if I'm going to be ready in under an hour," Annie said.

Elvin left the room, and Annie blew out a sigh. She should have guessed that Graham wouldn't leave her alone. She consoled herself with the knowledge that this would be the one and only time she dined with him and his wife; getting it out of the way on the first night was probably a good thing.

She opened her suitcase and hoped that Serena had packed something that she could wear for a formal dinner.

In fact, she hoped she had packed a lot of things. It was only now that Annie realised she'd boarded the ship with the clothes she was wearing and a hope that someone else's case would contain everything she needed.

Annie quickly started to empty the case onto the bed. There was a toiletry bag which, thankfully, had everything she needed including the essentials and what looked like a brand-new toothbrush.

Next, she found swimwear, shorts, skinny jeans, tops, dresses, and underwear.

Annie ruffled her nose. She hadn't thought of that. She didn't want to wear Serena's underwear; that was just *too* weird. She'd have to see if there was a place on board where she could buy new pairs.

Serena's taste in clothes was slightly different to

Annie's. Her outfits were more revealing than Annie would usually favour. The dresses had plunging necklines and short hems. The shorts were a couple of inches shorter than Annie was used to.

"Good thing I'm not shy," Annie muttered.

Every article of clothing was classy, something her previous wardrobe sorely lacked. Diego was constantly buying clothes for her, dressing her up like a doll. Sadly, his tastes were tacky, and it showed in the clothes he purchased and requested she wore. He spent large amounts of money on designer labels, but that didn't mean that the result looked anything other than cheap.

Serena's outfits were different, certainly revealing but in the style of a movie star rather than a hen night.

She held up a couple of dresses to her body in front of the full-length mirror beside the bathroom door. Admittedly, it was going to be tiny bit fun to play at being Serena Rubio for a while. She didn't like lying to people, but she'd never see these people again anyway. It would be exciting to wear a celebrity's clothes and swan around like she was an opera singer for an evening.

"So, with all of that being said, we hope for a very smooth departure from Barcelona this evening," Captain West's voice drifted from the television.

"It better be," Annie replied. "I didn't pack my sea legs."

A knock on the door indicated that Elvin had returned. Annie opened the door, and he entered with a silver tray with a mug, a sugar bowl, some milk, and a carafe of coffee. He placed it on the desk.

"Would you like me to pour for you?"

Annie was about to say no, but he looked so eager to be helpful that she changed her mind and nodded. She'd already decided to give Elvin the almightiest tip when she left the ship.

She held up a black, floor-length dress. There was a slit up the right leg to her hip, and the straps were very thin. The front and back of the dress plunged down, exposing a lot of skin.

If I'm going to eat in the main dining room, I might as well splash out and wear something really elegant, she thought.

"What do you think, Elvin?" She held the dress in front of her body and turned to face him.

He beamed at her and nodded rapidly. "It's beautiful, Miss Serena. Very nice." He gestured to the tray. "Milk or sugar?"

"Just some milk, please."

Elvin fixed the drink, glancing up at the television as he did. "You are keeping an eye on the weather?"

More like the captain, Annie admitted privately.

"Yes, to see if these sunny conditions will continue," she said. "And calm seas. I'm not good on the water."

"Captain West is an excellent captain. She will make sure we are safe," Elvin assured.

"Have you ever met her?" Annie asked.

Elvin held out the mug for Annie to take. "A few times. She talks to the crew a lot at meetings and parties, but she is very busy, very in demand with the passengers."

She took the mug and sipped. "I bet she is. Are there many female captains?"

Elvin shook his head. "She is the only one for this company. There are others, but not many. She is the best."

Annie chuckled. "Better than the men?"

"Of course," Elvin said.

"Good answer," Annie said.

He grinned. "Can I get you anything else?"

"No, I better get ready before Graham gets here."

"So sorry again—"

"Nothing to be sorry about, you were just doing your job. Don't worry about it. Will probably do me good to get out and get some food," Annie reassured him.

"I will clean your room while you are at dinner," he said.

"Thank you, then I suppose I'll see you tomorrow. Thank you for the coffee."

"If you need anything else, please just call." He smiled at her again before making his way out of the stateroom.

Annie thought he really was the sweetest man. He was very kind and obviously adored his job. She wondered if she was lucky and had encountered the best stateroom attendant by chance, or if everyone on the ship was as dedicated as Elvin.

She looked at her watch again and realised it was time to hustle if she was going to be presentable in time for dinner.

When Graham Shelby did arrive, Annie was very glad she opted to dress up. He wore a dinner jacket, the whole suit probably costing more than his fare on the cruise. Louise was beside him, wearing a tasteful blue gown with lace-capped sleeves.

"Oh my, you look lovely, dear!" Louise said. "Doesn't she look lovely, Graham?"

"You look magnificent," Graham said.

"Thank you, you both look lovely as well." Annie stepped into the hallway.

They started walking, Graham leading the way and Louise taking hold of Annie's arm.

"The menu looks exquisite. They always have lovely food in the main dining room," Louise said. "Do you know how it works?"

"No."

"There's a choice of eight dishes for each course, a starter, a main, and a dessert. So, you're bound to find something you like. We have the drinks package, do you?"

Annie had no idea. "I'm not sure, I didn't book it."

"Show me your pass card," Louise requested.

Annie unlinked her arm from Louise's and dug through her small clutch bag and produced her pass. Louise looked at it and tapped it.

"Yes, you see that there? That's the code for the drinks package. That means you can go anywhere on the ship and order whatever you like, alcohol, coffee, wines, beers, milkshakes. Anything, and it won't be an extra charge," Louise explained.

Annie silently thanked Serena, or Serena's manager, for the convenience of an unlimited bar. Even if she probably wouldn't use it that often.

They all stepped into the elevator, and Graham pressed the button.

Annie looked out of the glass windows at the other elevators and floors. Everything was either glass or open-plan, and she could see people milling about in all manner of clothes. Some people were in swimwear, presumably heading for the pool deck, some in shorts and T-shirts, some in dresses, some in ballgowns. It really was a diverse mix.

"We're members of the Captain's Circle," Graham said.

"Oh, lovely," Annie replied. He sounded boastful, and she wasn't particularly interested in what clubs he had acquired access to through multiple cruises.

"Going on seven years now," he added.

She was saved from having to come up with another reply by the doors opening. They all filed out of the elevator and walked the short distance to the main dining room entrance.

"Ah, Mr and Mrs Shelby, how lovely to see you again," the greeter said. "And your guest, Miss Rubio, a pleasure."

"Thank you," Annie said, adding a little flourish to her hint of an accent.

They were guided along an opulent, large corridor with multiple awards hung on the wood-panelled walls. Up ahead, Annie could hear the bustling of muted conversation and realised that the dining room was absolutely packed solid.

Suddenly, her assumption that she would be able to easily fool everyone into thinking she was Serena Rubio seemed foolish. There could be hundreds of people in that dining room, potentially some Rubio mega-fans.

I'll be fine as long as I stick with the Shelbys and then get back to the room as soon as possible, she reminded herself.

Graham led the way, conversing with various staff members as he went. He cut through the dining room towards a large table in the middle of the room. Annie frowned. The chairs were high-backed and padded with red velvet, with a brass ring on the back to allow the multitude of waiters that surrounded the table to pull the seats out with ease.

It was then that Annie realised something critical.

She was heading straight for the captain's table.

CAPTAIN WEST

CAROLINE GOT to her feet to welcome Mr and Mrs Shelby and their guest. Graham and Louise were platinum members of the Dream Frequent Cruisers Club, members of Dreams Plus, and every other special club that Dream could come up with to flatter monied cruisers. As such, they were very well known amongst the crew.

"Captain West, a delight to see you," Graham greeted her with both hands on her upper arms and a small kiss to each cheek.

"Lovely to see you again, Mr Shelby," Caroline greeted. She turned to Louise. "And so nice to see you, Mrs Shelby, what a lovely dress."

"Thank you, Captain," Louise said. She gestured to the woman stood behind her. "This is our guest, Serena Rubio."

Louise took a small step to the side, and Caroline had to remind herself not to stare. Serena was magnificent in a black, floor-length gown which clung to her body. The swooping neckline left little to the imagination. She realised that Serena was holding out a hand in greeting and quickly reciprocated. Her hand was warm, soft, and very gentle.

"Welcome aboard, Miss Rubio. Is this your first time on *Fortuna*?" Caroline asked.

"It's her first time on a cruise at all," Graham said. "She's an opera singer. Performed with orchestras around the world, even won a Grammy."

Serena narrowed her eyes at Graham. He didn't notice as he was too busy taking his seat to Caroline's left. Louise graciously gestured for Serena to take her seat to Caroline's right, opting to seat herself on Serena's other side. This was presumably so she could talk with Mrs Martin who already sat at the table. The two women often had a strange game of one-upmanship about which of their children were the most accomplished.

Graham quickly introduced Serena to the rest of the table, and everyone sat down. The waiters approached, placing the linen napkins on the diners' laps and handing each of them a menu.

Caroline couldn't help but glance up at Serena Rubio. She was a breath of fresh air to her table. She was young, incredibly attractive, and there was something about her that Caroline couldn't quite put her finger on.

"Are you travelling alone, Miss Rubio?" she asked.

"She is," Graham immediately replied.

Caroline maintained eye contact with Serena, seeing in her eyes that she had already had enough of Graham speaking on her behalf.

"I am," Serena agreed. "My manager booked a trip for me, to rest and relax before my next tour."

"She's performing in Madrid in two weeks," Graham said.

Serena's eyes flashed with anger, and Caroline knew she had to diffuse the situation.

"Graham, have you told Mrs McGregor about your visit to Alaska?" she asked, gesturing to the woman beside him. "I know she spoke about being interested in hearing more about that side of the world."

Graham turned like lightning and started to explain to Laura McGregor when and how she should make arrangements.

Caroline turned back to Serena, who offered her a smile and mouthed a "thank you."

"Welcome aboard, I hope you find plenty of opportunity to rest," Caroline said. "As well as visit some interesting ports."

Serena smiled and then looked down at her menu. Caroline felt surprised. Usually people were happy to engage her in conversation, even wanting to continue talking long after she was ready to leave.

"Do you have any excursions booked?" Caroline tried again.

"No," Serena said, keeping her head down.

"You will have to read our daily newsletter to see if anything appeals," Caroline suggested.

Serena looked up. "Newsletter?"

"Yes, every evening you'll have the latest edition of *DreamFinders* delivered to your room. It will tell you about the next day's port, the weather, all the ship activities. Everything. It's very useful. With a ship as big as *Fortuna*, it's easy to miss out on something."

"I'll look out for it," Serena said before returning her attention to her menu.

Caroline blinked. For some reason, she was being ignored. She didn't know if Serena had an issue with her or simply wasn't interested in her, but Caroline was fairly certain that it was the first time in her career that someone had sat at the captain's table with absolutely zero interest in the captain.

She'd find it infuriating if she didn't find it so intriguing.

"So, you're a performer?" she tried again. She'd spoken with many celebrities in the past, and they were always more than happy to discuss themselves. Sometimes a star felt that their own celebrity was dulled in the presence of the captain and enjoyed the opportunity to reassert their authority.

"I am," Serena agreed. "A singer."

Caroline had expected a little more than that. "Impressive, and a Grammy winner?" Surely, Serena would jump at the chance to mention her awards and accolades.

"Yes." Serena gestured to the menu. "Do you have a recommendation for a good wine to pair with the fish?"

"The Sauvignon Blanc," Caroline replied. "I can order if you'd like?"

Serena nodded. "Please, that would be lovely."

She turned to the assistant waiter. "A glass of the Sauvignon Blanc for Miss Rubio, water for myself."

"Ah, no drinking on duty?" Serena asked.

"Occasionally I indulge, but not often," Caroline admitted.

Graham turned his attention back to them and started

to talk to Caroline about Serena's many performances. Serena had a face like thunder, which Graham completely missed. Caroline nodded along politely, but her mind was focused on Serena.

A celebrity who didn't want to talk about herself was unusual. A young, attractive woman at the captain's table was also unusual. Caroline was fighting to tear her eyes away from Serena. There was something about her that intrigued Caroline.

She hoped it wasn't just her looks. It had been a long time since she'd been seeing anyone, but she prayed she hadn't stooped to the level of drooling over someone purely based on their looks.

She took a sip of her water, listening to Graham and watching as Serena focused on her menu, ignoring the man's snobbish behaviour. There was something about Serena Rubio, but she just couldn't put her finger on it.

LOST AT SEA

Annie barrelled through the door to her stateroom. She tossed her clutch onto the sofa, kicked off her heels, and started to pace the room. The door clicked shut behind her, the automatic closure denying her the satisfaction of slamming the door in frustration.

"Why's it so bloody dark in here?" she wondered aloud.

She patted the wall, searching for the light switch.

After a few moments, she found it and turned on all the switches to illuminate the room. Her bed had been made, the curtains drawn, a towel had been folded into the shape of an elephant on her bed, and a piece of paper and an envelope lay beside it.

"Ah, this is the second round of housekeeping," she realised. "Elephants and post."

She picked up the piece of paper and saw that it was the *DreamFinders* newsletter that Captain West had spoken about. She opened it up and saw a hefty list of activities, opening and closing times for restaurants and bars, shore excursions, drinks offers, and more. She put it on the desk and turned her attention to the envelope.

She ripped it open and pulled out the card.

"An *art auction*?" she said. "This place has an art gallery, too? Does it ever stop?"

She tossed the card and envelope onto the desk and flopped down on the bed.

Dinner had been terrible. Well, not terrible exactly. More like terrifying.

She couldn't believe out of everyone on the ship, out of all the thousands of people, she had been sat right next to the captain, the one person who could presumably smell an imposter *and* have her imprisoned.

The odds of sitting at the captain's table were long, but to be sat next to the woman herself. Able to smell her perfume. There was no escape; every time she dared to look up over her menu, she saw curious eyes watching her.

Annie grabbed a pillow and held it tightly to her chest.

Everyone in the dining room had been watching her. Or rather, watching the captain. But as the person right beside the captain, she could feel the eyes of so many people burrowing into her.

So much for a nice, quiet, relaxing time. So much for hoping that no one would recognise her. So much for trying to keep a low profile.

She was going to kill Graham Shelby. Her fingers dug into the soft pillow. The man had clearly Googled the shit out of Serena Rubio and now knew far more about Serena than Annie did. He was dining off her celebrity, showing off about all the awards that Serena had won and all the places she had performed. As if he had something to do with any of it. Or as if he were a personal friend.

When he was no one.

No, that wasn't quite true.

He was a bully. He'd pushed Annie to a dinner she didn't want to attend so he could be the person who invited a star to the captain's table.

Captain West had softly put him in his place a couple of times, guiding him to talk to someone else, changing the conversation, and even proposing a toast once while he was in the middle of talking.

Of course, Graham was too dense to know what was happening. He was too busy lapping up the praise from the other diners for finding a world-class opera singer and bringing her to them.

She'd felt like a prize bird, some rare species that Graham had managed to trap and show off to all his contemporaries.

Annie unclenched her fingers from the pillow and wrapped her arms around it in a full-body hug.

That part had been horrible, but it could have been far worse if it wasn't for her guardian angel, Captain West.

Caroline was impressive. Commanding, as one would expect from a captain, but also thoughtful, sensitive, and intelligent. Annie felt bad that she had spent most of the evening attempting to avoid talking to her.

It was obviously part of the captain's job to ensure that everyone was having a good time, and Caroline had continued to try to engage Annie in conversation.

The few times that Annie did cave in and talk to the older woman, she noticed a couple of subtle tell-tale signs of attraction. Dilated pupils, licking of lips, wandering eyes. Annie wouldn't be at all surprised if Captain West were a lesbian, or bisexual. She was definitely somehow interested in women.

Seeing someone like Caroline show interest in her had resurrected long-since-buried feelings in Annie. She identified as bisexual and had dated both men and women up until the time she got involved with Diego.

After her relationship with Diego had fizzled out, and she'd been content to simply be in his entourage, she hadn't even thought about dating anyone. Subconsciously she must have known that to bring anyone into that environment would be unfair, even if she hadn't fully realised it herself.

She felt as if she had woken up from a dream. When she looked back, she didn't recognise herself. Only now was she slowly putting together the pieces and realising what a crazy situation she had been in.

She'd genuinely thought she was happy. Now that she was out, she realised she'd been trapped. Her father had always gently chastised her for being impulsive, her mother encouraging her to be spontaneous but never reckless. Somewhere along the line, Annie had gotten muddled.

She groaned. Why did she ever think she could get away with this? She didn't know anything about opera, and now she was stuck on a seven-day cruise with Encyclopaedia Graham who knew everything about her and more.

On top of that, she'd sat next to the captain for two hours, during which time she'd been invited to a multitude of other events. Everything was spiralling out of control. It was only a matter of time before everything came crashing down.

"Stop it," she told herself. "Just… stop."

She took a couple of deep breaths to calm herself down.

"This is better than being in Barcelona," she reminded herself. "At least you're safe for a while. You can do this. Pretend you're an artist. They're flighty, sometimes rude. You just bat people away when they get to close. You can do this."

She swallowed and stared up the ceiling. She wasn't at all sure if she could do it, but she had little choice now.

Running away from Diego Ortega by sea was a lot safer than doing it on land. But at sea, she had to be Serena Rubio and she was stuck in a confined space. Okay, that confined space was one of the biggest cruise ships in the world, but it was still a bubble from which she couldn't escape.

Somehow, she'd managed to take the mess she'd been in and replace it with an entirely different one.

Annie jolted awake. She tossed the pillow to one side and sat up, gasping for breath. It was the nightmare she'd had every night for the last couple evenings. It was a blow-by-blow re-enactment of what she had seen, from the moment she had barged into Diego's office without knocking, to seeing the blood, to running.

In her dreams, she didn't get very far, being tackled on

the stairs long before she managed to leave the luxury townhouse. Luckily, in reality, she had managed to get a lot farther.

She stood and picked up a bottle of complimentary water from the desk, downing half of it in a few short gulps.

Exhaustion must have hit her thick and fast; she'd fallen asleep in an awkward position, still wearing her dress from dinner. Now she felt wide awake. Adrenaline coursed through her, fight-or-flight mode fully engaged.

Unfortunately, she was trapped in a stateroom with nowhere to go.

She put the cap back on the bottle and returned it to the desk, eyeing up the closed curtains. She crossed the room, throwing the curtains open. For some reason, she was surprised to see darkness. Logically she knew it was nighttime, and she knew they were in the middle of the ocean.

Still, the utter absence of light confused her.

She opened the balcony door and stepped outside. She approached the railings and peered out in front of her.

Nothing.

Absolute darkness.

It was unnerving.

It was also cold.

The sound of the ocean hitting the hull of the ship caused her to swallow. She'd tried to get over her fear of the water many times over the last few years, but the addition of the darkness made the sound all the more eerie.

She went back inside, closing the door behind her. She

looked at the bed but knew she was restless, and she'd not be able to sleep.

It was a good time to do something useful, like unpack. She'd had to get ready in a hurry earlier; now she could have a look and see exactly what Serena had packed. And to see how much of it was usable and what Annie would need to try to purchase on board.

She opened the wardrobe door and began to hang up dresses and blouses, fold jeans and shorts, and places shoes in the bottom of the wardrobe.

Serena's feet were slightly smaller than Annie's, so she knew she wouldn't be wearing many of the shoes for any longer than she absolutely had to. She'd quickly slipped off the high heels under the captain's table as soon as she was seated.

After a few minutes, everything was unpacked, and she slipped the empty case under the bed.

"Now what?" she wondered.

She felt claustrophobic, like she needed to get out. She'd never been great at confined spaces, and she wasn't happy with the dark either. She tapped her fingers against her thigh as she looked thoughtfully at the clothes she had put away. There were a pair of thick jeans, a long-sleeved blouse, and a cosy-looking sweater.

She pulled off the dress and put on the comfortable, warmer clothes. If there was ever a time to inspect the ship, surely when everyone else was asleep would be the best time to do so.

She picked up her pass card from the table and slipped out of the room.

A STROLL IN THE NIGHT

Annie took the elevator to the top deck, deck seventeen. The pictogram beside the button promised beach balls, parasols, and waves. It was three o'clock in the morning, and she'd already passed a few people staggering around the ship. Nothing to do with any weather conditions, solely the open bars.

Luckily, the drunken passengers were few and far between. They were also chaperoned by staff members helping them get back to their staterooms.

She hoped the pool deck would be quieter, so she could enjoy a brisk walk around the ship and blow the cobwebs of horrifying dreams straight out to sea.

The elevator doors opened, and she walked through the lobby towards the external sliding doors. She pulled the sleeves of the sweater down over her hands and stepped outside.

The cold wind immediately whipped around her, and she shivered involuntarily. She could hear waves crashing below, and the sound of the water constantly churning.

Crossing over to the railing, she looked down at the sea. Again, everything was black. She saw the occasional sparkle of light being reflected from one of the ship's lights, but after a blink of the eye it was gone.

She lifted her gaze to where the sky should meet the ocean and could see absolutely nothing. It was unsettling to be in a complete absence of light, but she couldn't tear her eyes away.

The sound of a cart rumbling along the deck caused her to turn. A crew member was pushing a large trolley.

"Good evening," he greeted her.

"Hello," Annie replied.

He paused and reached into the trolley and lifted up a pale blue blanket, holding it out to her.

Annie gratefully took the blanket. "Thank you."

He nodded and carried on about his business, leaving Annie to wonder what kind of shift patterns the crew members worked. She unfolded the blanket and wrapped it around her shoulders.

She took a step back from the handrail and walked along the deck. She'd come up to the top deck to explore, not get lost staring at the seemingly black waters below. With so many passengers on board, she assumed that there would be plenty to keep them occupied during days on end at sea.

She quickly came across two pools, one on either side of the deck in front of her. Each was surrounded by whirlpools. In the middle was a large, open space surrounded by handrails, similar to the ones on the edge of the deck.

She crossed towards them and looked down.

"You have got to be kidding me," she breathed.

Around six decks below her was a garden; fairy lights, trees, plants, restaurants, and much more filled an enormous space carved out in the middle of the ship. On each side were countless balconies looking down into the garden area.

"A garden," she whispered. "On a ship."

She took a step back and continued to explore the deck. There were ice cream machines, bars, two more pools, more whirlpools to the point where she ended up losing count of them. At the front of the ship was a large bar with a layered glass roof for protection against the wind.

Near the front was another lobby with a set of elevators. Annie cut through to warm up a little. She passed by an arcade, bathrooms, a shop, and a restaurant.

"And this is just one floor," she mumbled to herself.

She exited the lobby through the other automatic doors and walked the length of the ship, wanting to see what on earth she might find at the rear of the ship on the deck.

She passed by the lobby where she had entered and stumbled upon yet another pool, this one attached to an enormous water slide. On the other side of the deck was a mini-golf course.

Towards the back was a flight of stairs, leading up. Annie was eager to know what else they could possibly dream up for the ship.

She pulled the blanket a little tighter around her and climbed the stairs. At the top there was a spacious seating area and, of course, another bar.

And standing right in the middle, leaning on the railing and looking out to sea, was Captain West.

She'd changed from her white dinner jacket into a thick wool sweater. It was navy blue and ribbed; epaulettes on each shoulder top displayed her rank.

Annie knew she should leave, but she also suspected that the captain wasn't entirely unaware of her presence. She noticed how Captain West had clenched her hands a little and how she was steadfastly staring into nothingness.

She decided to approach, taking her own place at the handrail but still giving the woman some space.

Caroline looked up and smiled. "Hello, Miss Rubio."

"Captain," Annie greeted.

"Can't sleep?" Caroline enquired.

"I might ask you the same thing."

"Maybe I'm on duty?" Caroline suggested.

Annie turned and looked at her thoughtfully. "No, I don't think you are."

Caroline grinned. "What makes you say that?"

"You're the most important person aboard the ship. I doubt you have a shift where you'd be expected to work at three in the morning. You have too many lunches and dinners to attend to. And the back of the ship, open to the elements, seems a strange place to be on duty."

"All true," Caroline confessed.

Silence fell between them, and Annie felt guilty at being so unfriendly over dinner. She didn't want to be rude to Caroline; she'd done nothing to deserve that. Maybe this was the opportunity to make amends; it didn't have to mean anything. Just a peace offering, a signal that Serena Rubio wasn't a complete bitch.

"I've been having trouble sleeping lately," Annie admitted. "At least here there is a lot to see when I'm unable to sleep."

"That's also true," Caroline agreed. "What do you think of *Fortuna*?"

"Honestly?"

Caroline nodded.

"It's a bit bonkers."

Caroline burst out laughing. "How so?"

"There has to be five hundred sun loungers on this deck, four pools... no, five! I lost count of how many whirlpools there are. There's a golf course. A *golf* course. At sea. It's all insanity."

Caroline leaned on her elbow and turned around to look at the ship. "Yes, it is a bit much. But we have five thousand six hundred and thirty-seven passengers on board to entertain."

"Did you just make that up?" Annie asked.

"Make what up?"

"That exact number."

"No." Caroline frowned in confusion. "That is how many passengers we have this sailing."

"And you just happen to remember the exact figure."

"Absolutely. I'm responsible for their safety. I need to know how many people are on board, and I need to ensure that every time we leave a port, everyone is accounted for. I also know that we have two thousand one hundred and eighteen crew members."

Annie blinked. "Wait a minute, so there's... seven thousand..."

"Seven thousand seven hundred and seventy-five souls on board," Caroline said.

Annie shook her head and leaned on the railing. "No wonder you're not asleep."

Caroline took a step closer. "It's not the busiest sailing we've had."

Annie got the message. Caroline didn't want to talk about her lack of sleep, and that suited Annie perfectly. She didn't want to talk about her own nightmares and fear of closing her eyes at night.

"I'm sorry about Graham Shelby," Caroline said. "He can be rather—"

"A boastful, arrogant show-off?" Annie suggested.

"Your words, not mine." Caroline grinned, indicating she agreed wholeheartedly.

"He saw me board and latched onto me," Annie explained. "I'll be happy if I don't see him again."

"That would be a shame," Caroline said.

Annie furrowed her brow in confusion. "Why?"

"Graham loves to bring a guest to the captain's table. If you don't see him again… then I might not see you again."

Annie felt a tingling in her stomach. She was pretty sure that Caroline West was flirting with her, which was wonderful and terrible all at once. Wonderful because Caroline was exactly the kind of woman that Annie was interested in. She adored older women, especially confident ones.

Terrible because Caroline was flirting with Serena Rubio, and Annie was most definitely not a world-class opera singer. There was also the tiny matter that Caroline was the captain of the ship and could report her to the authorities and have her arrested.

There was, of course, the chance that Caroline was just being polite. Part of her job was to socialise and schmooze with the guests. It was late, Annie was tired. There was a good possibility that she was reading too much into the comment.

"I'm sure we will see each other around," Annie said. "Does Mr West ever attend dinner with you?"

"There's no *Mrs* West," Caroline explained, efficiently giving Annie an answer to the gay-or-not dilemma. "Not sailing with Mr Rubio?"

"I'm single," Annie replied. Ordinarily, she'd indicate that she was interested in all genders, but she didn't want to encourage Caroline. Not when she was in the position she was currently in and unable to take things any further.

"I imagine it must be hard to find a partner when you tour as often as you do. How many nights are you away from home?"

Annie's mind went blank. She didn't know where Serena lived or how often she toured. This was dangerous territory, and she was too tired to be able to skilfully navigate the conversation with no facts to hand.

She faked a yawn, smothering it behind a hand. "Many nights—oh, I'm sorry. I don't mean to be rude, but I've suddenly come over very tired."

Caroline stepped forward. "Allow me to walk you back to your cabin."

"Oh, I'll be fine," Annie said. "I wouldn't want to take you out of your way."

"What deck are you on?"

"Fourteen."

"That's the deck the bridge is on. I'll accompany you down."

Annie had no choice. She pushed away from the railing and walked along the deck with Caroline.

"I would have thought the bridge would be on the top deck, so you can see everything?" Annie asked.

"It needs to be in the middle, so we are not disrupting the guests and they are not disrupting us. We're right at the front, but you can't see the bridge from any of the guest areas, only when you are off the ship."

They stepped into the lobby, and Caroline pressed the call button for the elevator.

"There's a lot I don't know about cruising," Annie said.

"Maybe you'll enjoy it and sail with us again in the future?" Caroline suggested.

Annie knew that was extremely unlikely. Her future consisted of running away and certainly not travelling under Serena Rubio's identity.

"Maybe," she said.

The elevator arrived, and they got into the car. Caroline pressed the button for the fourteenth floor. Annie noticed that someone had changed the panel in the floor. It was now Monday.

"Mallorca tomorrow," Caroline said, clearly trying to make conversation.

"Yes, I'm looking forward to it," Annie said.

"Have you been before?"

Annie had no idea. "I think so," she said. "The places… blend… into one." She wanted to wince.

Why did you say that? 'Places blend into one?' You're so

stupid, Annie, she chastised herself.

"You can refresh your memory when we arrive," Caroline said, thankfully ignoring Annie's ridiculous statement.

"I will." Annie rushed out of the elevator and into the long corridor of staterooms, Caroline right behind her.

She paused by her door, only then realising that she still had the blanket around her shoulders. She removed it and wondered what to do with it.

"Would you like me to take that for you?" Caroline offered.

"You can't do that. You're the captain," Annie said.

"I assure you, I've done a lot worse than return a blanket for a guest." Caroline held out her hand.

Annie reluctantly handed the blanket over. "Thank you."

"You're welcome. I do hope you enjoy the rest of your cruise with us, Miss Rubio." Caroline inclined her head, then spun on her heel and walked away.

Annie bit her lip, watching the woman leave. She hated the feeling that it was farewell, that she might not see Caroline again.

Even if it really was important for her to *not* see Caroline again.

Annie knew she couldn't keep up her façade with the woman. She liked her, probably more than she should, and she got the impression that Caroline liked her back. Even in the short amount of time they'd been together, something sparked between them.

Which was dangerous.

Annie sighed, pulled her pass card out of her pocket, and entered her stateroom.

HARMLESS FLIRTING

CAROLINE WALKED ONTO THE BRIDGE, bleary-eyed and frustrated. She entered the Security Command Centre at the back of the bridge and looked at the screens over the shoulders of the team working in there.

She felt on edge, annoyed with herself, a feeling she hadn't been able to shake off since the early hours of that morning.

After escorting Serena Rubio to her stateroom, Caroline had gone to her own rooms and proceeded to mentally kick herself for her poor choice of words during their conversation.

Caroline had never been one to sit and stew over discussions. She was far too busy to dwell on things that couldn't be changed. But this particular conversation had stayed with her.

On the deck in the middle of the night, she had said some things that may well be misconstrued. Suggesting that she was disheartened at the prospect of not seeing Serena at the captain's table again could have been interpreted as flirting. And quizzing Serena over the possible difficulties of finding a partner was clumsy.

She wanted to wince but maintained a steely expression. The bridge of *Fortuna* was not the place to have a personal crisis.

She was intrigued by Serena, and in other circumstances she would possibly consider attempting to identify the attractive woman's sexual preferences. She might even reach out to her.

But this wasn't other circumstances.

Serena Rubio was a guest aboard, and the last thing she needed or deserved was the captain sniffing around her like some puppy in heat. Not to mention that Caroline must have been deluded to think that someone like Serena would toss her a second glance even if she were interested in women.

The late hour, the darkness, the surprise arrival of the fascinating woman had all combined to make Caroline see something that clearly wasn't there. As a result, she'd said a couple of things that may have been taken as flirting despite her best attempts to remain professional.

"Why have those papers not been filed yet?" She pointed to the engine room reports which were now five minutes late.

The crewman jumped up and grabbed the papers from the file. "Sorry, Captain, I'll do it now."

She stalked away from him, focusing her attention on the navigation station instead. She was annoyed with herself and taking it out on the team, which wasn't fair but was an unjust perk of being the captain.

Thomas stood beside her. "Everything okay?"

He could always read her, knew when she was in a foul mood. He also never let things go. She'd learnt a long time ago that it was better to be honest with him from the start.

"Just something I said to a guest," she said.

"Will there be a complaint?" Thomas queried.

Caroline snapped her eyes up to him. "I certainly hope not."

The idea that Serena would make a complaint hit her in the gut. Not just because she'd have to explain herself to management, that she could deal with, but the thought that Serena would be so uncomfortable with Caroline's awkward phrasing that she'd feel compelled to object in an official capacity.

She would never want to be the source of such discomfort, never had been in the past, and couldn't have ever imagined it happening, but there was something about Serena that just knocked her off kilter.

"What did you say?"

"I…" She looked around the SCC, cautious of the fact they could be overheard. She took his arm and walked him onto the bridge, to one of the wings where they could speak privately.

"I was talking with a guest," Caroline said slowly, stalling.

"Yes?" Thomas folded his arms and looked at her, a grin on his face. He knew it was embarrassing, and he was revelling in it.

"And I might have said something that might have possibly sounded… like I… was flirting."

She turned away, looking towards the port of Palma that was fast approaching.

"Were you?"

She turned to glare at him. "No!"

He chuckled and held his hands up. "Just asking. You are allowed, you know. There's no rule against a bit of harmless flirting."

"There are rules about harassment," Caroline reminded him.

"I very much doubt you harassed anyone. I'm sure it's fine."

"It's not fine, she may have taken it the wrong way," Caroline explained.

"Would it be the end of the world if she thought you had flirted with her?" Thomas asked. "Is she *really* ugly?"

"No!" This time she slapped his arm to stop the teasing.

He grinned knowingly. "Oh, she's really not. Is she hot?"

"I'm not having this conversation with you." She looked towards the port again. It was time to prepare to dock. "We better get ready."

He softly put his hand on her arm. "Seriously, I wouldn't worry about it. Whatever you said, it can't have been that bad. And if there was a misunderstanding, then you only have to avoid her for the next six days."

She inclined her head in agreement. He walked back towards the centre bridge controls and started to issue orders, preparing the team for the docking procedure.

He was right. What she had said wasn't that bad. If she were honest, what bothered her most was the fact that she felt a little unhinged in the presence of Serena. Something about her fascinated Caroline. In many ways she wanted to learn more about her; in others she wanted to avoid her and focus on the other guests aboard.

There was something different about Serena, something almost dangerous. Caroline could sense it, and she was somehow drawn to it, which unnerved her greatly. She wasn't used to feeling this way. She'd been alone for years, happily so. It was unexpected, to say the least, for her to suddenly take an interest in someone. Especially someone so obviously out of her league like Serena. She had to be half her age, and a famous singer at that.

Caroline snorted a little laugh to herself. It was ridiculous. She just needed to push all thoughts of Serena Rubio to one side and get on with her job.

GOOD MORNING

CAROLINE STOOD by the navigation console, watching the harbour pilot struggle with the overwhelmingly technical systems aboard *Fortuna*.

It wasn't unusual for ports to want to send their own team aboard to assist with docking the ship. Ports were expensive places, and docks could be easily damaged by a large ship hitting the mooring too hard.

As guests in the country, it was sometimes up to the able command team to step aside and allow the locals to steer the ship safely into position.

However, Caroline always felt as if she was teaching a toddler to drive a car, watching the dribbling youngster not know what they were doing and almost driving them into a tree.

Fortuna's systems were very different to other ships. Technological advancements in steering and fuel consumption had made the ship almost indecipherable to the average harbour pilot.

She, and four members of her crew, stood by and

watched the pilot try his best. They were all ready to jump in and avert disaster if needed.

After a lot of back and forth, the ship was almost in position. It was mere centimetres from being in place, but it looked like the pilot was about to push the incorrect button. Caroline couldn't stand the dithering any longer. She stepped forward and pressed a couple of buttons and took control of the stick to gradually press the stern of the ship where it needed to be for the mooring ropes to be attached.

"Thank you for your assistance," she said to the pilot. "I believe Lucia has your paperwork."

She gestured for Lucia to take the pilot into the SCC so the rest of the crew could get on with the job of securing the ship, preparing paperwork, clearing customs and security, securing the gangplank, and advising the passengers that they were able to depart the ship.

The moment he was out of the way, everyone sprang into action. Caroline stayed back, overseeing and observing as her team did their jobs. Now and then she stepped forward and offered advice, but for the most part she allowed Thomas to take the lead on things.

The bridge was full of activity for the next twenty minutes, and soon enough they received word from the port that they had completed all the necessary procedures. Passengers could go ashore to the Spanish island of Mallorca.

"I'll go to my office and make the announcement," Caroline told Thomas.

"Great, I'll catch you later on for the meeting with Dom."

She swiped her card and left the bridge. She walked down the narrow corridors in the forward crew-only section of deck fourteen towards her own rooms.

A few seconds later she entered her office. Her window had the perfect view of the Mallorca port, and she sat in her high-backed, upholstered leather chair. She shook the mouse to wake up her computer; her inbox was already out of control, but that was something she'd deal with later.

She picked up her telephone handset and called the telecoms room.

"Good morning, Captain West," the operator answered quickly.

"Good morning, can you patch me through for an all-rooms announcement?" she asked.

"Yes, ma'am. The countdown will begin… now."

Little beeps sounded through the earpiece, and she counted them down knowing that when they stopped, she would be broadcasting to every part of the ship, every public area, and every stateroom.

"Good morning, good morning, good morning," she greeted.

She'd said the same thing every morning since she started doing such announcements. She knew some people would be in bed, some people would be eating, some would be in the shower. The repetition was a polite and friendly way of postponing the content of her announcement, allow people to stop what they were doing if they wished to listen to her.

"This is Captain West, and it's my pleasure to welcome you to the beautiful island of Mallorca. It is eight-fifteen, and the gangway is now open on deck three for you to disembark and enjoy all the sights, sounds, and of course foods of Palma."

She swivelled in her seat to look at one of the many screens embedded into the wall behind her desk. It displayed everything from weather reports, to operational systems, to the ship-wide CCTV system.

"The weather today will be a comfortable twenty-four degrees, so don't forget the sun lotion. Remember, if you are going ashore today to take your pass card and a form of photo identification with you. If you have any questions about any of our excursions, you'll find many knowledgeable and friendly members of our shore excursions team around the ship this morning. Make sure you are back aboard by three-thirty. That's three-thirty for all aboard. Thank you and enjoy Mallorca."

She ended the call and picked up a remote control and started to scroll through some of the camera views on the CCTV screens. Guests were already waiting by the gangway, even though they had docked fifteen minutes earlier than stated in the itinerary. Some people were eager to get off the ship and spend as much time as possible in the destinations.

She scanned through a few decks, checking that everything was in order. Having access to every single public area of the ship was a fantastic feature of the newer cruise liners. In the past, she'd had to go to the security office. Now she could pinpoint any area, or just browse to check everything was in order at any time.

Her thumb hovered over the button she'd been clicking.

Serena Rubio was already on the sun deck, taking advantage of the early Mediterranean sun. Caroline swallowed hard. She really was an extremely attractive woman. The swimsuit she wore highlighted what the dress from the night before had only hinted at. Long, toned legs, a flat stomach, and ample breasts.

She quickly changed the camera and looked away from the screen entirely.

She shook her head, furious at herself for even looking. In all her time as captain she had never, ever used the CCTV system for anything other than security purposes. She'd immediately fire anyone who gawked at a passenger in the way she just had.

"What is it about her?" she wondered to herself.

She turned back to her desk and opened up a browser window. She typed Serena's name into the search bar. Perhaps finding out more about the woman would satisfy her curiosity, and she would be released from whatever pull Serena unknowingly had on her.

The first thing that came up was a Wikipedia page. Caroline clicked the link and started to hungrily read all the information it provided, which admittedly wasn't much. She stared at the pictures on the profile, turning her head to the side as she looked even closer.

"Has she had work done?" she mused.

She let out a long sigh and closed the window down. She had work to do; she didn't have time to research one of the passengers, not to mention that it seemed wrong to do so. With another sigh, she turned her attention to her email inbox.

DINOSAUR ON BOARD

"Can I get you something from the bar?"

Annie opened her eyes and raised her hand to shield her gaze from the sun. The staff member wore a crisp, white polo-necked T-shirt and dark blue shorts. He spun an empty drinks tray on his finger.

She'd been outside for a couple of hours and had to admit that sitting in the sun was thirsty work.

"Sure, why not. Can I have a piña colada?"

"Absolutely. Can I have your pass card?"

She handed it over, and he glanced at it and smiled. "I'll be back in a couple of minutes, Miss Rubio."

"Thank you." Annie lay back down on the sunbed. She let out a moan of pleasure as she enjoyed the hot rays of sun beating down on her.

Around five o'clock that morning, she had come to the conclusion that if she was going to be found out and either arrested by Caroline or killed by Diego, she might as well be well rested.

She was on a luxury cruise ship for the first, and probably last, time in her life, so she might as well enjoy it a little. It could be the last opportunity she had to sunbathe, the last piña colada she'd drink. She might as well enjoy herself while she could. Recent events had proved that she really never knew what tomorrow might bring.

With that stomach-churning realisation, she'd gone to the on-board shop and purchased some swimwear. As with the underwear situation, it felt wrong to wear Serena's swimwear. Now she was decked out in Dream merchandise and enjoying some quiet rest and relaxation.

The ship seemed to be fairly empty, many people having disembarked to look at Palma and the rest of the island of Mallorca. The few who did remain were spread out among the restaurants or on the sundeck.

Annie had noticed a couple of people looking in her direction. Paranoia had started to seep in. She didn't know if they were just looking around, as people tended to do, or if they had heard who she was supposed to be.

She'd already decided to spend the afternoon in the ship's internet café to conduct some discreet research on Serena. If everyone else was Googling her, she better do so as well.

"Here you are, Miss Rubio, one piña colada."

She took the drink and her pass card. "Thank you so much."

"You're welcome." He winked and walked away, continuing to spin the empty drinks tray as he did.

He was cute but definitely not Annie's type.

As if on cue, Caroline West and another officer passed the waiter. They were deep in conversation, but Caroline looked up and their eyes met. Annie saw the hesitation in them and wondered what Caroline would choose to do.

It became quickly clear that the war between Caroline's desire to escape and her courtesy was won by her sense of duty when she paused at a polite distance from Annie's lounger.

"Miss Rubio," Caroline said.

"Captain West," Annie replied.

"This is my staff captain, Thomas Barridge," Caroline introduced her conversation partner.

"Two captains?" Annie asked.

"More like about eight," Thomas replied. "Pleasure to meet you, Miss Rubio. I'll leave you to it, Captain; I have a meeting in the engine room."

Caroline looked as if she was going to argue, but Thomas had already continued walking. Caroline turned to look at Annie before averting her eyes and looking behind her, over the railings.

"Did you decide not to sample the delights of Mallorca after all, Miss Rubio?" Caroline enquired, still not looking directly at her.

She's embarrassed, Annie realised. It was adorable that someone as confident and commanding as Caroline was so clearly afraid of a bit of skin on show. Annie sat up a little and draped a towel over her shoulders, covering herself a little to save Caroline's blushes.

"No, I thought I'd enjoy the sun in case the weather turns," Annie replied.

Caroline's eyes flickered down, meeting Annie's. Her pupils were dilated, and Annie had to hide her smirk at how she seemed to affect the captain.

"You can tune in to channel 41 for my weather round-up. I'm afraid it's rather boring for some, pressure systems, wind speeds, that kind of thing, but I do also give some information on temperatures."

"I know. I've been watching," Annie admitted.

When she'd returned to her room the previous evening, sleep had continued to elude her. In the end, she'd turned on the television and fallen asleep listening to Caroline talk about the fast-moving high pressure in the Balearic Sea.

Then she had woken up a couple of hours later to the announcement that they had arrived in Palma.

Good morning, good morning, good morning, Annie thought, remembering waking up to the rich voice coming through the speaker in the ceiling. Caroline West was fast becoming a fixture of Annie's day.

"Well, then you'll know that we have some strong winds expected tonight and that Marseille will be quite windy," Caroline said.

"So, I heard. Luckily, I intend to stay on the ship at Marseille," Annie said.

In truth, she intended to stay on the ship as much as possible. It seemed safer, if anything could really be considered safe anymore. Her only concern was that it might appear a little strange if she never ventured off the ship, but she'd deal with that when she got to it. Only yesterday she'd decided to never leave her room. Now she was sunbathing on the top deck.

Impulsive Annie Peck, striking again.

"You toured there, didn't you?" Caroline asked.

Annie wasn't sure if this was a fact that Graham had

mentioned at dinner or if Caroline had been conducting her own research. Panic flashed through her like a cold bolt of lightning. She pulled the towel a little tighter around her and shrugged.

"I don't recall. My manager books things, and I am so busy... places merge into one," Annie said.

Caroline looked confused and opened her mouth to say something when a crew member approached her.

"Captain, we have a twenty-sixty on deck two," he said.

Caroline nodded. "I'll be there in a moment."

He saluted her and left.

"What's a twenty-sixty?" Annie asked.

"A code word to prevent passengers from knowing what is happening," Caroline explained with a grin.

"I bet I can guess." Annie sipped at her piña colada.

Caroline chuckled. "You can try, if you like."

"Man overboard?"

Caroline shook her head. "On deck two? With no windows?"

"Maybe not," Annie agreed. "Fire?"

"No."

"Dinosaur," Annie said confidently, nodding.

Caroline's smile grew wider. "Dinosaur? Is that what you're going with?"

"Absolutely, there's a dinosaur rampaging through deck two. That or a stowaway."

"More likely that we'd have a dinosaur on board," Caroline said. "We don't get stowaways; security is too tight."

As a child, Annie wouldn't have been able to resist

such temptation. She would have had to announce immediately that she had managed it, done the impossible, broken through the defences, and then be in an enormous amount of trouble.

Adult Annie knew better, but the itch to say something bubbled in her and had to be tampered down.

"So, what would you do if a stowaway did manage to get on board?" she fished.

"I'd put them in the brig and drop them at the next port," Caroline said in such a casual way that Annie really did believe that it had never happened.

"And a dinosaur?" she asked, her heart pounding.

"Same thing, just a bigger brig." Caroline grinned.

Annie smiled. "I should let you go and catch that dinosaur then. It was good seeing you again."

"You, too." Caroline hesitated a moment. "Don't forget to top up the sun lotion." An almost imperceptible wince crossed her face before she turned on her heel and walked away.

Annie picked up her piña colada and took a few gulps. Why did she keep talking to Caroline? It would have been far more sensible to ignore her entirely. Caroline seemed to be a kind person and obviously very dedicated to her job. If she knew who Annie really was, then she would surely lock her up and throw her off the ship at the first opportunity.

If she handed Annie over to any local authority, it wouldn't be long before Diego would find her. His network had links with the police all over Europe.

It was clearly stupid to keep talking to Caroline West;

the risk of discovery and the resulting actions were far too high.

But Annie liked her.

She was capable and kind, funny and a little adorably awkward. There was something comforting about her. While Annie knew that it was foolish to talk to her, she also suspected that she'd continue to do it.

No, she told herself firmly. *Try to avoid her. Be polite, but nothing more.*

She sipped some more of her cocktail and tried to push aside the image of Caroline West's endearing flushed cheeks as she attempted to look away from Annie's swimsuit-clad body.

She is cute, though, she allowed.

PERFECTLY WELL-JAZZED

CAROLINE STABBED at the keyboard key which refreshed the passenger manifest list. It was five minutes until the gangway was supposed to be closed, but there were still three hundred and seventeen people not accounted for.

It was the same at every single port. There would be some who left it to the very last minute to return to *Fortuna*. Some who would happily delay the whole ship, without any consideration for others.

Thankfully, the all-aboard time was at least an hour earlier than they technically needed to set sail to allow for this exact situation, but it still irked Caroline that so many people were disorganised and late. It seemed careless at best.

Technically, as master of *Fortuna*, she could choose to go without them, as long as they weren't on any of Dream's managed excursion, but the publicity and corporate backlash would be too extreme to even think about it. She had only ever left passengers behind at ports in matters of extreme emergencies.

In the past, she'd waited nearly three hours for someone when their tour bus had broken down. Another time, she'd sent a member of the crew in a taxi to find a lost couple who had called the ship in a terrified panic.

Every day at sea was a new surprise.

She pressed the button again. More were aboard, but there were still more than she liked unaccounted for considering the time. She turned to look out of her office window; coaches were pulling into the port, hopefully filled with her missing passengers.

There was a knock on the door. She turned back to face her desk. "Come in."

Dominic walked in, looking as laidback and relaxed as ever. "How are we doing?"

"Just under three hundred unaccounted for," Caroline said. She gave him a look that told him that she blamed him entirely.

"Hey, it's not my fault." He sat in one of the visitor's chairs.

"Can we make the signage at the port a little bigger?" she asked. "Emphasise the all-aboard times?"

"We could write it in the sky to an orchestral piece, and no one would take any notice," Dominic told her. "As more people start cruising, they become more casual about the whole thing. A first-time cruiser rarely leaves the port unless they are on a planned excursion. Someone on their tenth cruise will push it to the limit. Not a lot we can do about human nature."

She stabbed the button again. The number would turn from red to green when the numbers balanced. She didn't need to read the exact number unaccounted for; it was still red and that was all that mattered.

"I thought we'd do something different for the welcome aboard tonight," Dominic suggested.

"Why?" Caroline knew she sounded petulant, but it was the one event she had any say over.

"Jazz it up," he said.

She slowly met his gaze, exhausted with the constant need for everything on board to be dialled up to ten.

"It's perfectly well-jazzed. Can't we leave it as it is?"

"But if we—"

"Dom, remind me what it's called?" Caroline interrupted.

"The welcome aboard—"

"No, say the whole thing."

He sighed. "The Captain's Mix and Mingle Welcome Aboard Gathering."

"There," Caroline said. "*My* mix and mingle. Mine. And I like it the way it is. It's elegant and perfectly balanced. People mix and mingle, everyone is welcomed. We gather. It's faultless the way it is."

"Okay, but at least when I welcome you, let me get the crowd—"

"No, whatever you're about to suggest, no. Let's just leave it the way it is, shall we?" It may have been phrased as a question, but she knew Dominic was left in no doubt that it was anything but.

Caroline stabbed the button again. Still red.

Dominic was forever trying to change certain events, tweaking things based upon customer feedback. Caroline usually didn't mind, but this was *her* event. She got to introduce the key members of her team, welcome the guests properly, and then talk with them one on one.

For an hour, she had the entire promenade to herself. She controlled the music, the speeches, the drinks. Everything.

If Dominic had his way, the bridge crew would probably be asked to arrive on a float of golf buggies with glitter cannons firing from the sides. Or possibly a conga line.

She shuddered.

"Fine," he allowed. "I do need to talk to you about the drill tomorrow. You said eleven, but I was wondering if we could make it ten-thirty? We have a round of lightning bingo starting at eleven."

Caroline pressed the button again. She never thought she'd be in an environment where bingo would take priority over her crew safety drills.

"Sure, let Thomas know. He is organising the drill," she said.

Safety obviously came first, but the drill could easily be moved. Presumably the bingo schedule was already printed and in the latest edition of *DreamFinder*.

The phone rang and she picked it up. "Caroline West."

"Captain, we have a call from one of the buses. They're delayed."

Caroline looked at Dominic. "A delayed tour bus? I see."

Dominic mouthed an apology and then jutted his thumb towards the door as he stood up to make his escape. She rolled her eyes. Tour buses, delayed or not, were definitely his remit.

As he opened the door, Thomas entered, and the two men passed each other. Caroline gave instructions to the crew member on the end of the phone and then hung up.

"A bus is delayed," she explained. "They think they'll be ten minutes delayed."

"So, about thirty minutes then?" Thomas asked.

"At least."

Thomas nodded. "Okay, I'll keep an eye on it. What did Dom want?"

"He wanted to jazz up my mix and mingle."

Thomas smothered a laugh behind his hand. "And?"

"I told him it's suitably jazzed, and we agreed to leave it. He also asked to move the staff drill tomorrow forward by half an hour because of bingo. I told him to talk to you about it."

"Okay, I'll let everyone know. Do you still want me to take your place at the early dinner tonight?" he asked.

"Yes, please. I need a couple of hours break before the welcome aboard in the promenade," she explained.

In truth, Caroline was hiding from Serena in case the Shelbys managed to twist her arm and encourage her to attend dinner again. For some reason she seemed to be getting tongue-tied around the woman.

It wasn't like she attended every dinner anyway; it was usual for her counterparts to take her place at any moment in case she had to deal with ship's business. Which was sometimes a cup of coffee in the blissful silence of her stateroom.

"No problem. Then I'll see you behind guest services to go up to the walkway around ten to eight?"

She nodded. "And, I think I'll take a couple of hours

ashore when we get to Marseille tomorrow. I have some shopping to do."

She didn't need a specific reason to go off the ship, but she always gave one, even if it was completely fabricated. She had no shopping to get; she just wanted a bit of time to herself.

She didn't mind admitting that the whole Serena Rubio business had unsettled her a little. Her reaction to the woman was unexpected. Caroline wasn't used to someone distracting her so easily. Some time off the ship and away from Serena would surely do her good.

"Get me something nice," Thomas quipped.

"I will," Caroline promised, her mind already on the tackiest possible souvenir she could find.

THE BEST HOT ROAST BEEF SANDWICHES IN THE WORLD

ANNIE SLAMMED her stateroom phone down. Graham Shelby was a persistent man, she'd give him that much. He'd left two voicemails and then called to invite her to dine with him and Louise that evening.

When she'd said no, he'd sounded very confused, and Annie had to admit she'd found that very satisfying. He'd floundered for a few minutes, explaining that he'd already, presumptuously, reserved a space for her at the captain's table.

Annie stuck her ground and said no. She even said she'd call him if she was interested in dining with them in the future and asked him not to call again. Then she'd hung up. Forcefully.

She didn't care about Serena's reputation; Graham was only interested in her for her apparent celebrity. To use her as a trinket to show off.

The whole thing made Annie feel cross. It was too similar to what Diego had done with her, using her youth and looks as an adornment for himself. Unfortunately,

Annie had been in a bad place when she'd met Diego, and so she'd gone along with whatever he'd suggested.

Looking back, she was disgusted with herself.

A knock on the door pulled her away from her thoughts. She looked through the peephole at Elvin's smiling face. Annie couldn't help but feel delighted at seeing him.

She opened the door. "Evening, Elvin. How are you today?"

"I'm good, Miss Serena. Did you have a nice day? Enjoy Palma?" Elvin held out an envelope.

Annie took the envelope. "I stayed on the ship. Enjoyed the sun. Do you get to do that?"

Elvin nodded. "Yes, when I am off work. I go to the quiet areas by the sports pool and sit on the chairs overlooking the water. Listen to music and watch the sea."

She tore open the envelope. It was an invitation to the casino.

"Would you like me to come back later to clean the room?" Elvin asked.

"You can do it now, if I'm not going to be in your way?" Annie suggested. She had no idea where she'd eat dinner or what her schedule would be. She didn't want to send Elvin away only to return at the same time he did later that evening.

He dropped a plastic doorstop to the floor and wedged it under the door. He entered the room and started to make the bed.

"I'm not eating in the main dining room tonight," Annie said. "Do you have any suggestions where I should eat instead?"

"Café Cruise," Elvin replied quickly. "It's on the promenade. They have the best hot roast beef sandwiches in the world."

Annie laughed. "In the world?"

"Yep." He smoothed down the sheets on the bed. "And I've travelled everywhere, so I know."

"Well, then Café Cruise it is," Annie said.

She opened the wardrobe and looked at her outfits. It was still surreal to be looking at someone else's clothes; each time she opened the wardrobe she expected to see her own outfits, but they were gone, probably ripped to shreds by an angry Diego.

She shook her head and returned her attention to the wardrobe and what she would wear that evening. The purchase of underwear, swimwear, and a new pair of heels in the on-board shop that morning meant that she now had everything she needed.

She was no stranger to going commando now and then, especially in a tight dress, but she wasn't prepared to do that for the entire cruise.

"Are you going to see Marseille?" Elvin asked.

"I wasn't planning to," Annie confessed.

"It is a very nice town," he explained. "Very... history."

"Historic?"

He snapped his fingers. "Yes, historic. Lots of boats in the marina. Churches, old buildings, museums. Very nice."

Annie pulled a pair of skinny jeans and a T-shirt from the wardrobe.

"Where are you from, Elvin?"

"Haiti, ma'am," he replied.

"How long have you worked for Dream?"

"Eight years."

"Wow, do you like it?"

Elvin stopped fluffing the pillow and looked up at her with a wide grin. "I love it. I get to see the world, meet all kind of people. This ship is like my family."

"Do you have a family back home?"

He nodded. "My parents. I Skype with them every day." He looked down and carried on making the bed.

Annie felt a tightness in her chest. She shook it off and sat on the sofa to remove her strappy sandals.

"Eight years. Have you been on *Fortuna* all that time?" she asked.

"No, only for three years."

"Always the same job?"

"Yeah. They try to promote me, but I like it here."

Annie chuckled. "You've turned down a promotion?"

"Every year they ask, every year I say no. I don't want to be supervisor, all the stress and responsibility. No, I like my life. I clean in the morning and then again in the evening. My nights I spend with my friends on the ship; in the afternoon I sometimes go ashore. It's perfect."

"It does sound pretty perfect," Annie agreed.

Elvin left the room to get something from his cleaning trolley. Annie looked again at the casino invitation he'd handed her when he arrived.

"Does everyone get these?" she asked when Elvin came back in.

"Not everyone, a lot of people," he admitted.

"So, I don't have to go?"

"You don't have to do anything; you're on holiday," he told her.

She put the invitation back into the envelope, folded the whole thing in half, and then placed it in the wastepaper bin.

"Tell me about your family," she asked. "They sound lovely."

THE MIX AND MINGLE

Elvin had been right. It was the best sandwich in the world. The view was pretty exquisite as well. Café Cruise was right in the middle of the promenade that cut through the centre of the ship on deck five.

Sitting at the table just outside the café, it would have been easy for Annie to have completely forgotten that she was on board a cruise ship. There were New York, Italian, and French influences as you walked along the promenade. The floor was designed to look like a stone walkway, the sculptures looked like trees, and the walls were heavily themed with murals.

Café Cruise was in the middle of the promenade, not too far from where Annie had entered the ship. Those doors were now sealed off; a mural of a Tuscan vineyard made the exit practically invisible unless you knew what you were looking for.

The ceiling was high, allowing for two extra levels of bars, each with a balustrade looking down onto the promenade. Portions of the ceiling were glass, letting in natural light from the garden which was located directly above them.

Annie knew precisely nothing about ship building, but she assumed the *Fortuna* was an incredible feat of design and engineering. She'd never expected a cruise ship to have so much open space.

Farther along the promenade, on the opposite side of the street, was an Irish pub. On a balcony above the pub a band was playing jazz music. Annie tapped her foot along to the tune while tucking into her second sandwich.

"Ma'am?"

She looked up to see a waiter with a tray filled with Champagne flutes. She looked around and noticed that other passengers were grabbing glasses and milling around the area.

"Thank you." She took a flute. He moved on to the next person before she had the chance to ask what the occasion was.

She shrugged and took a sip. It was nice, much nicer than the cheap Champagne that she'd been given when she boarded the ship.

Suddenly the band's speakers were cranked up, and they played some kind of introduction music that made Annie jump in surprise. On a balcony that crossed the promenade, a man wearing a tuxedo and holding a microphone appeared.

Annie had seen him on the television; he was something to do with the entertainment team, and his face was everywhere.

"Good evening, good evening, ladies and gentlemen, I'm Dominic Yang, your hotel director."

That's it, she thought. *Dom.*

She placed the flute on the table and took another bite of her sandwich, waiting for him to introduce whatever band or singer was about to perform.

"We are so pleased that you are here with us on *Fortuna*. We know you could have chosen other cruises; we know you could have chosen another ship. We're grateful that you chose us because we feel, and we hope that you'll agree, that we are the best."

Passengers around Annie started to applaud loudly.

"The best ship," Dominic said over the applause. "The best crew!" He shouted to more applause. "And of course, the best captain!"

Annie coughed around her sandwich. She looked up at the balcony, hoping that Dominic wasn't about to do what she thought he was about to do.

"Ladies and gentlemen, please put your hands together and welcome our wonderful captain, the best in the business, Captain Caroline West, the master of *Fortuna*!"

Caroline, clutching her own microphone, stepped out onto the balcony to thunderous applause. She wore the formal white jacket that Annie had seen her wear at dinner, black pressed trousers, and the ever-present crisp white shirt and black tie.

Annie looked around the promenade. Passengers were clapping loudly and even whooping with excitement, many staring up at Caroline with adoration. To these people, Caroline was as popular as any rock star.

"Thank you, thank you," Caroline said.

Annie turned her attention to Caroline, unable to stop herself from smiling. She'd tried to avoid the woman but somehow ended up with a front-row seat for some kind of captain's party.

"Welcome to *Fortuna*," Caroline said. "On behalf of all of the crew, thank you for choosing to sail with us. Believe it or not, there are five thousand six hundred and thirty-seven guests on board. And you come from thirty-nine countries."

The audience whooped in excitement.

"And a special 'welcome back' to the two thousand seven hundred Dreams Plus members who have again chosen to sail with us. Thank you for your loyalty; we appreciate it more than we can say."

Annie sipped her Champagne and watched Caroline's casual movements. The way she turned back and forth to address all the people in the promenade below her. The way she smiled and waved at people who waved to her. The way she seemed so poised and in control.

She's magnificent, Annie thought.

"While I'd like to take all the of credit myself…" Caroline winked. "I have to admit that I do have the best crew in the business. You've already met our fantastic hotel director, Dom, but now I'd like to introduce you to the core team that ensures this cruise will be the very best cruise. Firstly, please welcome my second-in-command, our staff captain, Thomas Barridge."

The band played some welcome music, and Thomas walked onto the balcony, waving to the applauding crowd below.

"Oh, isn't he handsome in his uniform?" Annie overheard an elderly lady saying.

"I bet he's handsome out of it!" another lady quipped.

Annie shook her head and laughed. The crew of *Fortuna* really were celebrities to everyone on board. It was fascinating to see. In the small ecosystem of the ship, there was still hierarchy.

Thomas gave a little speech about himself before introducing the activities director, who did the same before introducing someone else. Annie tuned out as the introductions went from person to person.

All she could focus on was Caroline.

Which irked her no end. She shouldn't be focusing on Caroline; she shouldn't be anywhere near her, but she couldn't bring herself to get up and leave.

In the end, a dozen people stood on the balcony, including five women, a man in a chef's hat, and someone in engineer's overalls.

The promenade was full of applauding guests, happily scooping up the free alcohol and toasting the people who made the ship run smoothly.

Dominic encouraged people to applaud more loudly before announcing that the captain and her crew would be entering the promenade to socialise with the passengers.

Annie's heart rate spiked.

She'd thought Caroline would remain on her lofty balcony, but now she was coming down to Annie's level. She didn't know if she should run or if she should stay and act aloof. She didn't even know if she *could* act aloof.

She was frozen in her inability to make a decision, watching as the crew members descended a staircase. Annie had practically made her mind up to leave when she noticed a woman in a white lab coat whisper in Caroline's ear as they approached the final step.

Caroline threw her head back in laughter, her eyes twinkling mischievously.

Who is she? Annie wondered.

The jealousy that surged through her was unmistakable. She snatched up her glass and sipped more Champagne, glaring at the mystery woman over the narrow rim.

Clearly a doctor, she thought.

Whoever she was, she was close with Caroline. They walked side by side, hands touching. Annie tore her gaze away. The flash of possessiveness was another warning sign that she was far too close to Caroline.

It angered her that she had no control over the feelings she seemed to have developed. It also fascinated her. She'd never been one to fangirl over people. She'd met Hollywood stars who had been holidaying in Barcelona and hardly gave them a second look.

But Caroline West was occupying her thoughts more than she should.

"Can I get you another drink?" a passing waiter paused to ask her.

The service aboard *Fortuna* was impeccable, and she felt that every member of staff she encountered genuinely wished to help her. She wondered how much of that was training and how much of that was the ethos that Caroline probably insisted upon.

She looked at the Champagne flutes and bit her lip.

"No, I've had a couple today, no more alcohol for me," she said.

"I can get you a coffee. Tea?" he offered.

Annie saw Caroline making her way around the

crowds. If she left now, there was a chance that Caroline would see her hightailing it away.

"Could I have a coffee? A latte if that's possible?"

"Absolutely, one latte coming up." Annie handed him her pass card, and he walked towards the bar area of Café Cruise to fetch her drink.

Annie felt something touch her foot. She looked down under the table and saw a cuddly giraffe toy.

She picked it up and looked behind her. There was a young toddler in a stroller facing her and giggling. Annie held up the toy.

"Is this yours?" she asked the toddler.

The mother, a middle-aged brunette, looked up. "Oh, I'm so sorry! Is she throwing her toys again?"

"She might have dropped it," Annie defended the girl, though she could see from the cheeky smile that probably wasn't the case. She handed the toy back. "How is she enjoying the cruise?"

"She's loving it; the kids' club is wonderful. There's a brilliant pool for toddlers as well."

"Cool, I never would have thought to bring a toddler on a cruise," Annie admitted.

"It's a pretty good vacation. The staff are great; there's lots of facilities. Do you have kids?"

Annie shook her head. "No, maybe one day."

Her latte arrived, and she continued talking to the woman. Over the next fifteen minutes they spoke about the ship and the amenities as well as the ports of call for the trip. It was the first time in a while that Annie felt like she could just relax and have a casual conversation with someone. The woman didn't know, or care, who she was. They were just two people talking.

Eventually the toddler, Ellie, needed to go to bed, and Annie said goodnight to them. She turned back to her table and was surprised to see Caroline standing right in front of her.

"Hello again, Miss Rubio," she greeted.

"Captain West," Annie replied. "I've been meaning to speak with you."

"Oh yes?" Caroline looked intrigued and little nervous.

"Yes, I wanted to complain about the sailing when we left Palma." Annie tried to cover her grin but couldn't quite manage it.

"Oh, really?" Caroline asked, a smirk on her face.

"Yes, it was terribly bumpy." Annie sipped her latte. "I think it was your steering."

Caroline laughed out loud before covering her mouth and composing herself so those around her didn't notice.

"I think you'll find that was the bridge officer on duty at that time. My piloting is exceptional," Caroline replied.

"Do you do much of that?" Annie asked.

"Personally? No. It's a team effort, and autopilot is very competent, probably better than a human for many things."

"So, you're a little redundant?" Annie teased.

"Completely," Caroline agreed readily. "Although autopilot isn't very good at welcoming passengers, so I have to do it."

"You do that very well," Annie admitted.

Caroline blushed a little. "Practice."

"Caroline," the female doctor cut in. She looked at Annie. "I'm sorry, I need to steal her away. The Barclays are asking after you."

Annie smiled tightly. "No problem."

"I'll be there in a moment, Mara," Caroline said.

Mara nodded and walked away.

"I'm sorry," Caroline apologised.

"It's okay. You're busy, and as we've already established, you can't send in autopilot."

"If only I could," Caroline muttered; a small exhale followed.

It was the first time her mask had slipped. Annie wondered if Caroline enjoyed the social aspect of her job. Being the captain of a large vessel and being the host seemed liked very different roles.

"At any rate, I apologise for the rough departure, Miss Rubio," Caroline said playfully. "We are expecting worse conditions this evening, but hopefully you'll sleep through them."

"I hope so."

"If not, please do report to me, and I'll be happy to try to make amends," Caroline continued.

I can't tell if she's flirting or not, Annie thought, *but my god, I hope she is.*

"I'll definitely do that. Good night," Annie said.

Caroline inclined her head in farewell and then turned to seek out Mara and the Barclays.

Annie watched her leave before shaking her head. This wasn't what she'd had in mind when she ordered herself to avoid Caroline.

THE STORM

CAROLINE HAD BEEN in her stateroom, half reading the latest crime thriller that Mara had loaned her and half watching the waves increase in intensity.

She trusted her bridge crew implicitly. She also knew that the buck stopped with her and that she had overall responsibility for the safety of the ship and all on board. It was one in the morning when she finally gave up on the book and left her stateroom and made her way to the bridge.

The weather reports had been saying for a while that the crossing between Palma and Marseille would mean encountering strong winds. Of course, the navigation team had done all they could to mitigate the weather front, but it was too big to avoid entirely. The best they could do was sail at a faster-than-usual speed out of Palma and then slow the ship to almost a crawl when they encountered the poor conditions.

She entered the bridge, the nighttime lighting illuminating everything in an eerie red glow.

"Did we wake you?" Thomas asked with a grin from his position at the navigation station.

Fortuna had been rocking slightly as the waves increased over the last hour; it was nothing Caroline hadn't experienced a thousand times before. But it was certainly more than most of the guests were used to.

"I noticed it was getting worse," she said.

"We're still a way away from the eye of the storm," he replied. He pointed to the charts and then indicated a printout of the latest weather report.

"It's going to get quite a lot worse, then," she muttered.

"Yep. We've navigated to here, but to be honest I don't think we'll feel much benefit. The whole area is being hit. The area of pressure is just too big."

"Agreed."

Caroline didn't want Thomas to think that she didn't trust him or believe in his abilities. She knew he was a fine captain. He may not have accrued as much experience as she had, but she'd put her life in his hands. As far as she was concerned, he was as capable as she was.

But that didn't mean that she didn't occasionally hover around when he was on duty. Not because of his ability, but because of her own desire to be in the thick of things.

"I'll be in the SCC," she said. "You have the bridge."

Technically she was still looking over his shoulder, but at least this way she would be in another room.

She'd never be able to sleep while the storm raged. The waters were rough, and soon the heavy gusts of wind would come which would make things worse, and louder. Everything had been prepared for the storm: the sun loungers had been locked down and the pools had been drained a little. Preparations had been made, and the staff were very used to dealing with all kinds of weather.

That didn't stop Caroline from wanting to keep an eye on things. Monitoring the situation from the command centre was preferable to doing so from her stateroom.

It was four in the morning, and *Fortuna* was sailing through the roughest of the conditions. Rain pelted the windows of the bridge, wind howled noisily all around them, and the ship swayed.

Fortuna had been through much worse, but Caroline was mindful that many of the guests on board hadn't. Most probably were having their roughest cruise experience to date. There was nothing that could be done about the weather, and she had done her best to warn people via the ship-wide television channels, but she knew those who weren't sleeping were probably frightened.

Thankfully, they predicted only another hour of poor weather. Then the sail into the Marseille port would, hopefully, be smooth in comparison.

She exited the SCC and leaned close to Thomas who sat in one of the operator's chairs on the bridge. "I'm going to head down to the promenade and grab some food. Would you like anything?"

Thomas pointed to a lunchbox under the console. "No, thanks. I'm all set."

"Okay, good job tonight," she acknowledged.

"Thanks, I was glad you were here," he confessed quietly.

Caroline had stayed out of the way, but Thomas had still entered the command centre every now and then to advise her of what he was doing. She had to prompt him to ask maintenance to lock some of the automatic doors and move some of the items on the upper decks, but on the whole, he'd followed protocol to the letter.

"It takes a team," she reminded him, as she always did.

She left the bridge and walked through the corridors in the crew section at the front of deck fourteen. The ship's sway caused her to reach out for the wall more than once to steady her balance.

She entered the guest area, mindful to close the door softly behind her. She walked along the corridor towards the stairwell, knowing better than to take the elevators in a storm.

No one wanted to be trapped in an elevator fourteen floors up, while the ship swayed. Certainly not the captain, in a glass elevator, where she could be observed by anyone who happened to be passing.

She hurried down the stairs, making sure to hold the railing as she did. Surges in the sea could be sudden, and she'd had her fair share of bumps and bruises in her career.

When she finally arrived on the promenade deck, she was surprised to see Serena Rubio. She was leaning on the wall with her hand on the glass of the locked automatic doors to the outside deck.

She looked exhausted and terrified. Her red-rimmed eyes stared out into the darkness; she flinched each time a strong wind sprayed rain against the glass door.

Caroline knew she couldn't leave her there.

"Serena?" she asked softly.

Serena turned and looked at her sadly.

"Are you okay?" Caroline asked.

Serena turned back to the glass. "I hate storms," she mumbled.

Caroline stood a little closer, mindful not to crowd her, and also to stand near a handrail. "I'm sorry. If it's any consolation, we'll be out of it within the next hour." She could see that fact would do little to calm Serena, who looked completely emotionally wrung out.

She couldn't tell if the woman had not managed to get any sleep or had been ripped from sleep in a terrifying manner as the ship lurched. The happy, carefree woman from the promenade a few hours ago was gone, and Caroline felt deeply for her.

"Why is the wind so damn loud?" Serena asked.

"There's nothing else out here to stop it," Caroline explained.

"Why can't we get outside? I feel I'd be happier if I could *see* what was happening. It feels like we're really rocking. It must be dangerous if we can't go out there, right?"

Caroline took a step closer. "It's simply because the deck gets wet with the spray; it's a slip hazard. Nothing more dramatic than that. And I know that it feels like we're moving a lot, but we're really not at all."

"So, no waves are coming up this high?" Serena clarified.

"Absolutely not. But even if they were, the stabilisation

on this ship can handle a storm ten times stronger than this. *Fortuna* is the safest place to be right now."

Serena rubbed at her tired eyes. "I'm sorry, I'm a mess. I just…" She trailed off, not able or not willing to explain any further.

"No need to apologise, I know many people aren't used to the conditions. It's completely natural to be… anxious." The word Caroline was trying to avoid was 'terrified.'

Serena smiled sadly. "You're sweet."

Caroline didn't know what to say to that.

"I just hate storms, they remind me—" Serena stopped and shook her head. "Never mind. I shouldn't keep you; I know you're busy."

"I have nowhere to be," Caroline said.

It was clear that Serena had been about to admit something, and Caroline ached to know what it was. She desperately wanted to know more about Serena; any additional pieces of the puzzle would be greedily accepted.

"Aren't you supposed to be on the bridge, turning the wheel and stuff? Don't tell me autopilot is dealing with this," Serena asked, wiping away a stray tear.

Technically autopilot *was* on—it was the safest way to navigate storms; limited input from the team, let the computer deal with the majority of things—but Caroline knew that Serena wouldn't be at all calmed to hear that.

"Thomas is on the bridge," she explained, "finding the smoothest route he can."

The ship surged starboard, and something crashed in the promenade. Caroline knew from experience that it was likely an unsecured chair at one of the restaurants. Everything sounded worse when it echoed through the large space.

Serena grabbed her arm, looking around her in fear. "What was that?"

Caroline placed her hands-on Serena's upper arms and forced her to make eye contact. She knew the fastest way to calm someone was to allow them to see that you weren't worried.

"Everything is fine. It's just a chair or something that's fallen over. Nothing to worry about."

Serena took a couple of deep breaths. She looked a little green and Caroline wondered if she was going to be sick. Either way, standing where they were was not going to help her feel any better. In one direction there was spray from the waves, in the other there was falling furniture.

"I think you should go back to your stateroom. I have the perfect solution for this," Caroline said. "Can I accompany you back?"

Serena quickly nodded, seemingly happy for a solution and possibly even the company.

Caroline placed her arm supportively around Serena's back and led her to the staircase. She held tightly onto her with one arm, her other hand on the handrail, and they slowly made their way up the many flights of stairs towards deck fourteen. They stopped a couple of times when the ship swayed a little too much and Serena started to lose her confidence rather than her balance.

Eventually, they made it to Serena's stateroom. Serena slipped her pass card out of her pocket and opened the door. Caroline walked in and turned on the light. The bed was unmade, an indication that Serena had at least attempted to sleep at some point that evening.

"Into bed," Caroline encouraged.

Serena didn't hesitate and got into bed, sitting up with her back against the headboard and wrapping the sheets over herself. She grabbed a spare pillow and held it to her chest.

Caroline entered the bathroom, grabbed one of the glasses from the shelf, and half filled it with water. She went back into the bedroom and placed the glass on the desk, she turned off the main light and opted for the soft desk light instead.

"This will show you how much we're moving. Because we're not accustomed to moving like this, our brain tricks us into thinking we're moving more than we are. You see the water in the glass? That's how much we're *actually* moving."

It wasn't technically true, but Caroline knew it would calm Serena, maybe enough to help her sleep, hopefully enough to calm her stomach.

Serena's light brown eyes focused on the glass. She remained silent for a full minute before slowly nodding.

"I'll leave you to it," Caroline said, suddenly aware that she was in Serena's bedroom and things were tense to say the least.

"Caroline?" Serena said softly.

"Yes?"

Serena got out of bed and placed the tiniest of kisses on Caroline's cheek.

"Thank you," she whispered, staring straight into Caroline's eyes. They were so close that Caroline could feel the heat radiating from her. Or possibly her own body heat being bounced back.

Before she could think of anything to say, Serena turned and got back into bed.

"You're welcome." She wished her voice didn't sound so shaky, but she didn't think Serena noticed as she stared at the water glass. "Sweet dreams."

"Good night," Serena whispered.

Caroline hurried out of the room as carefully and quietly as she could. Once she was in the hallway, she let out a long breath.

She didn't want to read too much into the kiss, but it was hard to ignore. Her heart was pounding, and her palms were sweaty. She reached up a hand and softly touched her cheek.

She shook her head and stood up straight.

"It meant nothing," she whispered to herself. "Nothing."

THE MORNING AFTER

"Good morning, good morning, good morning."

Annie groaned and rolled onto her back. She blinked and looked around the room before realising that the sound had come from the speaker in the ceiling.

"Welcome to Marseille," Caroline continued.

Annie sat up and rubbed at her eyes. She felt drained and disorientated. Caroline continued her welcome talk, starting with the temperature in Marseille that morning.

There was something just out of Annie's reach, a dream. Or a memory. She tried to tune out Caroline's voice and focus on what it was that she couldn't quite grasp.

She remembered something from the previous night. Waking up to the ship rocking, the sound of the wind whistling, the eerie darkness from her balcony.

She frowned. Another memory surfaced. She'd seen Caroline last night, or early that morning.

And then total recall hit.

She winced.

She'd kissed Caroline West. On the cheek, but she'd definitely kissed her.

"You idiot," she whispered to herself, placing her head in her hands.

Caroline's cheerful voice continued from the speaker, telling people what to expect in Marseille and when to be back on the ship. She sounded as professional as ever. Not at all like someone who had been awake most of the night and had had to accompany a complete basket case back to her room.

Annie lifted her head and looked at the glass of water on the desk. She couldn't remember falling asleep, but she knew that watching the slight roll of the liquid had played a part.

Caroline signed off her morning greeting, and Annie ran a hand through her hair. She felt terrible. She didn't know if it was from the lack of sleep or from the continuing sway of the ship even though they were docked.

The idea of going back to bed seemed appealing, but she knew she had ordered breakfast to be delivered to her room. That meant Elvin was probably on his way.

She got up and went to the bathroom to get ready. Twenty minutes and a lot of make-up later, she was ready. Just in time for Elvin to knock on the door and announce, "Breakfast!"

Annie let him in, and he rolled a breakfast trolley into the room.

"Good morning, Miss Serena."

"Morning, Elvin."

"Did you sleep well?" He put the brakes on the trolley

and got the chair from under the desk and placed it by the trolley.

"Not really," Annie confessed. "The storm kept me up."

It had done more than that; it had terrified her. But she couldn't tell Elvin that, she couldn't tell anyone aboard. To do so would definitely blow her cover.

"There was a storm?" He paused and looked up in confusion.

"Yes, last night. You didn't feel it? We were rocking all over the place, and the wind was so loud."

Elvin shook his head. "No. I sleep very well on the ship. I'm used to the rocking; it puts me to sleep like a baby."

He gestured to the seat and Annie sat down. "I wish the same was true for me," she said. "I still feel sick."

Elvin removed a couple of the lids from the breakfast, and Annie winced. "I'm not even sure I'll be able to eat."

"Would you like me to take this away?" he offered.

"No, thank you, it's okay. I'll try and eat something."

"You should get off the ship for a while," he recommended. "Be on solid ground for a while. Fresh air. You will feel much better. And Marseille is very nice."

Annie had promised herself that she'd avoid using Serena's ID as much as possible. Getting off the ship, and back on again later, would involve going past the security podiums on the gangway. Every time she used the ID, she risked getting caught.

Then again, she'd already checked in and passed through security to get on *Fortuna*. She'd had her photograph taken and surely the security officer would look at that image saved on file, rather than Serena's passport.

When she'd spoken with the mother at the mix and mingle, she'd said that they always left their passports in the safe in the room, which meant that she wouldn't need to use Serena's ID.

The churning in her stomach was uncomfortable, and she felt unbalanced, like the ship was swaying a lot more than it actually was. She hadn't been able to steady herself since she woke up.

And if that wasn't enough, she needed to avoid Caroline. For some reason, they spent a lot of time bumping into one another on the ship. Now that she had kissed Caroline and allowed herself to be seen when she was in such an emotional mess, she needed to hide.

The memory caused her stomach to lurch, but not with sickness.

She needed to get off *Fortuna* for a couple of hours. Dry land, fresh air, and space sounded heavenly.

She turned to Elvin. "What do you recommend I go and do in Marseille?"

CAN I BUY YOU AN ICE CREAM?

CAROLINE SIPPED from the takeaway mug, enjoying the taste of the expertly crafted cappuccino. The staff on board *Fortuna* did many things well; sadly, delivering speciality coffees was not one of those things.

It was a cool day in Marseille. The sun shone brightly, but its heat was quickly blown away by the winds that had taken over the area. The two in combination actually made for quite a nice day, especially as Caroline had opted for a summer dress and thick cardigan.

It was a very rare day that Caroline wasn't appropriately dressed for the weather. In her line of work, the forecast was checked constantly throughout the day and the night.

She'd only been off the ship for an hour, and she already felt rejuvenated. She'd grabbed a few hours' sleep in the morning, followed by a couple of meetings and then a quick lunch, and then she'd left her able team behind for the rest of the afternoon.

Whenever she came to Marseille, she came to the same

place. On a bench overlooking the old port, behind her was the Grand Hotel Beauvau, an elegant, nineteenth-century building. The port was U-shaped, surrounded on all three sides by impressive architecture. It felt timeless, like it hadn't changed much in the last hundred years.

Fortuna was docked four miles away in the newer, large commercial port. Here in the middle of Marseille, the old port was filled with much smaller local boats that specialised in tours or fishing.

Caroline loved the sights, sounds, and smells of old ports. She could spend hours watching the smaller boats bobbing away in the water. In fact, she often did.

Someone sat down beside her on the bench.

"You're probably enjoying some rare time to yourself…"

Caroline snapped her head around to see Serena beside her. She hadn't been expecting to see the woman and found herself completely at a loss for anything to say.

"But I saw you," Serena continued. "Because that seems to be a thing we do. Always… seeing each other. And, it felt rude to just walk on by. So, hello, thank you for last night, sincere *apologies* for last night, and goodbye."

Serena got up to leave, but Caroline instinctively reached out and grabbed her arm.

"Wait," she requested before she even realised what she was saying.

Serena paused and looked at her expectantly.

"You have nothing to apologise for," Caroline insisted. "And you're welcome to sit with me if you like."

The little voice in Caroline's head sighed. She'd

promised herself to keep a distance from Serena Rubio, and here she was, inviting her to sit with her at the first opportunity she got.

The previous night had been electric. Caroline hated seeing Serena in such an emotionally distressed state, but the closeness, and the kiss, had been seared into her mind.

Which was a problem. Caroline didn't like feeling out of control, and Serena made her feel that way, like she had no governance over her own feelings. Even though she knew it would be advisable to keep her distance, she couldn't help but invite Serena to join her.

Serena looked like she was mulling over the invitation for a few seconds before she eventually sat down. "As long as I'm not intruding?"

"Not at all. Good to have some company," Caroline said. Not that Caroline ever felt the need for company; she enjoyed being alone. Time with only herself for company was one of her most precious commodities but spending time with Serena had suddenly shot up her priority list.

"That's a lot of boats," Serena noted, nodding her head towards the marina.

"It is. Marseille has always been a harbour town," Caroline said.

"Lots of fishing here?" Serena asked.

"Yes, primarily sole, I believe."

The small talk was painful, nothing like the easy conversation and banter they usually enjoyed.

Serena worried her hands together in her lap. "I am sorry… for last night, I mean. I feel so stupid."

"It was an unnerving situation," Caroline said. "You were perfectly right to be unsettled by the conditions."

"Unsettled?" Serena snorted a laugh. "I was terrified."

Caroline didn't know what to say to that. She was too busy trying to put her finger on what about this woman intrigued her so much. Obviously, she was attractive, Caroline would have to be blind to not notice that, but she'd seen attractive women on the ship before and had never reacted like this.

There was definitely another factor, something about her personality. The way she spoke, her outlook, her sense of humour.

In that moment, Caroline struck upon it. Serena's persona didn't match her celebrity status. Plenty of celebrities had sailed on *Fortuna,* and Caroline had met most of them. While they were all very different people, they had their similarities. Namely, an air of fame about them.

Serena didn't have that.

Instead, Serena seemed real and tangible.

Like the celebrity version of Serena Rubio and the real person were completely different. Which was how Caroline felt when she was at work. Captain Caroline West was a completely different person to Caroline when she was off duty.

It was entirely possible that she felt a kinship with Serena. They were both playing two very different roles.

"Will it be that rough tonight?" Serena asked.

"No," Caroline reassured her. "The weather front has moved south, and we are sailing east. On top of that, we'll be nearer to the coast in much calmer waters."

Serena nodded. "Sorry for being a baby."

"You weren't anything of the sort," Caroline admonished her. "Clearly you have issues with rough conditions at sea. Many people do."

"Do you put them all to bed?" Serena asked, a playful smirk on her lips.

Caroline swallowed, swallowed the lump suddenly in her throat.

"It was the first time," she admitted.

"Lucky me," Serena replied, still watching the boats in the marina.

She didn't know if Serena was flirting or was simply making a joke to mask her embarrassment at the night's events.

"Do you recall Marseille?" Caroline asked, switching the subject to safer ground. "Now you've seen it again?"

"Can I buy you an ice cream?" Serena offered, gesturing towards the stand nearby.

"I… shouldn't," Caroline said. "I'm watching my weight."

Since she'd hit her early forties a decade ago, she'd had to be a lot more careful with what she ate. The fast metabolism of her youth had completely vanished, and now just looking at some of the desserts in the main dining room made her feel bloated.

"You look incredible," Serena said, her eyes trailing up and down Caroline's figure. "Come on, I bet they have a sugar-free option; everywhere does these days."

Serena was already up and holding her hand out to Caroline, ready to help her to her feet.

Caroline knew she shouldn't indulge in ice cream or more of Serena's vivacious company. But again, the woman's pull was too much for her. She threw away her empty coffee mug and took Serena's hand.

They crossed over to the ice cream cart, Serena practically dragging her. Caroline couldn't complain too much; the feel of the soft, warm hand in hers was quite welcome.

They approached the old-fashioned ice cream stand, and Caroline wondered when the last time was she'd even considered having an ice cream. It was a long time ago, not something that she'd think of doing by herself.

"There you go, sugar-free strawberry or sugar-free blueberry. Or you could just push the boat out, so to speak, and have a huge sundae with everything," Serena said. She'd released Caroline's hand to point at the menu. "Like, everything. With whipped cream, of course."

Caroline couldn't help the grin on her face. Serena was literally like a child in an ice cream shop. The thought caused Caroline to sober a little. She knew from Serena's online biography that the woman was twenty-six years old.

Exactly half Caroline's age.

The grin vanished from her face. She instantly processed Serena's age at various stages in her own life. Realising the woman she was most definitely attracted to was a foetus when she was signing up for her second deployment in the navy caused her breath to leave her body in a gasp.

"Are you okay?" Serena asked.

Caroline nodded and tried to look unaffected by the sudden comprehension. She felt stupid. Passers-by probably thought she was out with her *daughter*.

At that moment, Caroline's phone started to ring from

within her handbag. She quickly answered it, thankful for the distraction.

Dominic started wittering on about a small issue with the schedule. It was nothing important and could absolutely wait, but it seemed like the perfect opportunity to escape a suddenly tricky situation.

"I'll be back on the ship shortly," she told him. She hung up the call and looked as apologetic as she could muster. "I'm sorry, duty calls."

"I understand," Serena said, though she looked disappointed. "Maybe another time?"

"Maybe, yes," Caroline said noncommittally. "Don't forego a treat on my behalf, though. I'm sorry, I really must dash."

Caroline turned around and held her arm up in the air, signalling for a taxi. Thankfully, one appeared almost immediately. She didn't look back at Serena, feeling too embarrassed and too guilty to do so.

She got into the taxi and gave the address for the port, slumping into the back seat in relief. The car sped away, and she leaned her head back and stared at the ceiling.

What was she doing hanging around with such a young woman? She should know better. And a guest at that. Whatever was happening between her and Serena had to stop, and it had to stop now.

NO POINT DENYING IT

ANNIE CROSSED the port terminal at a sluggish amble. She should have been petrified of returning to the ship, worried that her pass would no longer work or that she had somehow been discovered while she had been ashore.

But she didn't care, as she was all-consumed with thoughts of Caroline West.

There was no point in denying it any longer: she had a massive and uncontrollable crush on the captain of *Fortuna*. She desperately wished that it wasn't the case, but continuing to lie to herself was becoming increasingly impossible.

When she'd seen Caroline on a bench by the marina, Annie had found her impossible to ignore. She wore dark sunglasses and a plain but elegant sundress, toned calves peeking out from underneath. She sipped at a drink from a takeaway mug, looking out towards the marina. She looked so elegant and mysterious.

Of course, Annie had walked away. She'd turned instantly and walked in the opposite direction with no goal other than to not be spotted by Caroline. After a minute or so, she realised she was being silly. *Fortuna* was on the other side of town, and she had to go past Caroline or swim through the centre of the marina itself.

She'd turned and gone back to the point where she'd spotted Caroline and watched her for a few moments again. Behind Caroline was a main road and then another wide pedestrian pavement; she could easily cross the road and pass Caroline without being seen.

Instead of making her escape, she watched Caroline a little more. People passed by her, and Annie thought it funny that they had no idea they were passing someone so incredible, the captain of one of the biggest and most impressive cruise ships in the world.

Pride bloomed in Annie's chest. *She* knew who Caroline was. She'd dined with her, conversed, laughed, and even kissed her. She winced. It may have only been a peck on the cheek, but still, it was embarrassing.

The obvious thing was to avoid Caroline, to walk around and get back to the ship, pretending she'd never even noticed her.

But Annie wasn't always good at doing the right thing. She was impulsive and dove into situations without too much thought. Most of her adult life could be explained by way of three or four impetuous decisions she'd made.

Things hadn't always ended up so well, but Annie couldn't change who she was.

And so, she'd walked right up to Caroline and sat down on the bench. She had every intention of apologising and then leaving, but she was willing to be convinced to stay if Caroline seemed amenable.

When Caroline had taken her arm and encouraged her to sit down, Annie had been in heaven. For a short while.

Right up until Caroline asked if she remembered Marseille. They were straying into Serena territory, and Annie didn't know what to say. Instead of answering the question, she'd dragged Caroline to an ice cream stand.

It was a great distraction, and who didn't like ice cream? Caroline had seemed happy with the idea until something happened, and she suddenly paled. A lost and sad look crossed her face; soon after, a phone call had come in and Caroline had all but run back to the ship.

If the call had arrived first, Annie wouldn't be walking back to *Fortuna* feeling like a lump of concrete was weighing down her stomach. She would have thought that Caroline's sudden withdrawal was just about duty and returning to the ship.

But the reaction had come *before* the call. Annie didn't know what had happened, but something had dawned on Caroline and had shaken her.

At first, she'd wondered if Caroline had sussed out her ruse in that moment, but it didn't seem likely. Caroline wouldn't have run off in the way she had if she'd realised that Annie was an identity thief.

Something else had happened. Something to make Caroline pull away.

It made Annie feel rejected, a terrible feeling that lay heavily on her shoulders and in her stomach. She felt like she was back in school, being dumped by Peter Lawson all over again.

She'd abandoned the idea of getting an ice cream and instead walked slowly back to the port. Most of the walk was through seedy industrial areas. It had taken a long time and she was in danger of missing the ship, but she didn't particularly care.

All she could think about was wishing that things were different.

What if she'd boarded the ship as Annie Peck? Would Caroline still have looked at her the way she did on the pool deck the previous day? Would Caroline even know she existed?

Probably not.

The thought gnawed at Annie because she had come to feel so close to Caroline in such a short space of time. Like somehow, she could see right into her soul and understand things about Caroline that others couldn't.

Annie could see the way Caroline so expertly socialised with the passengers; she was great at that aspect of her job, but there was a tiny part of her that looked like she didn't want to be there. It was so subtle that Annie was sure she was the only one to see it. But see it she did. And she felt it in her heart because she'd been doing the same for years.

As Diego's girlfriend, and later on a part of his entourage, she'd been expected to play a certain role. She'd had to act as if the sun rose and set on the man, portray an image that told everyone in their group that Diego was a god in her eyes.

On top of that, she'd had to socialise with Diego's colleagues, associates, and even his enemies. She'd had to smile and make small talk with the worst people on the planet.

It was all an act, but no one could ever know.

She wondered what her life would have been like if she

had met Caroline rather than Diego five years ago. Things could have been so very different. But she was a mess back then, someone she didn't recognise anymore.

She walked up the gangway ramp and into the ship, holding out her pass card and wondering if this would be the time she was discovered and, strangely enough, not particularly caring. She felt too heartbroken to really care. It would just be another thing on top of the huge disaster that was her life at the moment.

"Welcome aboard, Miss Rubio," the security guard said.

"Thank you," Annie mumbled.

She passed the security desk and walked around the corner to the elevators. The feeling of sickness was back, but this time it wasn't from the choppy waters.

THE BEST FRIEND SPEECH

Caroline entered the royal box of the on-board Aldridge Theatre, which housed a show twelve times a week. It included live singing, dancing, acrobatics, and aerial stunts. It was probably tremendously impressive to those who hadn't seen it twice a week for the last three years.

The problem with *Fortuna's* schedule was that Caroline ended up seeing the same thing time after time. It was impossible to mix it up and one day change her mind and attend the ice-skating studio instead. The schedule was the same week in, week out, and the people who liked to be seen with the captain expected it to remain the same.

The royal box was already full of the people who had received invitations that day, invitations chosen by Dominic, primarily based upon the pecking order of how many previous cruises the guest had been on.

It was one of the things Caroline disliked about the cruising industry, the hierarchy. The more you cruised, the more benefits you were given. Time with Caroline was considered a benefit, and therefore she was made to spend her time with whomever had cruised the most in the past.

More often than not, those people were terrible snobs.

"Tell me, Graham, where is the lovely Serena Rubio? I didn't see her at dinner," Margaret Whitchurch asked.

"She's been busy," Graham said, "but I'm hoping to be able to convince her to do a little performance to just a select few. Maybe in the Dreams Plus Champagne lounge."

"Oh, that would be a delight!" Margaret said.

Caroline took her seat beside Mara at the back of the box, not wishing to interrupt the conversation.

"If she wears what she wore at dinner that first night, it would be more than just a delight," Jonathan Spires spoke up.

Caroline pinned him with a glare, but he didn't notice.

Margaret playfully slapped his arm. "Oh, Jonathan!"

Apparently horribly objectifying statements could be swept under the carpet with a chuckle and a tap. Caroline stared at the ceiling and willed herself to not say anything.

"Nice afternoon in Marseille?" Mara whispered.

"It was for a while," Caroline confessed.

"What happened?" Mara asked.

"Graham, you must get Miss Rubio to join us for the formal night tomorrow. We're at the later seating, so we can then take her to Sparkles and get a chance to have some photos with her. Maybe she can help our Theresa with her music lessons," Margaret suggested.

"Absolutely, maybe she could do a small performance there?" Graham suggested.

"As long as that doesn't interfere with a more private performance at a later date," Margaret said.

Caroline let out a small huff. She leaned forward into the group.

"I'm sorry to interrupt, but I have it on good authority that Miss Rubio is here to rest and won't be performing at all. I think asking her to do so may put her in an awkward position," she said.

"Serena and I have been speaking, and I'm sure she won't mind a little—" Graham started.

"She would. She's here on holiday, and I would very much appreciate it if she was left to enjoy that holiday."

The group half-heartedly agreed, but Caroline could tell that any one of them would happily take any given opportunity to solidify a faux friendship with the singer in order to get their wishes.

"If you'll excuse us, I just have to borrow Captain West for a couple of moments," Mara said, standing up and gesturing for Caroline to follow her out of the box.

Caroline did as she was asked and then followed Mara behind an inconspicuous door to the crew-only area.

"What was that?" Mara demanded the moment the door closed behind them.

"What?"

Mara folded her arms. "You know what I'm talking about. Jumping to Miss Rubio's defence at the risk of upsetting Plus guests. That's not like you, Caroline."

Caroline turned away in frustration before quickly spinning back. "I have a... complicated relationship with Miss Rubio."

"Define 'complicated'," Mara asked, her tone softening.

Caroline wished it were that easy. It would be wonderful to be able to put whatever was happening into words.

"There's… a tension between us," she explained.

"A bad tension?" Mara frowned in confusion.

"Depends on your perspective. She's, well, I think she's been flirting with me. And we keep bumping into each other, and she's very… intriguing."

Mara chuckled, and Caroline glared at her.

"I'm sorry." Mara held up her hands. "I'm sorry, you have a crush on her, I assume?"

"Crush sounds a little juvenile," Caroline argued.

"Fine, whatever appropriate word you'd like to replace it with. Do you have one of them?"

Caroline shrugged her shoulders gently. "I don't know. I'm just… drawn to her. I enjoy talking to her, I can't stop thinking about her. But it's more than a crush. If it even is a crush. I don't know. I'm not making any sense. I'm losing my mind." Caroline put one hand on her hip and held her forehead with the other. "And she's twenty-six. Half my age. I've been alive twice as long as she has. What am I doing? It's insanity."

"I saw a video on Facebook the other day about an adorable lesbian couple with something like a thirty-five-year age gap between them." Mara reached for her bag to get her phone.

Caroline held up her hand. "I don't need to see it."

"Is she gay?" Mara asked.

"I don't know." She didn't know anything anymore.

She felt like she was crawling out of her skin. "I think she's been flirting with me. She offered to buy me an ice cream."

"Aw, that's cute!"

"Mara, I swear to you, I will throw you overboard," Caroline threatened.

Mara tried to compose herself, clearly enjoying the fact that Caroline was struggling with whatever was happening between her and Serena. "I'm sorry. Okay. Firstly, there's no rule against you dating a guest, so that isn't an issue. Secondly, I can't remember the last time you were with someone, so it's really about time."

"Mara," Caroline warned.

Mara removed her glasses. "If you knew that she was interested, like she said she was interested, what would you do?" she asked.

Caroline shook her head. "I'm not talking about this, it's… just ridiculous. This sailing will be over in a few days, and then things will go back to normal."

"Yes, you're absolutely right," Mara agreed. "You should just ignore the chance to actually hang out with someone whose company you enjoy. God forbid you have any fun."

"Mara," Caroline said with exasperation.

"Caroline, this entire ship is dedicated to having fun. It employs over a thousand people, an army, to ensure that people have a good time on board. Can't you take just a little bit of that spirit and enjoy the fact that you've met someone who intrigues you? Someone who might be interested in you?"

"I just don't understand how someone like her could

be interested in someone like me. I must be misreading the signals. Projecting my own... crush... on her." She pinched the bridge of her nose. There, she'd admitted it. She had a crush on Serena Rubio. "It's ridiculous."

"Why?" Mara asked.

"I hardly know her. We set sail on Sunday, it's Tuesday! And I can't stop thinking about her."

"It happens like that sometimes," Mara said.

"Not to me," Caroline argued.

"Well, no, but to us mere mortals it has been known to happen. Why do you think there are so many stories of people's eyes meeting across a crowded room? Sometimes you just know."

"But it seems so... pointless. A few more days and she'll be gone. And we could never last. As I said, I'm double her age."

"Things rarely last forever. You have to enjoy life when the opportunity presents itself. It's not marriage, Caroline. It's just enjoying someone's company. Maybe a drink, maybe a kiss. Maybe more. You don't have to have a five-year plan before you even decide if you have a crush on someone or not. Just enjoy yourself. You obviously feel something for her; take that as a sign and enjoy that time together."

Caroline wanted to argue, but she realised she couldn't. Everything Mara said made sense. It was Caroline's overthinking that was making things balloon out of control.

"Fine," she agreed. "But I won't seek her out."

"I'm not saying you should," Mara agreed readily. "But if you do see her, have fun. Maybe flirt back a little. Don't deny yourself the chance to be happy for a while. Explore opportunities whenever you can. Who knows where they might lead?"

"Did you read that quote online?" Caroline asked.

"Yes, I shared it. Twenty-seven likes."

"Why am I not surprised?"

They heard the band start up, indicating that the show was about to start.

"We better get back. Do you feel you can stop yourself from throttling Graham?" Mara asked.

"It will be a struggle," Caroline admitted. She took a deep breath and stood up straight. "Let's do it."

Mara nodded and opened the door for them to return to the guest area. Caroline followed her back to their seats in the royal box, her mind swimming with thoughts of Serena. The high-flying aerial acrobatics couldn't hold her attention as she considered all of the interactions they'd had and what they could possibly mean.

She found it almost impossible to make sense of it all, and she would keep to her word and not deliberately seek her out. But if their paths did cross again, maybe she would take Mara's advice and see where it led.

GOOD MORNING

"Good morning, good morning, good morning."

Annie grabbed a pillow and put it over her head to muffle Caroline's traditional morning greeting. She could hear the welcome speech continue in the background regardless and realised it was pointless. She slowly lowered the pillow.

"As you know," Caroline was saying, "La Spezia is the gateway to Pisa and Florence, so there is plenty to see and do at this port. Please remember that all aboard is at eight this evening. Have a lovely day, whatever you decide to do."

Annie let out a sigh. Caroline had made it very clear that she wasn't interested in her for whatever reason. Maybe some rule about not being allowed to date passengers, knowing Caroline. It was her sense of duty that somehow made her all the more attractive to Annie.

It didn't matter because Annie knew that she shouldn't be flirting with Caroline anyway. It was a disaster in the making to continue down that path. Not fair on Caroline, and dangerous for her.

So, in some ways, it was a blessing that Caroline had put a stop to things. At least, that was the way Annie had interpreted her behaviour and sudden need to run away, back to the safety of *Fortuna*.

It certainly felt like rejection, and Annie knew she had to accept that.

She padded out of bed and grabbed the *DreamFinder* newsletter, looking for some kind of distraction. It was the third day of the cruise, nearly halfway done. Annie had found distraction in Caroline and had conveniently pushed aside the bigger issue facing her.

Now time was running out, and she needed to decide what she was doing. The next day the ship would stop in Rome, the day after in Naples, and the day after that was a full day at sea before returning to Barcelona early in the morning.

Annie was torn. She knew Barcelona; it felt like home to her. She had a couple of contacts she might be able to trust, and she knew where everything was. It was also far more likely that she would be seen and identified in Barcelona before she had time to properly escape. Returning to the burning building, even if it was her home, seemed like a very bad idea.

Which left Rome or Naples. Unless she was going to swim to Corsica on the sea day. An image of Caroline being furious at having to turn the ship around due to a woman overboard flashed through her mind.

No, she'd have to leave at a port.

Naples seemed like the better idea. More time to plan.

She needed to get Serena's stuff back to her without alerting anyone to the fact that she wasn't Serena herself. It was all becoming rather complicated.

She wiggled her tense shoulders. There was a lot to think about, and she was becoming more tense as *Fortuna* slowly crawled its way around the destination ports. Every port brought a possibility of escape, but its own challenges as well.

Getting off the ship the previous day had helped to calm her. Being away from the goldfish-bowl existence on board was a nice relief. She looked at the excursions for La Spezia; most of them involved a long journey to Florence or to Pisa.

The last thing she wanted was to go from feeling cooped up on a large ship to being confined to a seat on a coach for hours on end to view a poorly constructed tower that was slowly falling over.

She crossed to the curtains and pushed one to the side, peeking out at La Spezia. There seemed to be shops and restaurants not too far from the ship. It certainly seemed like a lively enough port town that she would be able to find something to do ashore.

"Lunch in town, I think," she decided.

She lowered the curtain, feeling a pull in her shoulder muscle as she did. She winced. Before then, she needed some distraction and maybe some exercise. Stretching out her back muscles before she permanently injured herself had risen to the top of her to-do list.

A GREAT VIEW

CAROLINE ENTERED the bridge a little later than she had been anticipating. It had been a hectic morning with the early arrival into La Spezia and then a handful of meetings with various departments. Caroline often considered *Fortuna* akin to a swan, both gliding effortlessly through the water, but behind the scenes it was utter mayhem.

She crossed the bridge, looking out of the large expanse of windows towards the port of La Spezia. It was her second favourite port in Italy. The dramatic landscape of beautiful, luscious mountains framed the view. In front of her, the port contained many beautiful buildings in various pastels, and the industrial port and the small marinas could be seen directly below them.

La Spezia showcased the beauty of Tuscany perfectly.

Or maybe she was just in a very good mood. She'd slept well for the first time in a long time. It was possible that her mini meltdown from the evening before had exhausted her enough to finally help her sleep.

The much-needed rest would hopefully allow her to

push all thoughts of Serena to one side for a while. She had a few more hours of meetings aboard the ship and then she had some time to herself ashore. She already knew exactly where she was going and exactly what she would eat when she got there.

The joy of going to the same places again and again was the opportunity to discover the real gems that no one else got to see. Caroline had her favourite spots in each port, and when she did get time off the ship, she loved to spend some quiet alone time in them.

Something caught her eye, and she glanced downwards. The health and fitness centre was located three decks below the bridge, and every week they held a yoga class right at the front of the ship. On the emergency helipad.

The helipad was never used. The logistics of trying to get a helicopter to land on a ship bobbing on the water meant that both the ship and the helicopter had to perform some skilful manoeuvring. On top of that, there were very limited times when the ship was close enough to land to be accessible by a helicopter. Most of the time they were out of the helicopter's limited reach.

Not to mention they had a well-stocked hospital on board, which was often technologically advanced to match the nearest hospital on land.

And so, once a week, a yoga class was held on the usually restricted bow of the ship. Caroline watched as the yoga instructor stepped into the middle of the large, white H in the green circle that made up the landing pad and unrolled her mat.

Maybe I should take up yoga again, she thought.

"Did you get that email from Luciana about the stop at Napoli?" Thomas asked, coming to stand beside Caroline.

She nodded. "Yes, as usual, Luciana overestimates how much free time we have on our Napoli stop. I suggested it would be better to do it tomorrow at Civitavecchia."

"Exactly, it's often up to ninety percent of passengers who disembark tomorrow, much fewer at Napoli. I don't want to do a system reboot when so many passengers will be on board," Thomas said.

"Agreed. Check with Dom to see how many passengers we know will be off the ship for excursions tomorrow and then the following day," Caroline suggested. "Hopefully with the raw data we'll be able to convince Luciana to bring her plans forward one day. Every single time we've done this, it's caused mayhem. I'd like to minimise the disruption to the passengers if we can."

Thomas agreed and started to talk about something else. Caroline had no idea what because she was suddenly completely and utterly distracted. It was as if Mara had somehow managed to plan an epic joke, something she wouldn't put past her friend at all.

Down on the helipad, in full view of the bridge, was the yoga class. One member of that class was Serena Rubio.

Of course she's here, Caroline thought to herself. *Just as I'm trying to forget about her and get some work done.*

Thomas was looking at the iPad in his hand, so he thankfully was unaware that Caroline's gaze had dropped from the mountain range to a quite different set of hills.

She coughed lightly and turned her body away from

the sight of Serena doing the famous downward-facing dog pose. Her eyes had refused to look away, and the only way Caroline could assure her body of complying with her brain was to walk away.

Luckily, her crew were used to her strutting along the length of the bridge to look at different stations and take in different views. Thomas followed her, continuing to talk about something to do with the next refuelling station.

Caroline stopped at the end of the bridge, still able to see the yoga class perfectly.

Damn them! Why did I ever agree to yoga on the helipad? she wondered.

She'd seen the yoga classes every week for the last four years and had never once found them to be as interruptive as then and there. She angled her head in another direction but strained her eyes to look to the side, trying to look without seeming as if she were watching.

Serena wore a strappy tank top and tight leggings. Her hair was pulled up into a messy bun, but some strands had come loose. She was obviously a seasoned yoga enthusiast as she contorted her body with great ease.

Caroline's mouth was dry, and she could feel her cheeks burn with a deep blush. She never ogled women. Ever. It was disrespectful at best, but she honestly couldn't stop looking. Her body betrayed her. She was appalled with herself for watching but also turned on beyond all belief.

Serena was stunning. Stretching her body to its limits, the sunlight twinkling on the tiny droplets of sweat on her skin.

Stop watching! she screamed to herself.

In a show of Herculean strength, she turned around fully, presenting her back to the window and trying to focus on whatever it was Thomas was reading from the iPad.

"What do you think about that?" Thomas asked, looking up at her.

"What do you think?" she countered; she had no idea what he had said.

"Well, it's obvious that we're going to need to consider the timing—"

She mentally congratulated herself on not getting caught. She took a step away from the glass and turned to give Thomas her full attention. As she tried to focus on what on earth he was talking about, she noticed something over his shoulder.

At the other end of the bridge, a junior officer was openly staring out of the window. She followed his gaze; he was unquestionably looking at the yoga class.

Caroline narrowed her eyes and stormed past Thomas towards the junior officer. She felt fury pulsing through her veins.

"You're dismissed," she said loudly.

He jumped so hard it was entirely possible he pulled a muscle.

"C—captain?"

"You heard me. Get off my bridge," Caroline ordered. She spun around and looked at the other half a dozen crew members. "I will not accept anyone on this bridge acting in an unprofessional manner. The yoga class on the helipad are not there for our entertainment. If I see anyone else watching them in that manner, then I will write them up. Understood?"

Everyone quickly acknowledged her. The junior officer attempted to apologise, but one glare from Caroline and he realised it was futile to speak with her now.

Caroline's heart was pounding. Anger had flared in her quicker than she'd ever known it to before. Now it was fading away and guilt was taking over. Her double standards were inexcusable.

"He was looking at the yoga class?" Thomas asked, disgust clear in his tone.

"Almost drooling," Caroline said.

"I'll speak with him."

"Do that," Caroline agreed. "Now, where were we?"

Thomas picked up where he'd left off, but Caroline still couldn't focus. She couldn't understand what Serena Rubio was doing to her. Her world seemed off kilter and she didn't know how to right it.

NO ESCAPE

La Spezia was just as hectic as Annie assumed it would be. There were mopeds racing around the streets everywhere she looked. It was a very busy, very industrial town. There was nothing necessarily wrong with that, Annie just wanted something a little calmer to soothe her mood.

She'd encountered a couple of people she recognised from *Fortuna,* and they had recommended she get a taxi to the castle on the hill. Apparently, the views were breathtaking, and there were a few smaller restaurants up on the hilltop.

When she arrived at the top of the hill, she was glad she'd taken their advice. It seemed that most of the tourists stayed in the town and didn't want to venture up the hill.

Which meant they were missing out.

Tuscany was beautifully mountainous, which meant there was something to see in every direction. From the castle area, she could see down to the port and up into the mountains behind her. To either side were more gorgeous landscapes.

She sucked in a deep breath of fresh air. This was a place where she could rest, where she could relax and take time to think. Away from the constant bustle aboard the ship.

She started to walk around the area, in search of somewhere quiet to have lunch. She wanted a glass of wine, a homecooked meal, and some time to think about things. She passed a couple of restaurants but deemed the crowds dining a little too noisy for her liking.

She saw a sign promising a café down a small, cobblestoned passageway. She didn't know what she would find but decided to take the risk. If she had hesitated before walking down the narrow path, hopefully other people had, too.

The gamble paid off. She found herself in a small courtyard with a beautiful, ivy-covered awning shielding a handful of tables from the sun. It looked absolutely idyllic, just what she had been hoping for.

A woman gestured to her to come farther in. "English?"

Annie nodded. *How do they always know?* she wondered.

"Welcome, welcome." The woman pulled out a chair for her and placed a menu down on the table. "To drink?"

Annie turned the menu over and quickly scanned through the wine list. She pointed to a Chianti that she'd heard of.

The woman nodded and hurried away to get the drink.

Annie looked around the space. It was quaintly perfect. A little rundown but it still held its charm. And it was completely empty. Everything on the menu looked delicious, and she felt a world away from all of her worries.

She let out a content little sigh and relaxed further into her seat. A glass of wine appeared on the table.

"Thank you," she said.

"I leave you a while," the woman replied, nodding to the menu in Annie's hand.

Annie smiled. She took a sip of the wine and then closed her eyes. She leaned her head back, feeling a few soft shafts of sunlight on her face through the ivy screen above her. She couldn't have stumbled upon a better location if she'd tried.

Just as she was starting to congratulate herself for her find, she heard footsteps softly echo from the passageway she'd entered by.

Great, she thought. *Hopefully just a delivery. Or someone who lives in the courtyard.*

She didn't want to share her tranquil little escape. Not for a while at least.

The footsteps got a little louder, and Annie opened her eyes.

"You're kidding me," she muttered to herself in shock.

Of all the people to run into in La Spezia, the odds were incredible. Captain Caroline West was walking out of the passageway and preparing to take a seat in the restaurant. She must have felt someone's eyes on her and paused before taking her seat.

She looked around, quickly making eye contact with Annie and looking as surprised as Annie felt. Caroline nodded a brief greeting to her before taking her seat.

So, we're sitting apart, Annie thought. She wasn't sure

how she felt about that. The rejection still stung, but there was a little excitement at seeing Caroline. She wondered if Caroline knew about this place or if her instincts had brought the captain here in the same way her own had.

Awkwardness permeated the atmosphere. What had been a nice little haven a few moments ago was now tense. It was ridiculous that they were sitting apart. Annie knew it, and she knew that Caroline probably knew it as well.

Caroline suddenly stood up. Annie fixed her attention back on her menu, trying to ignore her but secretly wondering if she was leaving. She hoped she wasn't.

"Hi."

Annie looked up. Caroline stood to Annie's left, holding onto the back of the chair with almost white knuckles. She wore a casual variation of her work uniform: black trousers and a white short-sleeved shirt, which was unbuttoned at the top with no tie.

"Hello," Annie greeted her in a polite but cold tone.

"I... we... seem to be at the same establishment. I wondered, and please don't feel in any way obligated, if you'd like to dine together?" Caroline asked.

Nervousness radiated from her, but Annie couldn't fathom why the usually put-together woman was suddenly on edge. However, she had made the first move and was making an effort—something that Annie couldn't ignore.

"I'd like that," she admitted.

Caroline pulled out the chair and sat down. "I'm sorry again, about yesterday."

"It's fine." Annie took a sip of wine.

The waitress appeared, handing Caroline a menu.

"*Grazie*," Caroline replied.

Annie sipped her wine again. Maybe Serena was on to something with this whole fate nonsense. What else could possibly explain the endless coincidences of them bumping into one another?

"I'll admit," Caroline spoke as her eyes focused intently on the menu in her hands, "that I feel rather guilty over my behaviour yesterday. I'd... suddenly begun to think it was unprofessional of me to monopolise your very enjoyable company. The call from the ship came in at the right time for me to run away like a coward."

Annie blinked in surprise at Caroline's honesty. Caroline remained fully focused on her menu, tense fingers around the edges of the leather binder the only thing that indicated her nerves.

"We seem to be bumping into each other often," Annie admitted. "And I can't complain about that. I enjoy your company. A lot."

Caroline glanced at her from over the top of the menu. "Likewise."

"Then there's no reason for us not to have lunch together," Annie said.

Caroline smiled. "I'm glad you agree. And, again, I'm sorry about yesterday."

"It's fine," Annie said. "Besides, it's worked out well. At least here I don't have to fight with the legions of your fans aboard the ship. I have you all to myself."

Caroline chuckled. "It's I who has to fight through your fans. You're the star."

Annie deflated a little. The reminder that it was all a lie was too real for her. She wanted to enjoy this time with

Caroline and be able to talk without mentioning Serena Rubio at all.

"How long have you worked for Dream?" Annie asked, wanting to keep to topics she was comfortable with. Talking about Caroline was definitely preferable to talking about herself.

"Five years," Caroline replied.

"What did you do before that?" Annie asked, interested in unravelling the mystery that was Captain West.

"I was in the Royal Navy," Caroline said. "I started out in the security service and worked my way up."

"And then... left?"

Caroline smiled. "Well, it isn't quite that simple."

"It never is," Annie agreed. "Want to tell me about it?"

Annie had expected a fairly quick no. She got the feeling that the change from naval officer to cruise ship captain wasn't exactly a simple one. It was possibly a long story that Caroline wouldn't want to tell someone she hardly knew.

To her surprise, Caroline seemed to give the matter some thought before slowly nodding. "Why not? You might as well know..."

IN A PREVIOUS LIFE

THEY ORDERED their meals and Caroline ordered some fruit juice, mindful of being on duty and the very strict alcohol policy that she enforced with an iron fist aboard *Fortuna*.

Seeing Serena in the hilltop restaurant had been a shock, so much so that she had foolishly sat down at another table. She'd agonised for a few moments over what would be best to do. Eventually, she pushed her anxiety to one side and walked over to Serena's table.

She was so pleased that she'd taken the gamble. Within a few minutes, the air had seemingly cleared. An apology was issued, a confession made, and now things had returned to normal.

Caroline's previous relationships had been volatile, with both parties under an enormous amount of work stress and taking it out on the other. Serena's laidback, carefree attitude was a breath of fresh air.

Of course, she had asked the one question which Caroline knew she would struggle to answer: how did she find herself as the master of *Fortuna*? In some ways it was good that Serena had asked so early on. It allowed Caroline the chance to get the sorry saga out of the way. To explain exactly how her life had been turned upside down and how she had ended up in her new life that she was still, even after five years, trying to settle into.

"I joined the Royal Navy the very moment I left school," she explained. "My father had been in the navy, died in service even. But that didn't stop me, it encouraged me if anything."

Serena offered condolences through facial expression alone, offering Caroline a clean run at what was so obviously going to be a difficult tale to tell.

"I worked hard, progressed quickly. I'm insatiably curious, which led to roles in security. I was with the Surface Fleet and eventually commanded a frigate. Do you know what that is?"

"It's a type of boat," Serena joked, looking very pleased with herself.

"It is," Caroline agreed. "Frigates are all-rounders, quite agile. They take on roles from antipiracy to humanitarian aid missions."

Serena's eyebrows rose in surprise. Caroline wasn't surprised. Being in charge of a cruise ship was considerably different from her previous career. She certainly wasn't drinking Champagne and wondering why they were serving lobster for the third night in a row when she was in the Royal Navy.

"I continued to progress. Ship to ship, command to command. I earned a huge amount of experience and honestly thought I'd never leave the service. I was in, what I thought was, a long-term, committed relationship with a… with a woman who was based in Portsmouth." Caroline sipped at her juice. She'd already made the comment about a lack of Mrs West, but this was a lot more direct and it made her a little uncomfortable. Over half a century old and coming out still felt like an ordeal.

"What happened?" Serena asked, fascination clear on her face.

"I was on an operation in the North Sea. We'd heard of human traffickers using a particular route and had been sent to intercept them. We got there, and this ship was overflowing with people, with literally no food and no drinking water. Conditions were horrendous. We called for backup, knowing that we couldn't take all the people as well as the traffickers."

Caroline leaned on the table, her head in her hand. She looked at Serena and let out a small sigh. "Do you ever have that feeling when you know something terrible will happen, but you just don't quite know what? Not an anxiety over a situation, but a concrete certainty that something is about to happen?"

Serena quickly nodded. "I know what you mean." She ran her hand over her bare arm. "The hairs on your arm stand up. You get goosebumps."

"Exactly." Caroline sat back. "I knew something was about to happen, but I never could have predicted what. The backup ship arrived, and the commanding officer was drunk."

"What?!"

"He was out of control, and let's just say the only

reason he was in the role in the first place was because of family connections."

"What happened?"

Caroline swallowed. "He was on my ship, and I decided I needed to relieve him of his duties. He didn't agree. He tried to fight his way out of the situation, and all of my bridge officers became embroiled in this ridiculous attempt to get him under control. We lost control of the situation. Security was called, and one of the cells wasn't locked correctly. One of the traffickers decided to use the distraction to his benefit to escape."

Serena covered her mouth in horror.

"He killed a member of my crew to take control of the bridge of the vessel we'd seized. He attempted to engage the engines and sail away, but we'd tied the boat to our ship. It was mayhem. We started to lose control, and the engines on the other vessel started to overheat."

Caroline tucked her hair behind her ear. She decided to cut the story short, the graphic details not needed to explain the overall outcome. "The trafficking vessel capsized. There were bodies everywhere, from all sides. A number of people died. The press got hold of the story, and it spread like wildfire: 'Royal Navy ship attempting to save people from being trafficked, actually ends up killing them in botched rescue'."

"But that wasn't your fault," Serena argued.

"It was by the time it was investigated. The higher-ups decided that they couldn't admit to the drunken behaviour of the other commanding officer; it would be too embarrassing for him and his wider family. They wanted to sweep that under the carpet, and what better way to do that than to pin it on one person? Me."

"But—" Serena looked outraged. "That… that's so unfair."

"It was. I was, essentially, asked to take the fall, for a large sum of money. If I fought it, I'd never command my own ship again. They told me I could step down and consult for them, quietly, in a few years' time." Caroline chuckled at the memory. "I almost considered it. I was so indoctrinated into the culture I couldn't imagine life outside it. I went to my partner to speak to her about it, but she wanted nothing to do with me. She thought that being associated with me would hurt her own prospects. I was poison at the time. Everyone wanted to be rid of me, and all the years of commendations and good conduct were wiped out because of someone else's mistake."

Serena's jaw dropped; her eyes widened. "She said that it would hurt her own prospects? I'm sorry, it's all terrible, but for your partner to say that? That blows my mind."

"She was seeing someone else while I was on deployment. I later found out." The pain was as raw in the ivy-covered courtyard as it was then. She'd thought she'd been in a loving and committed relationship; finding out that it was all a lie was soul-destroying.

Serena shook her head and blew out a breath. "Whoa. Okay, so, I get why you left the whole situation. That sounds *horrible*. I am so sorry that happened."

Caroline casually shrugged. "It was a long time ago."

"Five years is nothing," Serena said. "You don't get over something like that in five years, trust me."

She sounded like she was speaking from experience,

but Caroline didn't know what experience it could be. She'd read Serena's biography on her website and on Wikipedia but knew that such things were often heavily edited.

"Well, time heals all wounds, right?" Caroline laughed. "I'm sure dramatic things happen in your line of work, too."

"Yeah, we're often helping out with humanitarian aid," Serena joked. "You've not explained how you got to be captain with Dream."

"Oh, that was a stroke of luck. I'd been working with a good friend designing new navigational systems for years before. That friend worked in the cruise-line industry. Evolutions in technology are always being made, and all seafaring organisations work together as it benefits us all. After my—very public—sacking, he contacted me and asked what I thought of cruise lines. I said something that was probably rather unkind."

Serena chuckled.

"He told me that Dream was having a bit of a MeToo problem. A lot of men, some not very well behaved." Caroline rolled her eyes. "As is too often the case. Anyway, they were coming under quite a lot of scrutiny from the worldwide press, so they wanted a woman, someone perfectly well qualified to be the captain of one of their flagship vessels, but also someone who was female. Someone who could take some of the PR pressure off. I had experience with the new systems being installed on *Fortuna* at the time. And I was unemployed. Captains usually sign up for a twelve-week term. I did that and then kept resigning up. For five years."

"So, you're the token woman?" Serena asked, not unkindly.

"I'm the token woman," Caroline agreed. "But I'm being paid a tremendous amount of money to do the job, and I get to make changes to the organisation from the *inside*. Many of the men who were causing problems have been kicked out, more women have been hired. So, I may have been a temporary fix for them, but I managed to make a few more permanent changes. So, it worked out rather well. In some respects."

Caroline couldn't pretend that she wasn't extremely bitter about the turn of events. The payoff from her previous job had helped to provide for her future, but she'd had to take the fall for something she hadn't done. Meanwhile, the actual perpetrator was now cruising even higher up in the ranks.

"So, you are only hired for twelve weeks at a time?" Serena asked.

"Yes, captains at my level are twelve weeks on and twelve weeks off."

Serena blinked. "So, what happens to *Fortuna* when you're off duty? What happens to you when you're off duty?"

Caroline smiled. "*Fortuna* has two captains—well, we refer to ourselves as masters. But she has two: myself and David Gillingham. For twelve weeks, I am on board in the role of captain, and at the end of that period, David will take over. I usually spend my twelve weeks off work at home, but sometimes I'll do some travel or even some consulting if I wish. It's not your usual nine-to-five."

"No, it really isn't," Serena agreed. "It must take some getting used to."

"It did," Caroline agreed. "Especially the off periods. When I'm at sea, on *Fortuna*, I'm on duty constantly. I could get a call any time of day or night. I work every day; I don't get days off. Which is why cruise schedules work the way they do. And then there's the time in the Caribbean."

Serena blinked. "What do you mean?"

"Oh, *Fortuna* isn't in Europe the entire year. It gets too cold to do this route in the winter months. There's a rescheduling cruise in late October that takes her to Miami. From there, she will do weekly tours of the Caribbean until late March, when she'll come back to Europe."

"Definitely not your average nine-to-five," Serena agreed.

"It must be the same for you," Caroline pointed out.

"Kind of," Serena said. "So, what do you do in the winter? Do you go with *Fortuna,* or do you stay in Europe?"

"Mostly I stay with the ship; there's nothing keeping me here." Caroline sipped at her juice and looked at the tablecloth. The nomadic lifestyle was a constant source of worry for her. How could she ever be in a relationship when she split her time between two locations thousands of miles apart? Who would be willing to live that kind of life for her?

"You said you were a master? I've heard that before. What's the difference between a master and a captain?" Serena asked.

"Essentially they're the same thing. Officially I'm the master of *Fortuna*, but the average person would refer to me as the captain."

The waitress returned with a pizza for Serena and a plate of penne carbonara for Caroline. It wasn't a meal that she would ordinarily treat herself to but had thrown caution to the wind at Serena's insistence. She mused that they really must have appeared to be classic tourists.

They thanked the waitress and started to eat.

"You don't like talking about yourself, do you?" Caroline asked. Serena had studiously avoided her questions and returned the attention to Caroline at every opportunity.

"No, I don't," Serena admitted. "Sometimes I find it hard to know what to say."

Caroline didn't quite understand but didn't want to push the issue. If not talking about herself made Serena happy, she could accommodate that easily enough.

"Then we'll just talk about the beauty of La Spezia," Caroline suggested. "How did you find this restaurant?"

"Complete chance," Serena admitted, slicing her pizza into thin wedges. "I wanted somewhere off the beaten track and saw a sign. You?"

"I've been here a couple of times; it was suggested to me by a member of the crew. They said the food was authentic and that it was often quiet. I do sometimes wonder if I'll come here and find it has closed down."

"Do you think we're the lunchtime rush?"

"I fear we might be."

"We'll have to have dessert," Serena suggested.

Caroline smiled at the casual invitation to spend more

time together. "We must," she agreed. "Do you have plans to see the castle?"

Serena shook her head. "I hadn't planned on it, should I?"

Caroline moved some pieces of pasta around the bowl with her fork. "It is beautiful, though sometimes a little crowded."

Serena took a bite of pizza and moaned happily. She chewed for a while before swallowing. "Best pizza ever," she announced. "I'm not really in the mood for crowds; I might just wander around."

"There is a church towards the top of the hill," Caroline suggested. "Wonderful views from up there, and the church is open to the public but nearly always empty at this time of day. I could give you directions."

Serena looked at her thoughtfully for a moment. "Maybe you could show me?"

Caroline's heart beat a little quicker. She thought back to Mara's suggestion that she just enjoy time with Serena. Her anxiety about their difference in age was waning, as she didn't technically know what Serena was thinking.

Maybe the younger woman simply enjoyed her company. She thought there had been flirting, but it had been so long since she'd been in a relationship that she had no idea if she was misreading all the signals.

"I'd like that," Caroline admitted.

"Good, so would I," Serena replied. She ate another bite of pizza and looked around the small courtyard. "It really is beautiful here."

"It is," Caroline agreed. "I love Italy. There are so many

hidden gems like this down small passageways and over rickety old cobbled streets. I plan to retire out here."

Serena chuckled. "You're a long way off from retirement, Captain West."

Caroline grinned. "Maybe, but my job pays well, and I fully intend to retire early."

"Good for you," Serena said. "We don't get long on this earth, and it's important that we enjoy the time we have."

The words were softly spoken and didn't feel at all like a pithy life lesson reposted a thousand times over social media. Caroline could easily sense the truth of the statement in Serena's tone. There was a story there, though maybe not one that Serena was willing to tell yet.

"Well, then we'll absolutely have to have that dessert," Caroline said, lifting the mood.

She was rewarded by a dazzling smile.

A PERFECT AFTERNOON

Annie laughed happily and freely, a simple pleasure that she couldn't remember doing much of lately. Caroline was telling a story about a famous politician whom she steadfastly refused to identify.

Apparently, the man had gotten so drunk that in the middle of the night, when he thought he was opening the door to his en-suite bathroom, he was actually opening the door to the public corridor.

"So, he was just…" Annie trailed off.

"Birthday suit," Caroline confirmed. "He had enough of his wits to realise what he'd done, but the door had closed by then."

"Wow, so… what happened?"

"He walked the corridor with nothing but an abandoned teacup to cover his modesty. Which, by all accounts, was ample. A member of his staff found him and helped him back to his room but not before the video was uploaded to Twitter by another passenger."

"That is priceless," Annie said through tears.

They'd had a wonderful meal together, and Annie had effortlessly encouraged Caroline to accompany her to the church at the top of the hill. Beside the church was a small park that offered beautiful views of the bay down below them.

Annie couldn't have imagined a more perfect afternoon if she'd tried. Caroline was impeccable company: attentive, funny, a great conversationalist, and a little bit of a flirt. Any feeling of rejection from the day before had completely vanished.

Something had changed between them, both seemingly accepting the invisible force that dragged them together time and time again. The little voice that reminded Annie how stupid it was to get more involved with Caroline had been pushed to the most distant recesses of her mind.

She was having fun. She felt safe and happy, something that she'd not felt for a very long time. Up until that very afternoon she had thought that her feeling of security had vanished forever the moment she last saw Diego.

Spending time with Caroline, someone who really did make her feel safe, caused Annie to realise that she hadn't felt that way for a very long time.

Caroline's phone rang, and she let out a groan. "I'm sorry, I have to get this."

"It's okay, I understand," Annie said.

She looked down at *Fortuna*, sitting in the port of La Spezia below them. It dwarfed the ships that surrounded it but looked tiny from their vantage point. She tried to give Caroline some privacy by taking a few steps away. She was still able to hear one half of the conversation and knew that their time together was soon to be cut short.

Not that she could complain. She hadn't expected to spend any time with Caroline that day, and she knew Caroline was incredibly busy. She was happy to take whatever she was offered when it came to the captain's time.

"I'm so sorry," Caroline said after she'd disconnected. "I have to get back to the ship."

Annie smiled. "It's fine, I've already taken up so much of your time today. I feel a little guilty, I know you don't get much time to yourself."

"I'd rather spend time with you than by myself," Caroline quickly replied.

Annie beamed.

"Do you want to travel back with me? Or are you spending more time ashore?" Caroline asked.

"I better get back to the ship," Annie said. "We have to be back by a certain time, and the captain is a real hard ass about it."

"Sounds like a tyrant," Caroline commented.

"She is, megalomaniac," Annie agreed.

Caroline chuckled as they walked through the park towards the small side streets that would lead them to a main road where they could hopefully hail a taxi. Annie greedily hoped that taxis would be a little sparse so she'd get a little more private time with Caroline.

"I like you," Annie whispered, the words falling from her mouth without her permission.

"I… like you, too," Caroline said.

Annie paused and turned to face Caroline. She closed the gap between them in one step, took Caroline's chin in her hand, and placed a soft kiss on her lips. The impulsive move caught them both by surprise, and Annie quickly stepped back again.

"I'm sorry, that was… I shouldn't have done that," she apologised. "You have to get back to the ship, and… I'm sorry."

She wanted to kick herself for acting so rashly. Something had taken over her, and all logical thought had faded into the background.

"Absolutely no need to apologise," Caroline replied, grinning widely.

Annie blushed and looked away. At least she knew she wasn't dreaming up the attraction between them; it was there and most definitely mutual.

"Let's find that taxi," Annie suggested, walking again.

"Do you have dinner plans?" Caroline asked.

"I was going to ask Elvin to bring me a burger," Annie confessed.

"Would you like to dine with me? Unfortunately, it will include the usual suspects, including Graham Shelby. I understand completely if you don't want to spend any extra time with him."

"I can easily ignore them," Annie said. "I'd love to join you for dinner."

She snuck a look at Caroline's face, happy to see that she was grinning from ear to ear like the cat that caught the canary.

Annie slipped her hand into Caroline's.

There were a hundred reasons to stay away from Caroline, but not one of them could stop her right then and there.

A REAL DATE

CAROLINE STOOD in front of the mirror and evaluated what she saw. Her hair was thankfully behaving itself, the brown curls only just grazing her shoulders. She fidgeted with her white tie, wondering if she should have opted for black.

Her uniform allowed for some variation, but everything was white, black, or navy. The whole ensemble was built around the ever-present white shirt. From there she could choose black or navy trousers or a skirt. Then she could choose either her navy-blue dress jacket or her white dress jacket. For very formal events she had a white, low, horseshoe waistcoat and a black jacket. Choices in tie were, of course, black or white.

She was hardly going to win any prizes for best dressed.

It was the first night in a long time where she had actually agonised over what to wear. She'd changed outfits three times. Now she stood looking at her reflection, wondering if the white tie, white dress jacket, and black trousers were suitable.

She'd worn the outfit hundreds of times before but never on a night like tonight.

Tonight she'd asked someone on a date. Something she had never done in all her time aboard *Fortuna*.

Yes, she'd asked people to join her at the captain's table, but this was different. This was a date.

She'd surprised herself when the invitation tumbled out of her mouth. After she'd been called back to the ship, her first thought was that the following day they were in Civitavecchia and that meant she was busy for the entire day. There would be no accidental meetings in quiet little restaurants.

Suddenly the realisation that she might be saying goodbye to Serena, possibly forever, sat in her gut like a stone. Especially after that kiss. It had been brief, almost accidental, but it had set Caroline's pulse racing. It was unmistakeable proof that Serena had been flirting with her all along and confirmation that the attraction wasn't one-sided.

Guaranteeing herself some extra time with the woman had been essential. Mara's advice continued to ring in her ears, reminding her to enjoy life and have fun whenever the opportunity arose.

Serena was the very essence of someone who appeared to enjoy life. She'd encouraged Caroline to eat chocolate cake before dragging her around the hills of La Spezia in search of the best vantage point.

Caroline had often been referred to as stuffy and unimaginative—not things she appreciated being called, but descriptors that she could agree were woefully accurate. Serena seemed to pull her out of that, suggesting things that Caroline wouldn't have thought of.

Simple things, fun things. Like attempting to count the fishing boats in the marina, a seemingly pointless or even impossible task. But with Serena attempting to cover her eyes as she counted and loudly calling out random numbers to put her off, she'd descended into fits of giggles in a way she couldn't recall ever doing before.

A smile tugged at her lips. It was a silly, ridiculous way to spend an afternoon, and it seemed like that was exactly what she needed.

THE PERFECT AMOUNT

Annie picked up the high heels and looked at the strappy buckle. She frowned and held it up to the light.

"Damn," she mumbled.

She called Elvin.

In the few days she'd been on board, she'd changed from being an independent woman to calling her stateroom attendant at the drop of a hat. Elvin was fast becoming her best friend. He was sweet, funny, always smiling, and eager to help. And Annie needed help.

"Yes, Miss Serena?"

"Elvin, do you know how I could get a pair of shoes fixed on the ship? One of the buckles is broken."

"I will come and have a look, one moment."

She hung up the phone and put the broken shoe on the desk for when he arrived. She looked at her reflection and grimaced. Her hair was all over the place. The wind and the sea air had caused it to curl more than usual, and she didn't have time for the ninety-minute long production of washing and styling it.

Hopefully, she would do as is.

Elvin knocked on the door, and Annie opened it with a pout. "My shoe's broken." She held it out for him to look at.

"We can fix this. You want it for tonight?" he asked.

She hadn't thought it was possible to fix so quickly and had been planning to use one of Serena's instead. But the shoe was perfect for her outfit, and it fit her properly, unlike Serena's too-tight heels.

"Um, if that would be possible?"

"Sure." Elvin grinned. "I'll be back soon."

She didn't get a chance to say anything else; he was already hurrying off. She chuckled and closed the door, wondering what on earth she had done in the dark days before Elvin.

She returned to the mirror, smoothing out her dress. It was floor-length and tight. Very tight. It left nothing to the imagination. Annie bit her lip. It was classy but definitely a little risqué.

She'd noticed Caroline's lingering looks and hoped that she'd appreciate the dress.

The familiar sinking feeling started in her stomach. It was guilt, pure and simple. She hated lying to Caroline but couldn't pull herself away from the incredible woman. In fact, she'd given up trying.

She'd made a deal with herself: she could spend time with Caroline as long as she didn't speak about Serena. That way the lies were kept to a minimum. As long as they stuck to light and breezy topics, with no specifics, she wouldn't be lying too much. They were just enjoying each other's company and having fun.

It didn't sit well with her, but it was the best she could do. Coming out and telling Caroline everything was just too risky. Caroline would be duty-bound to chuck Annie off *Fortuna* and essentially send her to her death.

Diego no doubt had private investigators searching for her. Any sniff of her appearing on a news report somewhere, and they'd descend on her like a pack of hyenas.

She walked into the bathroom and fussed with her hair. Serena obviously didn't have the same hair type as Annie and had none of the smoothing products that Annie relied on. She decided she'd have to embrace the wild look and apply a darker, heavier make-up palette to accompany her new style.

There was a knock on the door. She walked through the bathroom and reached her hand out to open the door. "Come in, Elvin," she said.

She walked back into the bathroom, needing to finishing applying her lipstick or she'd be late. "I hate to be a bother, but could you have a look at the balcony door again? It keeps sticking, maybe I'm breaking it. But if you fix it again then I promise to do my very best not to break it ever again."

She heard Elvin walk across the stateroom floor and then the sounds of the handle of the balcony door being raised and lowered. She really didn't know why she struggled with the sliding door. It wasn't complicated, but it was heavy, and it did close with a sort of air-tight seal.

She finished applying her lipstick and entered the stateroom to again apologise to Elvin for being such a pain. How he put up with her was a mystery; his tip was growing every day.

Except Elvin wasn't in the room. Caroline was. And she was attempting to fix the balcony door.

"Oh, it was you!" Annie exclaimed. "I didn't mean for you to do that."

"It's not a problem," Caroline said. She turned around to say something else but stopped dead in her tracks. Her mouth fell open as she looked at Annie for the first time since entering the room.

Annie didn't say anything. She just stood there and allowed Caroline's eyes to rake over her.

"Hi," she said, offering a little wave.

That shook Caroline out of her stupor. She coughed, looked away, and then straightened the sleeves of her jacket.

"The door lock was on," she mumbled. "I unlocked it. It should be fine now."

There was a knock on the door, and Annie turned around to open it. "Hey, Elvin," she greeted him.

He handed her the shoe, which looked as good as new, beaming with pride as he did.

"That's fantastic! How did you do that?" She realised her accent was slipping but no one seemed to notice. It was probably a good thing as she was finding it impossible to remember.

"I have a friend in maintenance," Elvin said.

"Better not let the captain hear that you're having maintenance professionals fix my shoes," Annie said with a nod to the woman standing behind her.

Elvin's eyes widened in shock. "Oh, I… sorry… I didn't know—"

"It's fine," Annie reassured him. "Thank you so much for your help."

Elvin took the opportunity to rush away. Annie picked up the other shoe and sat on the sofa, putting them on and buckling them up. Caroline stood and waited patiently.

Annie stood up. "Will I do?"

Despite Caroline's deliberate appraisal of her, she still felt that she didn't deserve to be in the woman's presence. How she had managed another invite to dine with her, without the help of someone like Graham Shelby, was beyond her.

Caroline's eyes widened. "Will you do? You look magnificent."

"Not too much?" Annie asked.

"The perfect amount," Caroline reassured. She gestured towards the door. "Shall we?"

FUCK THE DOOR

Caroline allowed Serena to lead the way down the hall towards the elevator lobby. The corridor was spacious, but the housekeeping trolleys and other passengers meant that single file was advised.

Not that Caroline minded. It meant that she could follow Serena and enjoy the looks the other passengers gave her. Caroline felt divinely invisible for once; eyes were definitely focused on the beauty walking ahead of her rather than on the captain of the vessel.

They entered the elevator lobby, and Caroline pushed the call button.

"Thank you for fixing my door," Serena said.

"All part of the service," Caroline replied.

"My sofa squeaks," Serena observed, staring up at the floor numbers of one of the six elevator shafts.

Caroline hesitated. She didn't know if Serena was flirting or not. Or what the correct response would be. She was saved from having to answer when a young boy sped past the elevators. Both women watched him run through the lobby and then looked at each other.

Children were everywhere on the ship, but there was something about the boy that sparked Caroline's curiosity. A moment later, he returned. His eyes were wide, and he looked at the elevators with something akin to panic.

The bell rang, signalling the elevator's arrival. Caroline and Serena stepped into the car. The boy followed them. Caroline guessed he was no older than eight.

Caroline selected the floor number, and the boy studied the buttons, not picking one.

"You okay, buddy?" Serena asked.

The boy tore his eyes away from the panel and looked up at her. He nodded and then quickly stabbed a button, seemingly at random.

"You sure?" Serena asked again.

"I… think so," he said.

He didn't look okay. He looked lost. Caroline was about to say something when Serena took a step closer to him. "I'm Serena."

"I'm Billy."

"Nice to meet you, Billy. Did your parents get lost?" Serena asked.

"I think I got lost," Billy admitted.

Serena flashed him a dazzling smile. "You're not lost, you're here with me. We know exactly where you are."

Relief was palpable on Billy's face.

Serena gestured to Caroline. "She's the captain, she doesn't get lost. It's totally your parents who are lost. Should we see if we can find them?"

Billy nodded fast, happily seizing on the kind rescue.

Caroline unclipped her radio from her belt and used the call sign to reach a member of the youth team and have them meet her at the restaurant. They'd be able to see where Billy's room was and make sure he was safely handed over to his parents.

The elevator doors opened, and the three of them got out, Billy's hand snaking into Serena's. They waited outside the restaurant for the youth team worker to get to them.

"Have you been in the pool yet?" Serena asked.

"Yeah." Billy smiled.

"It's cool, isn't it? And the arcade, I've not been in the arcade yet, have you?"

Billy nodded.

"Do they have basketball in the arcade? I love basketball."

"Yeah, I got a high score yesterday. But it was in the morning. In the afternoon someone had beaten me," Billy said.

Caroline watched the pair interact; Serena was a natural with the boy, not talking down to him, not talking over him. Caroline had been on courses about how to deal with lost, scared, or even hurt children, and Serena was as competent as any of the teachers.

The youth team supervisor quickly turned up, and Billy went off to look for his lost parents with her.

"You were wonderful with him," Caroline said.

"I love kids," Serena admitted.

Caroline wanted to ask more. She wanted to fish for the answer to whether Serena would ever consider having children of her own, to talk about her own research into the world of adoption. Sadly, being outside of the restaurant and being the captain, they were soon swamped by people.

"We better go in and sit down," she whispered to Serena.

They entered the dining room, and Caroline could feel all eyes were on her. It wasn't unusual at all; in fact, she'd grown quite used to it. But for the first time she felt like she was sharing some of the limelight, like the load was being carried by two people instead of just one. Caroline didn't realise how wonderful that would feel until she experienced it.

Waiters pulled out their chairs, and they took their seats at the captain's table. The Shelbys weren't there; instead they were introduced to two new diners whom Caroline hadn't met before.

Once introductions were made, Serena leaned in closer. "Where's Graham?"

"Strangest thing," Caroline said, "he got an invitation to tour the bridge. Apparently, they are having a cocktail party and some nibbles up there."

Serena grinned. "Oh, really? That just happened to be scheduled for now?"

Caroline tried to look innocent, but knew she was failing judging from the look Serena offered her. She'd known that Serena would be uncomfortable with Graham's presence and had organised an offer he couldn't refuse.

Graham got to experience something so few got to, and Caroline was able to treat Serena to a meal where Graham wasn't reading her Wikipedia page word for word over the soup.

"Thank you," Serena whispered, gently placing her hand over Caroline's.

"I can't believe it's midnight," Serena said.

"Nor can I," Caroline replied. Somehow the evening had gotten away from them. Dinner in the main dining room followed by dancing at the nightclub. Drinks, non-alcoholic for Caroline, at one of the many bars, and then a moonlit stroll through the park.

Neither seemed to want to say goodnight, so they had gone from place to place, seeking out more ways to extend the wonderful evening.

Sadly, Caroline couldn't put it off any longer. She had a very long day the next day, and as much as she never wanted the night to end, it *had* ended.

In order to have a few more minutes with Serena, Caroline had offered to walk her back to her stateroom. It made sense, considering they were located on the same floor. But that wasn't the only reason.

Caroline had enjoyed every second of the evening, more than any other she had spent on *Fortuna*. For the first time in five years, she'd excitedly shown off some of the ship's facilities and enjoyed them in a way she'd never allowed herself to before.

Experiencing the nightclub had been a new feeling for her. She'd been inside, but usually during the day when the space was empty or used for other things. But when Serena had said she wanted to go dancing, Caroline had immediately agreed.

She'd felt out of place and almost suggested leaving, but Serena had taken her hands and pulled her onto the dance floor and led her around the space in a casual half-dance, half-walk.

Caroline had suggested a walk along the pool deck to watch the ocean, but Serena had requested something inside, stating that the wind would be too strong on the top deck. It sounded like a lie, and Caroline recalled the terrified look in Serena's eyes two nights ago. She wondered if Serena had some kind of fear of the water.

"I need help with my balcony door," Serena said as they approached her stateroom.

"I fixed it earlier," Caroline explained.

"Did you? I didn't see. Could you show me?" Serena asked, swiping her pass card.

"Of course."

Serena opened the door, and Caroline stepped inside and turned the lights on. She walked over to the doors, now hidden behind the closed curtains thanks to the second round of housekeeping.

"It's a simple error to make," she said. "There's a safety lock, in case there are children in the cabin."

"Caroline?"

She turned. Serena was beside her and looked a little exasperated.

"Yes?"

"Fuck the door, Caroline." Serena wrapped a hand around the back of her neck, threading her fingers through Caroline's hair. She took a step closer, pressing their bodies flush against one another.

Caroline knew a kiss was imminent.

"May I kiss you?" Serena asked huskily.

Caroline couldn't trust her voice so instead offered a quick nod. It was all the reassurance Serena needed. Soft lips were upon hers in a second, insistent and demanding. It had been so long since Caroline had been kissed that she had to remind herself to participate and not just stand there in a stupor.

She placed her hands just above Serena's hips, gripping firmly and pulling her the extra centimetre closer. Serena's arm wrapped around Caroline's back, clawing at her shoulders through the thick uniform jacket.

Serena pulled her lips away from Caroline's and started to make her way down Caroline's throat. She tugged on the jacket lapels. "I need this off."

Caroline's mind went blank. She wasn't a prude, but she certainly hadn't expected things to intensify so quickly. While some people, crew members included, thought nothing of sleeping their way around the Mediterranean, Caroline had never done anything like that.

Any doubts were pushed to one side as Serena slid the jacket down Caroline's arms and then turned.

"Help me with the zip?" She gestured to the back of her dress.

Caroline's fingers quickly found the tiny piece of metal, eager to dispense with the tight dress that had been taunting her all night.

"Eagle One?" Caroline's radio crackled to life.

"You are kidding me," she whispered in frustration.

Serena looked over her shoulder. "I'm guessing that you're Eagle One?"

Caroline nodded. "I'm so sorry."

Serena shook her head, indicating that she understood. Her lipstick was smudged, her eyes wide with unmistakable passion.

Caroline removed her radio, resisting the desire to rip the batteries out and take Serena back into her arms.

"Go ahead," she said, trying to not sound like she was out of breath but failing.

"Seventy-sixty in SCC," the duty officer said.

Caroline rubbed at her forehead with her free hand. She'd known that the duty officer wouldn't contact her unless it was important. And it was.

"I'll be right there," she replied into the radio. She gave Serena an apologetic look.

"None of that," Serena said. She took hold of Caroline's shirt collar and pulled her close for another kiss before releasing her and straightening up her tie. "Go deal with the fifty-fifty."

"Seventy-sixty," Caroline corrected.

"That, too." Serena walked away, sitting on the edge of the sofa and undoing the straps on her shoes. "I had a wonderful evening."

"So did I, I'm sorry to cut it short," Caroline said. "And I'm also sorry I won't get to see you tomorrow."

"You apologise a lot," Serena said. "I'm glad I got to monopolise your time for as long as I did."

Caroline wanted to point out that it wasn't monopolising in her eyes. If she had her way, she'd spend many more hours with Serena. Her eyes flickered to the bed, and she had to wonder what might have been.

And what would very likely happen if she stayed in the room another moment.

"Hopefully, I'll see you soon," she said. She picked up her jacket from the bed.

"You have my number." Serena winked.

She stood up, a little shorter than Caroline without her heels. She pressed a soft kiss to her cheek. "Good night, Caroline."

Caroline whispered, "Good night."

She let herself out of the stateroom, quietly closing the door behind her. She was glad that no other passengers were in the corridor; she had a feeling she probably looked a bit of a mess. At the very least, she knew she had a glassy look in her eyes.

She walked along the long corridor of deck fourteen towards the crew area, having every intention of quickly popping into her own room to check her appearance before going to the bridge. The call wasn't an emergency, she had a few minutes to get herself together.

In all her career, she had never had an evening quite like it. And the kiss was incredible. Unexpected, but incredible.

She couldn't believe that someone like Serena was interested in someone like her. Someone as old as she was. The thought had crossed her mind that maybe she was a fling to Serena, a conquest of sorts. Caroline hoped that wasn't the case but couldn't lower her guard enough to completely disregard the thought.

If it is all an act, she's damn good at it, Caroline thought.

She'd always been cautious, but this situation seemed to have gotten away from her. It was like she had no control as her burgeoning relationship with Serena raced ahead of her. She felt like she was running to keep up.

She wanted to know what Serena really thought about the whole thing. They hadn't discussed it, keeping the conversation light whenever possible. Caroline presumed that she was falling for Serena in a much deeper way than Serena was falling for her.

She tried to remind herself that she was supposed to be having fun and not looking ten steps ahead. They were simply enjoying time together, not planning for the future. As much as that killed Caroline because that was something she always needed to do.

She swiped into the crew area and then into her stateroom. Whatever was happening with her private life would have to wait.

She had a job to do.

GOOD MORNING

"Good morning, good morning, good morning."

Annie grinned. She looked up at the speaker. "Good morning to you, too," she said.

"And welcome to the Italian port of Civitavecchia," Caroline continued.

"Thank you," Annie said to the metal grill in the ceiling.

"The gateway to Rome," Caroline explained. "It is seven twenty-two, and I'm happy to announce that the gangway is open, and you are free to disembark the ship. Today, you'll be disembarking from deck number two, that's deck number two. Please be back aboard by seven-thirty this evening. Have a wonderful day exploring."

The moment the broadcast ended, Annie picked up the remote control and turned on the television. In a few moments, Caroline appeared on the screen, navigational maps forming a backdrop behind her. Annie had never before given a damn about the weather reports. To be honest, she didn't care about them now much either. But seeing Caroline some more, whenever she wanted, was a treat she wasn't going to deny herself.

She hadn't intended to kiss Caroline the night before, but she wasn't sorry that she had. Knowing that there was a price on her head, and that she may well be killed soon if Diego had his way, had started to change her outlook on things. Dying was going to be pretty terrible; knowing that she'd lived the last few days or weeks of her life to the fullest would make it slightly less so.

The ever-present impulsive side of her was becoming uncontrollable. The guilt was still there, making itself known every now and then by stabbing needles into her stomach lining.

She hated lying to Caroline, but things had gone so far now that she couldn't stay away if she tried. Half the time she forgot that she was living a lie when she was with Caroline. They didn't talk about Serena or her work; they talked about Caroline, or about food, movies, the weather, travel. It was easy to pretend that she wasn't playing at being someone else, because when she was with Caroline… she rarely was.

And the kiss.

Annie let out a dramatic sigh and giggled to herself. It had been such a spur-of-the-moment thing. Annie just felt she *had* to kiss Caroline in that moment, that she would never forgive herself if she let the perfect opportunity go to waste.

It had been a while since she'd kissed a woman. Now she was wondering why she'd ever bothered with men. She'd always known she was bisexual, even in school where she couldn't decide between the sexes.

In her late teens, she'd dated men. In her early twenties, she'd dated women. Then she'd met Diego.

The smile vanished from her face at the memory of him. She'd been so in love with him, or maybe with the idea of him. The relationship had burned hard and fast for a while, eventually faltering and turning into a sort of friendship. Or so Annie had thought.

In hindsight she understood that he kept her around to keep her under control. Annie hadn't questioned any of it. She'd become one of the many people who surrounded Diego, not within the inner circle but just a groupie.

She felt like a fool.

Being on *Fortuna* had been an eye-opening experience. Her fear of being found had dissipated, and with it had come a realisation that she had wasted five years of her life on a man she didn't love. A man she didn't even like.

Everything was such a mess. She wanted to rewrite her narrative, to be able to be herself aboard. To be able to tell Caroline everything. She looked at Caroline's smiling face, explaining weather patterns over Corsica.

Maybe she'd understand, she thought. *Or maybe she'd be rightly furious.*

The idea of hurting Caroline was more painful than the thought of being thrown in an Italian prison somewhere. She wanted to believe that Caroline would help her, but she knew that finding out the truth would hurt Caroline immensely. Annie hated the idea of that.

Moreover, her subconscious persistently reminded her that Captain Caroline West could never be interested in someone like Annie Peck.

She got out of bed and stretched her arms above her

head. She used the bathroom and tossed on some casual clothes before sitting on the sofa and studying the *DreamFinder* to see what she might do that day.

Elvin knocked on the door to deliver breakfast. Annie knew it was an excessive luxury, but she didn't want to spend too much time in the main dining room in case she bumped into people like Graham. Or any of the other people who pointed and stared at her when they thought she wasn't looking.

Being a celebrity, even a fake one, was zero fun.

She opened the door, and Elvin pushed the breakfast trolley in. "Good morning, Miss Serena! Did you sleep well?" he asked.

"I did. How about you?"

"Like a baby," he said. "Are you going to Civitavecchia today?"

"Elvin, I can't even *say* Civi…ta…whatsit." She poured herself some coffee, feeling guilty that he was serving her when she was perfectly capable of doing things herself.

"You must. People go to Rome, but you don't need to go that far. The port has amazing buildings," Elvin enthused. "Designed by Leonardo da Vinci."

Annie flipped over the *DreamFinder* to look at the information about the port.

"And on the piazza, there's a restaurant that does the best ice cream. And pizza," Elvin continued. "Even if you get off the ship for just an hour, you'll see so much."

Annie considered it for a moment. She didn't have any plans, and it did seem like a good place to spend some time. She knew she wouldn't see Caroline that day with her back-to-back meetings, so taking her mind off of things could be a good idea.

"You know, I think I will. It will be a good distraction."

"Distraction from vacation?" Elvin asked, looking confused.

"No, well…" She paused. She'd slipped up and wasn't sure what to say. Elvin continued to look at her expectantly.

"I heard from a friend," she started. "Well, I thought she was a friend, but she lied to me about something. Now I'm wondering whether to forgive her."

It was suitably vague, nothing that would incriminate her. Certainly not considering she was saying it to Elvin.

"Was it a big lie?" he asked.

Annie tilted her head to the side to think about the question. It was the biggest of lies, but then it also wasn't. She didn't continue to perpetuate the lie, wherever possible anyway.

"Yes and no," she finally said. "In some ways, it was a very big lie. But in some ways, it doesn't matter that much."

Elvin chewed his cheek and looked up at the ceiling as he considered the conundrum. "If she was a good friend, and she means her apology, then you should forgive her," he said. "People make mistakes. Maybe she lied for a good reason."

"I think she did," Annie agreed.

"Then you should forgive her."

"But she lied to me, and I feel hurt," Annie said. In her mind's eye she could see Caroline's confused and pained expression, something which kept appearing to her no matter how much she tried to push it away.

"Can you get over it?" Elvin asked.

That was the big question. It wasn't necessarily how big the lie was, whether it was done for good reason or not. It was all about if the person being lied to could get beyond it. Could they forgive?

"I hope so," Annie said.

A PRIVATE WORD

ANNIE STEPPED into the elevator and pressed the button for the second floor. She'd decided to take Elvin's advice and see what the port town had to offer. Maybe she'd take a few moments to learn how to pronounce its name

Probably not. Annie and languages didn't mix.

The doors opened on the next floor down, and the female doctor that she had seen on the promenade the second night stepped in.

"Good morning," she greeted.

"Hello," Annie said.

"It's Miss Rubio, isn't it?"

Annie nodded.

"I'm Mara Perry." Mara held out her hand, and Annie shook it. "Caroline mentioned you."

"All good I hope?" Annie asked, wondering if Mara was going to turn out to be some jealous competition.

"Very good. I'm glad you two have been spending time together. Caroline rarely allows herself to have any fun. She needs to be forced to enjoy herself from time to time."

Annie chuckled. The description matched up with what she knew of Caroline.

The elevator doors opened again, and Mara stepped out, wishing her a pleasant day. Annie patiently waited for the elevator to resume its course to the second floor. She wished, not for the first time, that she could stay in the cocoon of *Fortuna* forever. She felt safe, welcome, and happy.

But it was fast coming to an end. Annie cursed Serena's manager for not choosing a fourteen-day cruise at the very least.

The elevator arrived at the correct floor, and she followed the signage and got to the open gangway before coming to a dead stop. Caroline was talking to someone by the security podium. She was deeply engrossed in a conversation which sounded... Italian.

She wore her black trousers and just a white, short-sleeved shirt, with an open collar and no tie. It was as casual as Caroline on duty got, and it was disastrously sexy for Annie.

Caroline must have felt she was being watched and turned around. She grinned and went back to her conversation, finishing it up quickly, as she soon turned again.

"Miss Rubio," Caroline said, walking over to her.

"Captain West." Annie smiled.

"May I speak with you for a moment? In private?" Caroline asked professionally. She held her arm up, gesturing for Annie to walk away from the gangway.

Annie's heart rate picked up, and she started to panic. She had no choice and walked in the direction Caroline had pointed in. They rounded a corner, and Caroline swiped open a door to a crew-only area.

They stepped through the door, and Annie looked around in fascination. Carpeted floors and wood-panelled walls faded away; in the crew area everything was grey and white metal.

"Is something—" Annie started.

She couldn't finish the sentence as Caroline turned and pulled her into a kiss. It was quite a surprise and very unlike the adorably slow-on-the-uptake Caroline from the previous night.

Annie quickly sank into the kiss. She'd promised herself that she would enjoy every moment, and this was one of the moments which she fully intended to enjoy. She pushed her hands over Caroline's shoulders and interlocked them behind her head. She wanted to run her fingers through the thick, dark locks, but knew better than to dishevel Caroline while she was clearly on duty.

A door slammed in the distance, echoing down the long, empty corridor. They pulled apart, even though no one was close enough to see them. They both giggled at their behaviour.

"I'm sorry," Caroline said. She didn't look particularly apologetic. "I had just wanted to thank you for your time last night. I didn't get a chance to say that before I was called away. But then I saw you… and realised I might not see you all day…"

"Nothing to apologise for," Annie said.

"Dine with me this evening?" Caroline asked before quickly wincing at her outburst. "Unless you have plans. I mean you don't *have* to dine with me each night. I know it must get boring… and I can't guarantee that Graham won't be there this time."

"I would love to have dinner with you. And we could be surrounded by a hundred Grahams, it wouldn't make a difference to me," Annie confessed.

"What a terrible mental image," Caroline said.

"I know, I must really like you," Annie whispered.

Caroline opened her mouth to reply, but her radio crackled. "Come in, Eagle One?"

Caroline looked frustrated and apologetic at the interruption.

"What time should I expect you?" Annie asked, ignoring the fact that their time together had been cut short.

"Seven?" Caroline asked.

"Great, I look forward to it."

"I'm so sorry, I—"

"Have to work," Annie finished. "I know. I understand. Go and do whatever it is you do. I'll see you tonight."

Caroline opened the door and led Annie back into the guest-facing area of the ship where there were passengers and crew members.

"Thank you, Miss Rubio. Have a pleasant day in Civitavecchia," Caroline said.

"I will. Thank you, Captain," Annie replied.

She gave Caroline a cheeky wink before she turned and left, loving how Caroline's cheeks blushed as she did.

A NOTE

Caroline was getting ready for dinner when there was a knock on her stateroom door. She really didn't have time for any further delays. Every single meeting that day had overrun horribly, and she'd not had a moment to herself.

She opened the door; one of the attendants stood in the hallway.

"Sorry, Captain. A note for you." He handed over the Dream-issued envelope.

"Thank you." She took the note and closed the door. It wasn't unusual for her to receive notes; the passengers didn't have access to her telephone and therefore they had to resort to older-fashioned methods. Most of the time it was an invitation to an event or a private gathering which she often had to decline.

She tore open the envelope and took out the slip of paper.

Her jaw tensed. It was from Serena, saying she couldn't make dinner that evening.

Caroline let out a deep sigh. Her one highlight of the

busy and stressful day had been the thought of seeing Serena that evening.

There was no explanation as to why she was cancelling. Caroline wondered if she should go and knock on Serena's door and see if she was okay. Or maybe call? A small voice told her that could be considered overstepping.

Serena was not obligated to give a reason for cancelling. Caroline had to accept her wishes, even if they were entirely opposite to her own.

She looked at her watch; she was running a little late. Not that she had any appetite left.

Had she been dumped?

She snorted a laugh. Was it possible to be dumped from whatever relationship they had been in? Was it even a relationship?

The not knowing was stressful. Caroline liked things to be organised and easy to understand. Her… whatever it was with Serena was neither of those things.

She looked at the letter again.

There was a strong possibility that whatever it was had now ended.

There was a chance that Serena had decided enough was enough. She'd had her fun, and now she'd spend the last two days of the cruise doing other things. Meeting other people.

It was a fear that Caroline had always carried with her, the worry about not being enough, especially when work dominated so much of her time. She knew it was hard for anyone to be with her when the other person in the relationship was every single crewman and passenger aboard *Fortuna*.

It still stung, even if she didn't know the reason for the cancellation.

She folded up the paper and placed it back into the envelope. She didn't have time to overthink things; she had to get to dinner.

The end of the meal couldn't come quickly enough for Caroline. The moment it was socially acceptable, she excused herself under the guise of official business. She felt a little guilty to use the lie, especially considering everyone on board was technically ship's business.

Nevertheless, she'd made her decision. She needed to speak with Serena and find out what had happened. To see if the young woman was sick, or simply sick of her.

As she walked down the corridor towards Serena's stateroom, she could see that the door was wedged open and the housekeeping trolley was outside.

Caroline stopped and peeked inside. The attendant stopped what he was doing and looked up at her.

"Hello, Captain West," he greeted her, looking a little anxious at her presence.

"Do you happen to know where Miss Rubio is?" Caroline asked.

He nodded and pointed to the ceiling. "The pool deck, she wanted to watch the sunset."

Caroline hadn't expected him to know. It wasn't usual for passengers to tell their stateroom attendant their every movement. She'd expected nothing more than an apologetic shrug.

"Are you going to see her, ma'am?"

Caroline nodded. "If I can find her."

He held up a finger, asking her to wait a moment. Caroline frowned, watching as he came around the bed and disappeared out of sight by the wardrobe. He returned a second later with a thick hoodie.

"I told her to take this, but she forgot. She will be cold. Can you take this to her?"

Caroline took the soft garment and smiled. Clearly Serena had a much closer relationship with her attendant than most guests. She'd obviously made a positive impression on him.

"I will. Thank you, Elvin," she said, reading his name badge.

He smiled brightly and then bowed a little, backing into the room to get on with his work.

Caroline gripped the hoodie, resisting the urge to bring it to her face and inhale. She could smell Serena's sweet perfume drifting up from the garment already.

She walked towards the elevator lobby, trying to ignore how she had picked up considerable speed. The need to see Serena and find out what was happening was growing with each passing minute.

Luckily, she spotted Serena the moment she walked out onto the pool deck. She was standing by the railing, looking out at the sun as it raced down to meet the ocean. Caroline felt her breath catch in her throat. She truly was beautiful.

Caroline walked over, attempting to look casual. "Miss Rubio."

Serena spun around. "Caroline! I... I thought you'd be busy."

"Shall I leave you alone?" Caroline asked. She wordlessly held the hoodie towards Serena, noting the goose-bumped flesh on her bare arms.

"No, I'm glad you're here," Serena said. She took the hoodie and smiled. "Elvin?"

"He seems very fond of you," Caroline said.

"He is wonderful. You need to give him a raise."

"Not my department," Caroline replied.

"I'm sorry I couldn't make dinner," Serena said, tugging the hoodie on over her head. She seemed genuinely apologetic, and some of the weight on Caroline's shoulders eased.

"Are you okay?" Caroline asked.

Serena opened her mouth to answer but stopped dead, looking over Caroline's shoulder. Caroline turned. Someone was taking photographs of them, pretending that they were photographing the sunset behind them.

Caroline smiled at the passenger and then nodded her head to Serena in a silent suggestion that they walk farther along the deck. Serena quickly agreed, and they walked along the railing a little.

It was a particularly beautiful sunset; the sky was painted with pinks and purples, and more and more passengers were piling out of the restaurants and onto the deck to get photographs. In the distance, a violin was playing in the park; if Caroline wasn't so worried, she would have found the whole situation quite romantic.

"Sorry," Serena whispered. "I... I had a lot on my

mind. And I realised I needed to tell you something very important, but dinner wasn't the place to say it."

Caroline started to worry again. She was about to ask what was on Serena's mind and reassure her that everything would be fine, but more passengers started to gather around them. This group weren't interested in them but were standing close enough that a private conversation was impossible.

Serena took Caroline's arm and walked them away from the railing, towards the middle of the deck.

"Are you okay?" Caroline asked.

"Yes, I just…" Serena closed her eyes and rubbed at her face. "It's hard to explain. I…"

"Captain, can we have a photo with you, please?"

Caroline wanted to scream. Instead she turned around and offered the family of four her best smile. "Of course," she agreed.

The photo was taken, and the family moved on. However, they'd attracted the attention of other guests, and Caroline knew she would soon be mobbed.

"Can we take this to another location?" Caroline asked.

"Agreed," Serena said.

They walked towards the back of the ship, away from the crowds who were focused on the sunset. There were still passengers meandering around, but considerably fewer.

"What is it?" Caroline asked, desperate to know what was happening.

Serena looked pale, and not just because of the cold temperatures on deck.

"I…" She looked down at the floor. "I haven't felt this way before," she confessed. "I… this kind of thing doesn't happen to me. And now it has and I'm really messed up. I feel so many strong feelings for you, and I… I don't know… I just…"

Caroline licked her lips nervously. Was this all just a case of nerves? Had Serena developed serious feelings for her and been spooked? While she didn't want Serena to feel bad, it would be the best possible outcome.

"I feel the same way," Caroline blurted. "There's something between us, I feel it."

Serena's head snapped up. Her eyes were wide.

"I can't stop thinking about you," Caroline said. "I know it's ridiculous, we've spent so little time together. But I can't control myself."

"I feel the same," Serena whispered. "It's just—"

"I know, it's confusing," Caroline said. "But I'm so relieved that we feel the same way about this. I was going to ask you tonight if you'd spend the day with me tomorrow in Napoli?"

"What?" Serena looked shocked.

"Napoli, Naples," Caroline explained. The schedule, being written for the English-speaking market, listed the port as Naples and it often caused confusion. "It is my favourite town; I'd love to show you around. I have the whole day free. Please say you'll come with me? I have things I want to show you."

Caroline practically shook with nerves. It was a huge step. Napoli was like her second home. It was somewhere dear to her, somewhere she never took guests. But Serena wasn't just anyone, and she'd admitted that whatever was pulling them together wasn't just in Caroline's head. Serena felt it, too.

Napoli was also the place where she would be able to properly explain to Serena what her chaotic life looked like and try to figure out if they could possibly bend their schedules to have the chance at a future together.

Out of the corner of her eye, she saw an elderly couple whispering to each other and gesturing towards her. She knew it wouldn't be long before they came over to introduce themselves.

"We can talk about everything tomorrow," Caroline promised. "I know the best place to have lunch. Please?"

Serena nodded. "Yes, I'd love to. And… we can talk."

"Absolutely," Caroline said. She'd agree to anything after the surprise dinner cancellation. She'd been thrown for a loop, not knowing whether she was coming or going, but now she knew why: she had strong feelings for Serena. By some miracle, Serena felt the same.

"It's just, this thing has been swirling around in my mind," Serena said. "And I need to tell you—"

"I know what you mean," Caroline reassured. "I thought I was going mad. I've never experienced this."

Serena let out a breath and smiled. "I'm so glad you feel the same way," she said after a moment's silence.

"I wish I could stay here with you, but I have to get to a drinks reception," Caroline apologised.

"It's fine," Serena said.

"Napoli tomorrow?" Caroline searched her eyes for confirmation, getting a strange feeling that Serena was pulling away again.

"Absolutely. What time?"

"Pick you up at ten-thirty?" Caroline asked.

"Should I bring anything?"

"That hoodie. The wind can get up, and you look divine in it."

Serena laughed. "In this old hoodie?"

"Cuddly," Caroline admitted.

"Then I'll definitely wear it," Serena said. "You better go. That couple are building up their courage to come over and say hello to you."

"I know," Caroline agreed. "You're okay, though?"

"I'm okay," Serena reassured. "I'll see you tomorrow. I promise."

NOT WHAT SHE EXPECTED

Annie wasn't okay. She was very, very far from okay. But she kept the smile firmly on her face as she watched Caroline walk away. The moment Caroline was gone, Annie spun on her heel and walked as far as she could in the opposite direction.

Unfortunately, being confined to the ship meant that wasn't very far.

Over the course of the day, she'd felt more and more ill. Guilt was swallowing her whole. It was easier to push aside the guilt when she was with Caroline, being distracted by the woman's hypnotic personality.

But when Annie was alone in Civitavecchia, all she had been able to think about was how she was lying to Caroline. She was dragging Caroline down with her, messing with her feelings. It was painfully unfair that Annie had met Caroline when she was pretending to be someone else, but that wasn't Caroline's fault. It was Annie's.

She'd made her mind up. It was time to be honest.

As much as it frightened her, she'd decided to tell Caroline everything. Even if that meant that Caroline never wanted to see her again and got security to throw her off the ship.

She'd spent hours deciding what she would say, deciding that the next time she saw Caroline was the time when she would be honest about everything. The idea of sitting at dinner and continuing the lie for two hours before finally admitting everything seemed ludicrous. And she wasn't about to tell Caroline before the dinner, that was cruel.

So, she'd send a note to cancel. She'd expected to see Caroline the next day, having seen the packed series of events which included the captain's presence that evening in the *DreamFinder* schedule.

When Caroline had turned up on the deck, Annie felt every single practised word fall out of her brain, roll across the deck, and splash into the water below them.

Surrounded by people, with a curious and nervous Caroline asking if she was okay, Annie had stumbled on her words. She'd wanted to tell Caroline the depth of her feelings *before* telling her the truth, to try to salvage some of their relationship if at all possible. To explain that she was falling in love and tell Caroline what a wonderful person she was before breaking her heart by admitting that she wasn't Serena Rubio.

But she'd only gotten a small way into her prepared speech. She'd gotten as far as saying that she had strong feelings for Caroline before Caroline had swept in and said she felt the same.

It was the best news and the worst news at the same

time.

To hear that Caroline had feelings for her and also felt the strange pull that connected them was incredible. But those words, the crowded deck, and Annie's inability to confess meant that she never got to the second part of her speech. The important part. The bit that would destroy everything.

Now she felt sicker than ever.

She knew what she had to do; she had to be honest, and the time for that had already been set by Caroline. The following day they would go to Naples, and Annie would explain everything.

She leaned on the railing at the back of the ship and let out a small sob. Not for herself, she'd stopped caring about herself over the last few hours. It had become clear to her that she couldn't carry on the way she was. Running from Diego was a fool's errand. Playing at being Serena would have to end eventually. She would get caught. It was inevitable.

But that paled into insignificance compared to what she'd done to Caroline. She'd looked so happy and relieved when Annie had admitted her feelings. Annie knew that the truth was going to break Caroline apart. They'd not known each other long, but she knew that Caroline found it hard to trust people and even harder to date people.

She'd done both with Annie in a short period of time.

Annie knew that if she could do anything at all to make it easier for Caroline, she would. Letting her down gently and explaining her side of things wouldn't be easy, but knew she wouldn't be able to live with herself if she didn't at least try.

SERENITY

CAROLINE ENTERED the bar and picked up a flute of orange juice from the tray immediately offered to her. She thanked the waiter and glanced around the room in the hope of finding a group she could talk to that wouldn't be too taxing.

Being surrounded by holidaymakers twenty-four seven was hard work. They were often overly excited, loud, and very, very happy.

Which was good news because it meant they were enjoying themselves. But when you wanted a moment's peace and quiet, or when you weren't having the greatest day yourself, it could be hard.

"Caroline," Mara greeted. "I was about to send out a search party."

"I had a meeting," Caroline lied.

"Hmm," Mara replied, sipping some Champagne. "And I'm about to star on Broadway."

Caroline rolled her eyes. "Fine, I was talking to a passenger."

Mara regarded her carefully. "I feel like there's more to the story."

"How do you do that?" Caroline demanded. She wasn't used to her feelings being on display, but somehow Mara cut through all the bullshit and could see right into Caroline's soul.

"Years of practice," Mara replied. "Many, many years of 'I feel fine, doctor'."

Caroline glanced around the room before indicating with a tilt of her head for Mara to join her in a quiet corner.

"I was supposed to dine with Serena," she explained. She couldn't help the grin that was rapidly taking over her face. She still couldn't believe what had happened.

"Yes?" Mara urged her on.

"She cancelled at the last moment, sending a note with no explanation. I sought her out after dinner, and she said she'd had to cancel because she had to tell me something that had been resting on her mind, something that wasn't appropriate to tell me over dinner."

"Oh, dear," Mara said.

"No, quite the opposite. She told me she had strong feelings for me, which is exactly how I feel about her. I thought I was losing my mind, unable to stop thinking about her. But it seems she's feeling this, too." Caroline stopped to take a breath, the excitement just too much for her to pretend that she was unaffected. She'd not felt so young or excited in a long, long time.

Mara's eyebrow raised. "Caroline, that's wonderful news."

"I invited her to Napoli," she confessed. "To see

Serenity. I want to show her my life and see if she thinks we could be at all compatible."

Mara's eyes widened. "So, it's serious?"

"I don't know what it is, but it's *something*. And now I know that I'm not the only one feeling it, and it's exhilarating. And terrifying. But I'm taking a leap." Caroline took a sip of orange juice, gazing over the rim to check that they were still alone and able to speak freely.

"Obviously, I have no idea what I'm doing," she confessed, "but it seems like fate. Tonight she told me she has feelings for me, and tomorrow we arrive in Napoli. I want to show her *Serenity*, introduce her to Hazel, have her know something about my life when I'm not here doing this."

"Caroline, I'm so happy for you," Mara said, squeezing her wrist. "You deserve this, and Serena seems lovely."

"I know it appears fast," Caroline defended her actions, well aware of how it must have looked from Mara's perspective.

"It does. But I know that you know what you're doing."

"I'm not sure that I do. I just... I like her, and I want to try and see if we have a possibility of spending more time together. I'm trying to ignore the voice in my head that is telling me it can't possibly work."

Mara nodded. They'd discussed Caroline's fears of being alone for the rest of her life. While Mara was filled with positivity, even she had to admit that Caroline's lifestyle was hectic and unusual and not conducive to a long-term relationship.

"Go with your gut," Mara said. She gave Caroline a slight grimace. "Incoming," she whispered.

Caroline turned. Sure enough, they had been spotted, and a group were on their way to socialise. Caroline put on her best smile and counted down the hours until the next day and her date with Serena.

MEGARIDE

Annie hadn't slept very well. Not that she'd gone to bed with the expectation of getting any sleep at all, but she'd gotten a couple of hours and that short time was filled with sweet dreams of Caroline.

She'd even muted the in-room morning announcement, only allowing Caroline to get two of her three traditional *good morning's* out before silencing her.

Knowing that Caroline had feelings for her was such a dangerous double-edged sword. On one hand she was ecstatic, on the other she was left wondering how much of that sentiment was for Serena and not for her.

She'd managed to convince herself that maybe Caroline would be interested in her. They'd spent time together and talked about all kinds of things, and during that time she'd tried to be Annie as much as possible, batting away any mention of touring, singing, or her manager.

She knew she had to be brave and tell Caroline the truth, but she also had to be sensitive with her words and with her timing. Caroline had mistakenly believed that

Annie was declaring her feelings the previous night. Which, of course, Annie had meant to do. It was just that there was a whole 'I'm not who you think I am' attached to it that never quite made it past her lips.

Annie didn't want to hurt Caroline, and she certainly didn't want Caroline to think she was being played. That could easily appear to be the case if one night Annie was declaring her feelings, and the very next she was telling the hard truth and requesting Caroline's help.

So, Annie had decided that she needed to keep up her charade, while trying to remain as honest as possible, until an ideal moment showed itself. She would continue to not talk about anything related to Serena in the hope that the right time to reveal all would present itself.

A melodious knock on the door indicated that Caroline had arrived. Annie took a deep breath and took one final look at herself in the mirror. Skinny jeans and a tight, white t-shirt, the hoodie Caroline had taken a shine to tied around her waist. Simple but classic.

She opened the door. Caroline had a pair of sunglasses on the top of her head, pushing her hair away from her face. She wore a light-blue polo neck with the collar up and a pair of black jeans. She looked happy and relaxed as she handed Annie… a crash helmet.

"Thanks, flowers are more traditional, but it's lovely," Annie quipped.

"Let's go." Caroline nodded her head, clearly eager to escape the ship and the people Annie could hear approaching in the distance.

She grabbed her bag and left the room.

She looked at the helmet; it was the same colours as

the Italian flag. Did Caroline expect her to get on a bike? She prayed that Caroline didn't expect her to drive one because Annie had never done so or been interested in learning.

There were quite a few passengers around them as they entered the elevator lobby and made their way down to the gangway on the second deck. Caroline turned away from the usual exit and guided Annie through a crew area which was thrumming with activity.

Crew in all sorts of uniforms, from engineers, to maintenance, to chefs, to waiters, rushed past them. Some had trolleys, some had pallets filled with supplies. Being behind the scenes was eye-opening; Annie had had no idea how hectic it was below the passenger decks.

Caroline greeted everyone she came across. They all seemed happy to see her, and Annie felt a bounce of pride as she followed in her wake.

They turned and walked into a room that led to a ramp down to the dock. Annie gasped at the huge hole in the wall which seemed to be a loading bay. The staff members stood to one side and allowed Caroline and Annie down the long ramp to the dock.

"Hello, Captain, here she is," a crew member said. He turned and gestured to a pastel-green Vespa which had a helmet hanging from the handlebar.

A member of security approached them and asked to scan Annie's card.

Caroline thanked the crewman and put her helmet on. She turned to Annie and gestured to the helmet.

"Safety first," she said with a smile.

"You're going to drive a bike?" Annie asked.

"Yes, it's the best way to get around in Italy, if you want to actually get anywhere." Caroline got on the bike and patted the space behind her. "I always have my bike aboard the ship."

Annie had never been a fan of bikes, but for some reason she felt at ease with the idea of Caroline being the one driving. She knew she'd not take any risks, try to show off, or do anything to endanger them.

Annie strapped the helmet on and then straddled the back of the bike. She slid forward, pressing her body up against Caroline's and letting out a contented sigh as she did. Caroline reached around and pulled Annie's arm tightly around her body.

"I promise this is the easiest way to get places, not an excuse to wrap you around my body," Caroline said.

"I'm not complaining," Annie replied.

Caroline laughed and started the engine. She shouted over the noise to ask if Annie was ready. Annie called back that she was, and away they went.

Annie suspected that Caroline was driving more slowly than she usually would because of her nervous passenger, and Annie wasn't going to complain about that. They passed through the port buildings quickly, only slowing as they approached a large security gate. The guard on duty gave them a friendly wave, and Annie realised that Caroline was known by him, proving that this was a stop that Caroline frequently explored.

She had said that it was her favourite place, after all.

They weaved through some cars loading up tourists in the port car park before joining the main road. Caroline expertly navigated. Annie expertly held on for dear life.

She saw an imposing-looking castle and tried to focus on it for a few seconds and not the cars and other bikes whizzing by them.

She tightened her grip around Caroline's middle, feeling safer the moment she did.

Caroline won't let anything happen to you, she reminded herself.

She peeked over Caroline's shoulder. They were weaving in and out of the slow-moving traffic. Up ahead, there was a large tunnel. Annie could see hundreds of red lights from the traffic built up in the tunnel.

Luckily, they turned left, remaining outside as they rumbled over a large, cobbled road. Caroline increased the power from the engine as they were travelling at a steep incline, and Annie held on a little tighter.

They reached the top of the hill, and everything seemed to change. They were now on a much quieter road; it was wide and peaceful. To the left was a stone balustrade that looked out onto the ocean, and in the distance were some menacing-looking mountains that Annie guessed contained Mount Vesuvius. To the right were tall stone buildings which comprised of apartments, hotels, and restaurants. On the wide pavements were large fast-food carts selling everything from bottles of water to pastries to ice cream.

The activity of the port vanished, and suddenly they were in a seaside town. They drove for a while, following the coastal road. Annie sat up a little straighter and looked to the left and then to right, admiring the view of the sea on one side and the beautiful architecture on the other.

The road bore right, and to the left Annie saw a small

marina. Next to it was a narrow, paved street cutting through the ocean. It was lined with beautiful lampposts and led to an imposing stone fortress on a peninsula away from the mainland.

Caroline turned, and they slowly drove along the paved road. Narrow stairwells leading down to restaurants and the marina. In the distance, buildings scattered up the side of rolling hills.

She looked straight ahead at the fortress. It was made from stone and very impressive. Three cannons protruded from three holes above the arched entrance. She wondered if Caroline was planning to show her the fortress when they turned down a small street to the left-hand side of the castle.

The narrow passageway was practically empty. There were a couple of vehicles unloading, but aside from that it was peaceful. As they travelled a little farther, Annie started to see restaurants and gelato stands. She realised that the small area they were in, accessible only by boat via the marina or via the small pathway, opened up into a network of small roads and streets. Stone buildings rose into the sky, two or even three storeys high. There were restaurants all around and what looked like apartments up above.

It put Annie in mind of pockets of Venice, a small island packed with people and entertainment, surrounded by small stone walls to keep the ocean at bay.

Caroline stopped the Vespa and kicked the stand down. She hopped off the bike, removed her helmet, and held out a hand to Annie. Annie gratefully took it as she navigated her way off of the bike and pulled off her own helmet. She fluffed up her hair and looked around.

"This place is amazing!"

Caroline beamed. She took Annie's helmet and placed it on the bike. "It is, isn't it?"

"Where are we?" Annie asked.

"That is the Castel dell'Ovo." Caroline pointed to the walls of the castle. "And we're on Isolotto di Megaride, or rather, the peninsula of Megaride."

"Mega. Ride?" Annie asked, anglicizing the words.

Caroline looked at her. "Well, you could say it like that if you were British. I would have thought an opera singer would pronounce it nicely." She winked.

Annie felt a stab in her stomach. She'd only just remembered that operas were frequently in Italian. And she was supposed to be an opera singer. Which presumably meant she was supposed to be able to speak, read, and understand Italian.

She'd never really understood the term 'sinking feeling' before. Now she understood it perfectly. Her legs felt like they couldn't support her body. She leaned back casually against a wall.

"Just joking," she said.

Caroline laughed. She leaned forward and kissed Annie chastely on the lips.

"Good," Caroline said. "Joke away. I want to have fun today; I want to put work behind me and try to remember what fun and relaxation are. I think I'd forgotten what that was before you came along."

Annie tried to smile; she didn't know how fake it

looked, but she did her best. "Sounds like fun," she said. "Why here?"

Caroline let out a nervous breath. "Because this is home."

"Home?" Annie looked around at the white and cream buildings which looked bigger than they probably were because of the narrow streets.

Caroline took Annie's hand and led her into one of the courtyards. The ground-floor doors to one of the buildings were flung open, and the delicious smell of homecooked food poured out. Café-style tables and chairs were being set up outside by a young waiter.

"Hello, Caroline," he greeted her.

"Hello, Matteo," Caroline replied.

A woman exited the building. She was tall and thin, probably in her sixties, and looked very, very British.

"Why don't you ever call before you come?" she complained to Caroline. "I could cook something special for you!"

Caroline chuckled. "Serena, this is Hazel. Hazel, this is Serena."

Hazel shook Annie's hand. Annie tried to keep a firm smile on her face but being introduced to more and more people in Caroline's life under the wrong name was, to say the least, stressful.

"Sit down, both of you, I'll get some drinks. How about some bread? Freshly made, of course. And some olives." Hazel turned around, the decision already made in her mind that they were sitting down and eating.

Caroline chuckled and pulled out a seat for Annie. Annie sat down, and Caroline took the seat beside her.

They looked out at the courtyard, the castle walls in the distance.

"She seems nice," Annie said.

"She is. She runs the restaurant here. I own the building, and my apartment is on the top floor." Caroline pointed behind them.

Annie squinted as she looked up. All she could see were closed shutters, but behind them was Caroline's home.

"Ah, so you're her landlady," Annie said.

"Yes, and she looks after my apartment when I'm not here."

"Is this where you spend those twelve weeks off?" Annie asked.

"Most of the time. Sometimes I spend time in other locations, but this is my home port."

Annie grinned. "Home port?"

Caroline blushed. "Sorry, work jargon."

"No need to apologise, it's adorable," Annie reassured her.

Hazel reappeared with a tray. She placed a bottle of water and two glasses on the table, a bread basket, two plates, cutlery, and a bowl of olives. Two menus were placed on the table as well.

"Can I get you ladies some wine?" Hazel asked.

"Not for me," Annie said. She wanted to keep a crystal-clear mind.

"Don't feel like you can't drink just because I can't," Caroline said.

"Maybe I'll have something later."

"Juice?" Hazel offered.

"I'll have an orange juice," Caroline said.

"Same," Annie agreed.

Hazel nodded and rushed back into the restaurant.

"So, how long have you owned this place?"

"Fifteen years, I..." Caroline started. She paused and winced.

"What?" Annie asked.

"I just realised that I bought this building when you were eleven."

Annie was about to argue with Caroline's math but remembered last minute that she had a few years on Serena.

"So?" Annie asked.

"I'm a lot older than you," Caroline lowered her voice, almost sounding embarrassed.

"You're more mature than I am, you've had more life experiences than I have. It's part of what I l... like about you." Annie nearly kicked herself for the slip-up.

Caroline focused on the bread basket, a light pink tinge to her cheeks. "I bought it as an investment and holiday base many moons ago, but I started spending more time here once I left the Navy. Since then, it became my home. Sort of."

"What drew you to Naples?" Annie asked. The 'sort of' seemed to leave a huge weight on Caroline, so Annie steered away from it for the time being. She knew talk of home could be difficult.

"History and culture," Caroline said. "Napoli has a very cultured history, which led to it becoming a very vibrant city. There are so many sites of historical interest here, and in between them are museums, galleries, opera houses, theatres. And then there's the water. Multiple smaller marinas and the main port. It's great for my work. I can be here in ten minutes, and even though it's close, it feels like I'm much farther away."

Annie looked around the idyllic peninsula; it looked timeless, a world away from the busy city, which was obviously a very short distance away.

"It seems peaceful," she said.

"Not too peaceful," Caroline replied. "Of an afternoon, this place starts to fill up with people. All of these restaurants are full by the evening."

"So, you're out here partying the night away?" Annie joked.

Caroline chuckled. "No, sometimes I'm in my apartment, listening to music and catching up on my reading." She took a sip of water. "Boring, I know."

"Not at all," Annie said. "That would be my preference, too. I did my partying when I was younger. Now I prefer an evening at home."

Caroline looked at her in disbelief. "You're too young to say that."

"Are people defined by their age?" Annie asked, a little irritated at Caroline's presumption. "At what age am I allowed to say that?"

It was a little harsh, but Annie wanted to give Caroline a wakeup call when it came to the matter of age. It worked, as Caroline looked suitably chastised.

"I'm sorry... I—"

"I think," Annie interrupted, "that people are defined by their experiences. Someone can live to be seventy and have lived a happy and comfortable life, maybe too comfortable, and have experienced very little. Some people lose everything at a young age and have to rebuild their entire world."

"I agree, I'm sorry. I shouldn't make presumptions about you." Caroline looked deeply upset, and Annie knew the message had been received loud and clear.

"It's okay," she said. "You won't do it again." She winked, taking the edge off her words.

Hazel returned with the juices. She'd obviously heard the end of the conversation and was chuckling. "What's she done now?" she asked Annie.

"Making comments about how young I am," Annie said.

Hazel rolled her eyes. "Honestly, the way she acts you'd think she was ninety. Fifty is the new thirty."

"You're as old as you feel, right?" Annie asked.

"Precisely." Hazel looked at Caroline. "She's fitter than any of us. Goes to the gym every day, if you can believe anyone would hate themselves that much."

"Thank you, Hazel," Caroline said through gritted teeth.

"Any food for you ladies?" Hazel asked.

Annie shook her head. "Nothing at the moment."

"Maybe in a while," Caroline said.

"No problem, do you want the board?" Hazel asked.

Caroline hesitated.

"Board?" Annie questioned.

"Chess board," Caroline said. "I sometimes play, but it's fine, we can—"

"I haven't played chess for years," Annie confessed,

"but I'd love to play. I mean, I'll be terrible, but I know how to play if you want to thrash me?"

Caroline laughed. "Are you sure?"

"She doesn't take any prisoners," Hazel said. "She made my grandson cry."

"It's not my fault he's so competitive," Caroline argued.

"You're supposed to let children win," Hazel told her.

Annie laughed as the two women bickered. She realised this was Caroline's family. Her home, her friends, the place where she was no longer Captain West but just Caroline. She could be herself and not be in the goldfish bowl that was *Fortuna*.

She could imagine Caroline sitting in the courtyard, playing chess with the locals, or looking out the window at the marina, watching the sun set over the ocean. It struck her that this was Caroline's sanctuary, somewhere she probably didn't take many people. Annie felt blessed that in such a short space of time, she'd earned Caroline's trust.

She also felt the ever-present guilt bubbling away in her gut.

TENACIOUS, NOT VERY STRATEGIC

"You cheater!" Caroline exclaimed.

Serena laughed as she plucked Caroline's knight from the board. "How am I cheating?"

"You're distracting me," she complained. "You were seductively adjusting your top."

Serena held the piece in her hand and looked at Caroline. "Seriously?"

"You were."

"I wasn't," Serena denied, "but if I was, you shouldn't be looking anyway."

Caroline narrowed her eyes. She was fairly convinced that Serena had decided to use distraction as a technique after losing her second game in a row. The start of the third game had been filled with supposedly casual stretches. Then she'd started to bite her lip in apparent concentration. Caroline lost the gift of speech during the fourth game when Hazel had delivered their meals and Serena had started moaning as she took bites of garlic bread.

Caroline didn't like cheaters, but she realised she was completely happy to play chess with Serena, despite the younger woman's clear attempts to divert her attention. Serena wasn't a bad player; she knew the rules and had a very vague understanding of some strategy, but it was very clear that she couldn't think more than one move ahead. She played rashly, not thinking of the consequences of her actions until it was far too late.

"Can I win?" Serena asked with a frown, examining the board.

"No," Caroline said. "Not with those pieces."

Serena groaned. "I lost again?"

"You did."

"Four games in a row, how embarrassing," Serena said. "Sorry, I'm sure I'm not very interesting to play with."

"On the contrary, you're very interesting to play with. I've learnt a lot about you," Caroline confessed.

"That I call the knight a horsey?" Serena asked.

"That was one of the highlights." Caroline grinned. "You're tenacious, not very strategic, but a fast learner. I think if we played more, you'd eventually become a very formidable opponent."

"I enjoyed playing," Serena said. "I don't mind losing; my skills lie elsewhere."

The look she gave Caroline was pure filth, and Caroline nearly choked on her drink in response. She tried to think of a witty, flirty reply, but while she was considering the matter—her phone rang.

"Saved by the bell," Serena noted.

Caroline looked at the display. "It's the ship. I have—"

"To take it, I know," Serena plucked a piece of lettuce

from the salad and ate it. "I'll be here with the food, so, you know, hurry back if you want any."

Caroline laughed. She stood up and took a few steps away from the table. She knew that no one wanted to sit and listen to their lunch companion discuss work. Although, come to think of it, Serena never seemed to react when Caroline was called away for work.

She took the call, noting that Hazel had rushed out of the restaurant the very moment Caroline stepped away, no doubt about to grill Serena for information.

Caroline rarely brought anyone to her little sanctuary, so Hazel would know that Serena's presence was meaningful. She listened to the details of the call and provided her response, all while watching the interaction between Hazel and Serena.

Curiosity tore at her. She wanted to know if Hazel was trying to determine if Serena was good enough for Caroline, or to convince Serena that Caroline was good enough for her. Hazel was like a protective older sister at the best of times, but even Hazel would surely recognise that Serena was way out of Caroline's league.

She wondered, not for the first time, why she had brought Serena into her little private world. Serena had said she had feelings for her, but what did that actually mean? Was there a future for them or was Caroline being foolish?

"Caroline? You there?" Thomas asked.

"Sorry, the connection dropped, what did you say?" Caroline lied.

Whether they had a future or not, Caroline just wanted to *know*. She was struggling to function with the unclear landscape she was currently walking on. On the other hand, she preferred to live in ignorance for a few more hours rather than be presented with the certainty that nothing would come of it.

Delaying the inevitable wasn't her style, but she couldn't stand the idea of letting go of her worry-free time with Serena.

She turned away, knowing the call would take a while and realising that giving it her full attention would draw it to a conclusion all the sooner.

HOME

Annie liked Hazel. A lot.

Hazel clearly adored Caroline and was now doing her absolute best to convince Annie that Caroline was a catch, something that she absolutely didn't need to do. Annie was already very much aware of the fact that anyone would be lucky to be with Caroline.

Hazel probably thought she was being subtle, but she wasn't even close to it.

"She'd make someone a lovely girlfriend, if you ladies still use that title?" Hazel asked. "I mean, I know you're not girls. But woman-friend sounds weird, and lady-friend sounds, well, less said the better about that."

Annie sipped at her drink. She wasn't going to throw Hazel a life preserver out of this conversation. It was more enjoyable to watch her flounder.

"Very kind, funny when she wants to be," Hazel said, as if she had been asked to list Caroline's best qualities. "She can be strict, but she has to be. Part of the job. Did you know she was in the Navy?"

Annie nodded.

"They treated her horribly, and that ex of hers." Hazel made a face like she had a mouth full of lemon sours. "Awful."

Annie couldn't disagree.

"You seem like a nice girl… woman," Hazel corrected.

Annie looked over to Caroline, still on the phone over the other side of the courtyard.

"I'm not good enough for her," she confessed. "I'd love to be, but I'm not."

Hazel shook her head. "Nonsense. Caroline's a good judge of character."

"Not this time," Annie disagreed.

Hazel tilted her head and regarded Annie for a few seconds. Annie honestly believed that her secret would fall out of her lips under the intense scrutiny.

"Caroline sees something in you, maybe you don't see it in yourself," Hazel reasoned. "Give yourself a chance."

"Hazel, are you telling all my secrets?" Caroline asked, practically sprinting back to the table.

"She's telling me the cheese comes from a local farmer," Annie replied, this time willing to help Hazel out.

Hazel nodded. "Yes, that."

Caroline looked between them. "Why don't I believe that?"

"Just because you don't share our cheese fascination, don't knock it," Annie said.

Hazel gave her a dazzling grin before pointing back to the restaurant. "I have work to get to. If I don't see you before you go, it was lovely meeting you, Serena."

"You, too," Annie replied.

"I'm sorry," Caroline apologised as she put the phone back in her pocket.

"As I keep telling you, it's fine. I know I'm sharing you with a lot of other people."

"I wish that wasn't the case," Caroline said.

"Me too, but it is what it is. I'd rather have a part of you than none of you."

"I'd... like to show you something, if that's okay?" Caroline looked nervous.

"Sure." Annie shrugged. She trusted Caroline despite the obvious nerves on display.

There had been something in the air between them since they arrived at the peninsula, as if there was something Caroline wanted to say but hadn't quite built up to yet. Annie knew the feeling well.

She wondered if she was about to be led upstairs to see Caroline's apartment. And if when she was there, she'd be presented with something unexpected, like a collection of Dolly Parton memorabilia.

Caroline stood up, and Annie did so, too. "You probably won't be interested, but it's a big part of my life."

"Now I'm intrigued," Annie reassured her.

Caroline led Annie around the restaurant to the sea wall. She jumped up on the wall and then down onto the rickety wooden pier below.

"Oh." Annie turned and looked behind her. "I thought we were going to your apartment?"

"I don't really spend much time there," Caroline confessed. She held a hand out and helped Annie to climb over the wall as well. Annie looked around the floating pontoons of the marina.

"It's a boat, isn't it?" Annie guessed.

Caroline nodded. She led Annie along a walkway, passing countless boats of various shapes and sizes. Some were clearly fishing boats, and some hadn't been used in some time. Annie was so busy staring at the fish being unloaded from one of the boats that she collided with Caroline when she stopped walking.

"Sorry."

Caroline put her hands out to balance her.

Annie turned and looked at the boat they were standing in front of. Her jaw dropped open.

"That's... a yacht," she said. "I think. I know nothing about boats. But that looks... wow."

The sleek white boat bobbed away on the water. Annie just stared at it. There was a flat platform at the rear to step onto the boat. On either side there was a short flight of three steps leading to another floor, which seemed to have an outside seating area.

From her vantage point, she couldn't see much of it, but she could easily tell that it was a beautiful and impressive vessel.

"Come aboard," Caroline suggested. She stepped onto the back of the boat and held out a hand to help Annie.

"Is this yours?"

"Yes. I told you that my father died while in the service? Well, he had a substantial life insurance policy, and I don't have any siblings. I bought a house in London, invested wisely. Between that and my own... compensation when I was asked to leave the service, I had a nice little sum. So, I bought *Serenity*."

"It's beautiful..." Annie let out a breath as she stared in awe.

She'd been on yachts before, Diego and his associates had several, but none of them were as classy as *Serenity*. Diego had been interested in boats that would tear up the ocean and potentially capsize and kill them all.

Serenity was different. It was sophisticated and stylish.

Caroline walked up the short flight of stairs, and Annie followed her. They came to a deck with a built-in outdoor table and leather seats. Two more flights of stairs led up to the upper deck, which Annie assumed housed more seating and probably a place to enjoy the sun.

Caroline opened a set of glass double doors and gestured for Annie to step inside.

In the living area, Annie marvelled at the furnishings. There was a seating area with more built-in sofas, then a dining area and a kitchen. At the front sat two large black leather seats in front of a complicated-looking control panel.

Caroline closed the double doors behind them. She looked nervous, her eyes darting about and a soft sheen of sweat on her upper lip.

Annie couldn't figure out what Caroline was concerned about. She assumed there was more to discover. Maybe the Dolly Parton collection was downstairs.

"She really is my pride and joy. Some people have children, this is mine," Caroline said.

Annie strolled around the interior, taking in the personal touches of framed photographs, a small collection of CDs, and a much larger collection of books. She approached the cockpit and noticed a stairwell heading downstairs.

"Two bedrooms," Caroline explained. "And two bathrooms. And an office."

"May I have a look around?" Annie asked.

"Of course, I'll see what I have in the kitchen."

Annie walked down the stairs, admiring the plush cream carpeting beneath her feet. Everything was furnished in creams and whites, accented with light wood. She couldn't believe how much space was aboard. She poked her head into the office, which was full of charts, paperwork, and more books. All neatly filed.

She found one of the bedrooms, which looked like a guest room. It was more spacious than her cabin aboard *Fortuna*, which made her chuckle. She entered the master bedroom, and a small gasp escaped her.

It was exquisite, so homely and still so elegant. More personal touches were scattered around the room—photos, artwork, and a bathrobe hung on the back of the door. She noticed some clothes folded and placed on the top of the chest of drawers and frowned. She opened a drawer; it was filled with clothes. She looked in the wardrobe and saw that was also filled with clothes.

She opened the bathroom and confirmed her suspicions when she saw it was filled with toiletries.

Caroline entered the master bedroom. She wrung her hands and looked around. "I can make some tea, if you'd like?"

"Caroline, do you live here?" Annie asked, finally understanding the sense of hesitation emanating from the usually confident woman.

"Well, no… I mean, sometimes." Caroline looked around, anywhere but making eye contact with Annie.

"That's why you wanted to bring me here, isn't it? To show me your life? Hazel, the restaurant, and here, your home?" Annie guessed.

"Yes. I know it may appear quite odd, but I feel more at home here than anywhere else in the world," Caroline confessed. "I know some people find that strange. They need to be somewhere solid, have an address, a solid location, in a particular country."

Caroline sat on the edge of the bed. "I like being at sea. I like to feel the waves as I go to sleep. When I'm off *Fortuna*, I may spend a few days here and there in my apartment in Napoli, but to be honest I mainly use the apartment for storage. For the most part, I'm here. It may look luxurious at first glance but living here for any long period of time is… different to most living arrangements."

"You can't pop to the shop for milk," Annie said.

Caroline laughed. "No. That one is tough."

"Do you travel to other ports, or do you just go out in the ocean and park up?"

Caroline smiled, probably at Annie's lack of understanding of seafaring lingo.

"Both," she replied. "It depends on the weather and the time of year. Tides dictate where you can go. It's not a conventional lifestyle."

And there it was. The source of Caroline's nerves. She was opening up to Annie and trying to explain what a relationship with her might look like, like a single mother admitting they had a child or a carer admitting they had a sick sibling to look after. Caroline's need for the sea was a factor in any relationship she might have.

The yacht was undeniably luxurious, but anyone wanting to be with Caroline would have to live on it for long periods of time. And then be alone without Caroline for long periods of time while she captained *Fortuna*.

Annie felt sorry for Caroline; dating must have been impossible for her. Her years of solitude now made a lot more sense.

As did Caroline's anxious disposition. She was explaining her lifestyle to Annie, expecting this to be the end of everything, knowing that very few people would be able to live that way. Annie suspected this was a conversation that Caroline had endured before.

She stood in front of Caroline and held out her hands. Caroline placed her hands in Annie's, looking up at her curiously.

"Thank you for showing me *Serenity*. She's a beautiful ship."

Caroline chuckled bitterly. "But?"

"Why do you think there's a but?"

"Because there always is. Whenever I've explained to any potential partner what my lifestyle looks like, they can't picture themselves as a part of it." Caroline's cheeks flashed red, and she pulled her hands away. "Not that I'm suggesting anything permanent, I'm not racing ahead. I just wanted to show you… me."

"Anyone would be lucky to be with you, to have the opportunity to share this life with you," Annie said.

"I know that you don't like the water. Many people

don't, but being on the sea is such an important part of my life."

"It's not that I don't like the water," Annie explained. "It's, well, it's complicated."

Caroline looked away, staring at the floor between her feet.

"I don't have all the answers," Annie continued. "I don't know how it would work, but that doesn't mean that it couldn't."

Caroline's eyes met hers again, and an unsure smile graced her face. Annie realised that her hypothetical statement attempting to tell Caroline that she could have a relationship with someone had been understood as something quite different. A real statement that *they* could figure things out.

Which Annie would love to say, but knew she couldn't without saying something else first.

"Caroline, I don't know what this thing is between us. I know it's there; I can't deny it. I've felt an attraction to you from the moment I saw you. And I'll admit, I didn't want to at first. I pulled away. But the more we bumped into each other, the more I got to know you, the more I... fell for you."

Annie blew out a nervous breath. This was it. She was going to tell her. She had to.

"And I get that you have a very unique job and lifestyle, but that honestly doesn't bother me. I've never lived a very conventional life, I'm not... grounded by family or home," she explained. "In fact, I'm not—"

"But your work," Caroline said. "The chances of your tours lining up with my schedule—"

"Caroline, there's something I have to tell you." She grabbed Caroline's hands again, wanting to show the strength of her feeling through the grip.

Caroline's phone rang. Both women winced. Annie let go of Caroline's hands and turned around.

"I'll give you some privacy, I'll be upstairs," Annie said.

"I'm sorry," Caroline called after her before answering the call.

Annie rushed up the stairs to the main living area. She couldn't believe things had escalated so far. She was meant to stay in her cabin, not speak to anyone, and plan her escape.

Somehow, she'd thrown those simple instructions out of the window. Instead she had fallen in love with someone, and it seemed that person had fallen for her, too.

"No, not for you," she muttered to herself. "For Serena."

She paced the living area. There was no easy way out of the scenario. It wasn't like she could tell Caroline and they'd laugh it off. Caroline would be devastated, especially now that she was admitting that she had feelings.

Once she found out that Annie was, well, Annie, she'd no doubt be furious. She'd feel conned.

"I'm sorry."

Annie turned around; Caroline had silently walked up the stairs.

"Caroline, I have to talk to you," Annie blurted out.

"I have to get back to the ship. There's been a mistake with some of the customs forms, and a rebooting of one of the ship's systems. I need to leave, right now. I am so sorry."

Caroline looked broken, like a woman who desperately wanted just five more minutes but knew it was impossible.

Annie wanted to explain, wanted to lead Caroline to the sofa and sit her down and give her the two-minute condensed version, just to have it out there. But that wasn't fair. Annie knew she had to make it easier for Caroline to leave; it was the least she could do.

She tried to smile as best she could.

"I understand." She crossed the room and put her hand on Caroline's cheek, pressing a soft kiss to the other. "Promise me that we can talk at some point this evening, just you and me. Fifteen minutes. It's important."

"I promise." Caroline surged forward and kissed Annie briefly on the lips. "I swear, I'll give you an entire hour. More, if I can."

They exited *Serenity*, Caroline locking up.

"Can I give you a lift back to *Fortuna*?"

"Actually, I think I'm going to walk around," Annie said. She needed some time and some air. She'd put an exact time on her revelation now. It really couldn't wait another moment. She needed some time to think about things, plan her words carefully.

She owed it to Caroline to have thoroughly planned what she intended to say, to work out the way to cause as little pain as possible.

"Are you sure?" Caroline asked as they walked towards the peninsula.

"Yes, I want to explore Napoli. You made it sound so wonderful."

"Okay, make sure you're back on the ship by—"

"Eight-thirty, I know. I read my *DreamFinder* every evening." Annie winked.

"Dinner tonight?" Caroline asked.

"Of course, unless you're sick of me?" Annie joked.

"Never." Caroline kissed her cheek.

Annie walked with Caroline to her Vespa, watching as she put on her helmet and offered her a small, sad wave goodbye before heading off the path they'd entered on a few hours earlier.

"Goodbye, Caroline," Annie whispered to herself.

ANOTHER INTERRUPTION

Caroline stormed onto the bridge, still in her casual attire as a clear message to the incompetent team that she actually had a life off the ship. One she'd had to leave behind to come and clean up their mess.

The crew stood to attention and all attempted to look a little more on duty than they had before they'd noticed her arrival. She assumed that her mood had pervaded the atmosphere, but she couldn't be upset about that.

She was furious, and she didn't care who knew.

"Thomas?" she asked as she marched into the SCC.

"Caroline, I'm so sorry. The system crashed after the reboot, and then we realised we had—"

"To get my signature to make a change to the roster, I know." She didn't want to hear what had gone wrong. The result was still that she'd had to come back to sign paperwork and clear everything with the customs director.

All because the reboot she wanted to do yesterday had gone wrong today. Yesterday, she would have been on board and easily able to cope with the issue. Today, she had to walk away from one of the most important conversations she could remember having in her personal life.

The next day she would gather the bridge crew to talk about what had gone wrong and why. At length. But at the moment, she was too angry to speak.

She'd finally managed to convince herself that she might have found someone who could actually put up with her. Maybe more than put up with her. It was no secret that Caroline kept to herself and had long ago constructed a tall wall to keep people out. Being the centre of attention as the captain meant a lot of people tried to befriend her, often for bragging rights.

But it was a part of the job, so Caroline allowed the behaviour and simply modified her own. She trusted no one and presented a fake Caroline West which the passengers adored.

Serena had seen through her and hadn't cared about her celebrity. Presumably because she was one in her own right.

Caroline sifted through the paperwork that Thomas was drowning in, helping him to get the customs forms in order, manually, before they had to set sail that evening.

She took a couple of calming breaths, reminding herself that Serena had seemed understanding of her unique living arrangements. She'd wanted to say something, but the way she'd held Caroline's hands so tightly indicated that it wasn't an end to whatever was growing between them.

Just a few more hours, Caroline reminded herself, and then everything will be answered.

"Er, sir?"

Thomas turned to look at the crewman who was interrupting them.

"The hotel director wanted to make you aware of three unexpected VIPs boarding here."

"Got the paperwork?" Thomas asked.

Caroline heard an exchange of papers, too busy collating her own paperwork to care about what was happening behind her.

"Ooh, celebrities," Thomas said.

"Anyone I'd know?" Caroline asked.

"Movie star and her husband," Thomas said.

"Then, no," Caroline said.

They worked in silence for a few minutes before Thomas spoke again. "I'm sorry for calling you back. I seriously tried everything, but the computer wouldn't accept changes without your code and the customs director wouldn't either."

"It's fine," Caroline lied. "Besides, the reset caused other problems anyway. I take it the CCTV is out?"

A constant bug in the system had been causing havoc for the last year since a new piece of software had been added. Despite reassurances that a reboot would fix the sluggish systems, it often threw many other systems offline with it.

"Yeah, we're working to get things back up," Thomas said. "But that's not the point, we should be able to cope without you."

"I'm the captain, the buck stops with me," Caroline said.

It was the way things on board the ship worked. Everything passed through her. The bureaucracy was antiquated, but it was the way things were. She signed off on absolutely everything; no one could be fired without having a meeting with her first. Even if they had gotten blind drunk and punched a passenger, the rules were that every decision passed in front of the master of the ship.

Even if that meant having no social life whatsoever.

DIEGO ORTEGA

Caroline raced out of the crew area, still putting on her tie as she walked down the long corridor towards the elevator lobby. If she saw another passenger manifest or order form, she'd throttle someone.

Not to mention whoever designed the supposedly foolproof system which was supposedly unable to fail. The one which had now failed in some way a total of fifty-two times.

She'd hardly had a moment's peace, but she'd eventually managed to get everything sorted out to the satisfaction of the port authorities. Unfortunately, it meant a delayed departure, which meant planning a new route and burning more costly fuel in order to keep on schedule.

Thankfully the next day was an entire day at sea. If they'd had a port to get to then things would have been much worse. It was a lot easier to catch up to schedule when they had an entire day to cross water rather than just an evening to arrive at the next stop.

Caroline walked into the lobby and headed to the stairwell, knowing that it would be much faster to go down nine floors via the stairs than to wait for an elevator during the evening rush.

She greeted passengers on her way, knowing already that she'd owe Serena yet another apology for her tardy timekeeping. She'd cleared most of her evening so that she could devote two hours to her. Hopefully that would get her off the hook.

She dove into the ladies' bathrooms to check her tie and general appearance before quickly returning to the deck and entering the restaurant. She nodded at the waiters who greeted her and took long strides towards her table.

"I'm so sorry I'm late, everyone," she apologised.

Michael, her personal head waiter, pulled her chair out. She thanked him and then took her seat. She glanced around the table, her eyes quickly landing on Serena, sitting to her right as had now become tradition.

Serena smiled at her, and Caroline felt relief flash through her. She felt whole again, something she had always felt was a ridiculous saying. How could any one single person feel like they weren't complete? Now it made sense.

The empty chair beside Serena was slid out. A good-looking man in his forties sat down. He wore a tuxedo, had slick, black hair, and smiled warmly.

"Captain West, a pleasure," he greeted her in a heavy Spanish accent.

Caroline noticed Serena go stiff. All the colour drained

away from her face. Caroline's eyes flicked from Serena to the newcomer and back again. She wanted to ask what was wrong but also focus her attention on the gentleman greeting her.

"My name is Diego Ortega. I see you have already met my beautiful fiancée, Serena."

He placed his hand over Serena's, leaned in, and gave her a soft peck on the cheek.

Caroline felt the very moment her mind went blank. She'd never experienced anything like it in her life before. She'd made life-or-death decisions with frequency throughout her career. She'd been trained so as not to not succumb under torture techniques.

And yet, this simple moment had undone her.

Serena was engaged.

Her brain still wasn't co-operating as she scrambled to recall precisely *how* she knew the name Diego Ortega. But she was fairly sure he was in some way connected to a crime family; the name certainly sounded familiar. She knew it would come to her as soon as her heart stopped pounding and her brain finished its spin cycle.

"I couldn't join this sailing immediately, but when I saw an opportunity open up in my schedule, I flew to Naples and raced to the port to be with her." He picked up Serena's hand and placed a soft kiss to her palm. Serena turned to look at him, offering a tight smile.

The other diners around the tables oohed and ahhed at the cute display. Caroline wanted to be sick. Or upend the table. Or both.

She opted to stand up.

"If you'll excuse me, it appears I'm needed elsewhere. I

do apologise, Mr Ortega, it was a pleasure to meet you," she announced.

She didn't look at Serena, Diego, or anyone else. She simply walked around the table, through the centre set of double doors, out of the restaurant with every intention of walking until *Fortuna* would allow her no more room.

THE END OF THE ROAD

Annie watched Caroline walk away. Everything had happened so fast. One moment she was smiling at Caroline, the next she smelt the familiar cologne of the man from her nightmares.

Panic had swept through her so quickly that she'd thought she might pass out. In hindsight, that would be have been preferable. Surely Caroline wouldn't have walked over her lifeless body in her hurry to leave?

But Annie hadn't passed out. She'd been too busy wondering if she could turn to Caroline and beg her for asylum. If such a thing existed at sea. Or would Diego reach for the innocent-looking steak knife on the table and kill her before she had time to get away?

She looked at him. He was all smiles and charm, talking with the other guests at the table. The words echoed in Annie's head, and she couldn't focus on what was being said or by whom.

All she knew was that Diego was on the ship. And Caroline had left the table.

Only then did it occur to Annie that Diego was playing along with her ruse. He was referring to her as Serena. Which meant he knew everything.

Why is he here? Annie wondered. *Why not just push me over the railing or slit my throat as I sleep?*

Though Annie had not been intimate with him for a long time, she knew him better than most people. Even so, his behaviour confused her, and she scoured her brain to try to understand what he was doing. And, more importantly, what he would do next.

Diego had always had a flair for the dramatic. There was a chance that he was just trying to frighten her, or possibly prove to her that he could find her.

He'd done both, and now Annie was forced to sit beside him and smile and nod and play along with whatever he said.

"We haven't decided on a honeymoon location yet, have we, darling?" Diego looked at her.

"No," Annie whispered.

"It's hard, with her being a famous opera singer," Diego said. "Trying to find time in her busy, busy schedule."

Annie swallowed hard and nodded, trying to force the tears down again.

"But we'll figure it out, won't we?" Diego stared at her, a faux smile plastered on his face.

Annie nodded again.

She knew they wouldn't figure anything out. Diego wouldn't have come all this way himself to have a simple chat with her. He was a man who liked to ensure that certain problems were solved rather than rely on someone else to do his dirty work.

He liked to see with his own eyes that skeletons in his closet were well and truly dealt with and wouldn't come back to haunt him.

Annie realised that it was the end of the road for her.

SHE'S TAKEN

Caroline had walked around the top deck for a few minutes, dodging passengers, when she realised she'd find no peace there. She needed to get back to her own room if she was going to have the crying fit that she knew was coming.

She walked into the crew area on deck fourteen and approached her stateroom door. She hesitated and then turned around and walked farther into the crew area before hammering on another door.

The door opened, and Mara looked at her in confusion. "Is there an emergency?"

"No," Caroline said, tears starting to stream down her cheeks.

Mara quickly pulled her into her cabin and closed the door behind them.

"Caroline? What happened? Are you okay?" Mara asked, holding her upper arms and trying to meet her eyes.

"I never should have listened to you," Caroline said.

"Me?" Mara took a step back. "What's happened?"

Caroline started to pace the room, not sure where to begin. She couldn't believe she'd been so foolish to fall for Serena, and now she was crying. She couldn't remember the last time she'd cried.

"I took Serena to Megaride," Caroline explained. "Everything was so perfect; we had a wonderful afternoon."

"Okay," Mara sounded confused.

Caroline fell onto the sofa. "And now I just met her fiancé at dinner."

Mara blinked. She sat on the edge of the coffee table. "You're sure?"

"Oh yes, he introduced himself to me personally. Took her hand in his right there at the table. I… I ran away. I couldn't think." Caroline closed her eyes and rubbed her palms against her face.

"It doesn't make any sense. Serena Rubio isn't engaged. I stalked her online profile when she came aboard," Mara said.

"So did I. Apparently this hasn't made the media yet. Probably because of who he is."

"Who is he?"

Caroline looked up at her friend. "Diego Ortega."

Mara frowned. "Why do I know that name?"

"Probably from the news. He's part of a large crime family." Caroline hated the very idea of the man being aboard his ship, but it wasn't unusual for criminals to come aboard the floating paradise that was *Fortuna*. Very often, crime did pay, and crime rather enjoyed a holiday.

"This makes no sense at all," Mara said.

"It makes perfect sense. They are engaged to be

married, and it's being kept quiet because of her career. I can't imagine people would be very happy with her marrying into the mafia," Caroline explained.

As she'd marched as far as the railings of the ship would allow, she'd realised the answer was quite simple. Serena was having a little fun before tying the knot. It was all part of some kind of twisted game, a game that she never would have been a part of if it hadn't been for…

"I shouldn't have listened to you," she told Mara again.

"It's hardly my fault. She didn't say she was engaged, she flirted with you, not me."

"People have flirted with me before," Caroline said, "and I kept my walls up and ignored them. You convinced me to let her in, to have fun and see how things went. If I'd not listened to you, I wouldn't feel like… like some teenager whose boy-band hero just eloped."

Mara stood up and walked over to her desk. She grabbed her laptop and lifted the lid. "This doesn't add up. Why would she not mention him? Why has he turned up now?"

"I don't know. Nor care." Caroline lay down on the sofa, not caring about creasing her dress uniform.

"Did you take her to *Serenity*?" Mara asked, obviously knowing the answer.

"Yes," Caroline whispered. "I feel like such an idiot. I wanted to show her the real me before the sailing was over. So she knew more about me, so she could… I don't know…"

"You thought you had something with her, so you put yourself out there," Mara said. "It makes sense. She must have been very important to you."

"She was."

Caroline's radio beeped. "Eagle One?"

She groaned loudly.

Mara lifted Caroline's jacket and plucked the radio from her belt.

"Thomas, it's Mara. Caroline's occupied, what do you need?"

"I need permission to reboot one of the computer systems again. We were having issues with earlier, and it seems the only solution will be a reboot. It will reset a lot of the ship's systems," Thomas replied.

"For fuck's sake," Caroline muttered. She sat up and rubbed at her eyes.

"What do you want me to tell him?" Mara asked.

"Tell him I'll be there in ten minutes." Caroline stood up. She needed to get back to her room to get changed and freshen up. Spending some time on the bridge was probably just what she needed. She didn't relish the idea of more system failures and reboots, but the distraction was timely to say the least.

Mara relayed the message and handed the radio back to Caroline. She gestured to her laptop. "What was his name?"

"Diego Ortega," Caroline said. "Googling him won't help. It won't change anything."

"I'm curious," Mara replied. "And sorry. I know you really liked her."

Caroline sniffed, examining her appearance in the hallway mirror to see how bad the damage was. "It's not your fault, I just… fell for her. Harder than I expected. It's my fault."

Mara tapped the name into the laptop while Caroline tried to make herself presentable for the short walk to her own cabin.

"Well, I'm still sorry. You deserved to find someone."

Caroline hummed noncommittally.

Just one more day, she reminded herself. *And then this nightmare sailing will be over.*

A LIABILITY

Annie had never been on deck ten before, but that was apparently where Diego's room was and that was where they were going. He hadn't said a word to her since they left the dining room. He held her hand, painfully tightly, and led her to his stateroom.

She had thought that they'd go back to her room and that she might be able to contact Elvin and get help, but that brief light at the end of the tunnel was extinguished when Diego pressed the elevator button for deck ten.

They stopped outside a room. Diego practically threw her hand to one side, got his pass card, and opened the door. He put his hand on Annie's back and shoved her into the room.

She stumbled, almost falling to the floor but catching herself on the desk. "Diego," she tried.

He raised his hand to silence her before stepping into the room. He waited a couple of seconds, allowing the door to slam behind them, and then he backhanded her across the face. He'd never struck her before, but Annie had always known he was capable of it.

He grabbed her arm and threw her towards the sofa.

"You think you can run? From me?" he demanded.

"No, I—"

"Think you can tell someone everything that you think you saw that day?"

"No, I'd never—" She stood up to explain.

He punched her. Annie never saw it coming. She was shocked at how lightning fast his fist came at her. And then shocked at how painful it was. White-hot pain seared through her skull. How any movie could portray someone being punched multiple times suddenly seemed ridiculous. She had no idea the action could be so excruciating.

He paced the room, fury radiating from him. Annie remained in a ball in front of the sofa, not wanting to get in his way again.

"If you'd come to me," he said, "if you'd spoken to me, rather than this foolish running away, I could have helped you."

Annie knew Diego well enough to know that wasn't true. She'd seen too many people from the inner circle disappear to believe that he'd have allowed her to live.

"Who have you spoken to?" he demanded.

"No one."

He surged towards her. "Liar!"

"I haven't!" Annie shouted back. The pain in her face dramatically reduced her fear of answering him back. She knew she needed to fight for her life now. He was capable of anything, and she'd only experienced a tiny amount of his rage so far.

He ran a frustrated hand over his mouth, staring down at her and attempting to figure her out. "What is this Serena Rubio business? You know her?"

Annie shook her head ever so lightly, aware that every movement felt like a needle forcing her bones apart. "I bumped into her at the station, this was her idea. I never wanted to do it."

Diego perched on the sofa. He patted the seat, requesting she come and sit beside her. Once she hesitantly did, he placed a large but gentle hand on her back.

"My little Annie," he said softly. "I have great love for you, you know."

Annie knew that was a lie. They'd had a passionate affair at first. She'd been brave enough to talk back to him and he'd liked that. And she'd liked him for a while, he'd been charming and fun to be around. But that fizzled out quickly and Annie had become more of a sister-figure to him, a part of his entourage but not a lot more.

This meant she knew him well. She'd watched Diego for years; this softer persona was the one he used to keep people calm before he inflicted whatever punishment he deemed fit.

There was no way he'd take Annie home and forgive her. Not after what she saw, she was too much of a liability. And, of course, there was the matter of her running away.

She'd had a good run, but she knew that it was undeniably the end of the line. Screaming for help wouldn't do much good; Diego would silence her in seconds. His effortless charm had allowed him to get away with worse than murdering a nobody like Annie.

She couldn't see a way out and wondered if she was getting what she deserved.

ANNIE PECK

"Captain? Doctor Perry is calling for you again," the duty officer called across the security command centre.

"Take a message," Caroline instructed them without looking up from the engine output screen.

Mara had called twice since Caroline had arrived on the bridge. Caroline hadn't taken the call either time. She told herself that she wasn't being petty, she was busy. She'd decided to remain on the bridge for the delayed sail-away that evening.

The distraction of work wasn't doing much to take her mind off of events.

"We have clearance to depart," Thomas said. "Finally."

The port authority had decided to punish them for the problems with paperwork and the late departure. Even Caroline's goodwill earned over years of working with, and buttering up, the port director was useless. He'd managed to be as awkward as possible and come up with problem after problem to delay them.

Caroline made a mental note to pick him up a case of

wine from La Spezia on the next sailing and go see him personally to beg forgiveness. She knew his ego would feel appropriately stroked if she did, which would mean easier sailings in and out of Napoli in the future.

Cruise ships were like big bullies who came into the ports, demanding so much in a short space of time. They disrupted the ordinary workings of many ports, caused pollution, and were perceived as uncaring of anything but profit.

Caroline had learnt long ago that creating personal connections with the port staff meant they didn't see it as *Fortuna* arriving in port, they saw it as Caroline doing so. After the system issues, she'd have to rebuild that relationship.

"Sector four-one has left that door open again," Thomas noted. He turned to the crewman beside him and asked them to call down to the area and have the door closed.

"Again?" Caroline asked.

"Yes, twice earlier today and once ten minutes ago," Thomas said. "We have a maintenance call booked for tomorrow in case it's a dodgy sensor or lock. Getting sick of seeing it on the panel."

"I think we need to have another memo sent to all staff about the importance of keeping certain areas secure," Caroline said. "It's gotten lax lately."

"I've had twenty reports today," Thomas said. "It's more than lax."

"Start disciplining," Caroline instructed him. "We can't have doors left open or unlocked."

"Um, Captain?"

Caroline turned around.

One of the security team who guarded the bridge stood in the doorway to the command centre. "Doctor Perry is here to see you."

"Here?" Caroline confirmed. To her knowledge, Mara had never been on the bridge.

"Yes, she's requesting access."

Caroline breezed past the woman, through the bridge, and to the door which was being held slightly ajar by another security guard. Mara stood outside the door, in the secure corridor, rolling her eyes.

"Let her in," Caroline said.

Mara edged around him, her laptop clutched to her chest. Caroline gestured to the side of the bridge where leather armchairs were set up for guests to watch the best view on the ship.

"What is it?" Caroline asked, her arms folded across her chest.

Mara opened her laptop, placing it on her palm for Caroline to see. "I was looking up Diego Ortega," she started.

"I don't care." Caroline started to walk away.

"You will," Mara said with certainty.

Caroline paused and slowly returned to look at the laptop.

Mara clicked on a browser window and brought up a picture of Diego and Serena. They were at a party on a beach, smiling and laughing at something out of shot.

"I'm so happy for them," Caroline deadpanned. "Anything else?"

"Put the sarcasm away, this is serious," Mara instructed.

She clicked on another browser window, bringing up an Instagram account. "This is from the same party. I found some of the same people. You can see Diego's back in this picture. Agree?"

Caroline squinted. "Yes, that's him."

Mara clicked on another browser window. "So, from that Instagram account, I found a Facebook page. This is the account of the same woman. Here she is with…"

Caroline looked from the picture to Mara and back to the picture. "Serena."

"No. The woman in this picture is not Serena Rubio." Mara clicked to another picture. "This picture is tagged as someone called Annie Peck. And here is Annie's profile."

Mara clicked on the link, and a Facebook profile page appeared. Caroline frowned. It said Annie Peck, but the photos were Serena Rubio.

"A pseudonym?" Caroline asked, knowing that many celebrities used them.

"That's what I thought at first. Then I did a deeper dive. Annie Peck has an extensive social media presence, she's definitely a real person. And there's a video of her performing karaoke. She cannot sing. At all."

"Coincidence?" Caroline asked, still looking at the photos on the Facebook page.

"I don't think that both Serena Rubio and Annie Peck, who look identical, know Diego Ortega. In fact, I couldn't find a single thing connecting Serena Rubio and Diego, but there was plenty connecting Annie Peck and Diego. Then I did this."

Mara clicked some more buttons, and a series of pictures appeared. The women in the pictures looked similar, but side by side it was clear that they were not the same woman.

"Left, Serena. Right, Annie," Mara explained. "They are different people. And the woman aboard is *not* Serena Rubio. She is definitely Annie Peck."

It wasn't the first time that Caroline had dealt with identity theft, but it was the first time that she had been personally and completely taken in by it. Caroline tried to keep herself together. She was on the bridge, and while no one was actively watching them, she could feel their eyes on her.

"Right," she said.

There was nothing else she could say. Mara was looking at her, awaiting a reply to see if Caroline had heard her words. She'd heard them, but it would take a lot longer to process them.

"So, she's a fraud." Caroline swallowed. She couldn't believe she'd been so completely taken in by Serena. Annie. Whoever it was. The woman she'd kissed and started to imagine a life with. Anger sparked; she wanted to lash out but knew better.

"Caroline, I'm worried," Mara whispered. "She's something to do with Diego Ortega; I looked him up, and he is *not* a nice man. I've done a very deep dive into Annie's social media accounts, and she doesn't seem the kind of person who would do this sort of thing. Honestly, going back years. She works with charities; she blogs about books she has read. Identity thief, she is not. And to what end? Why does anyone pretend to be a famous opera singer in an enclosed space? It's a massive risk."

"Criminals get a kick out of this kind of thing. Fooling people," Caroline explained.

"I know this is more your area of expertise than mine, but I don't think so," Mara said. "Something is going on here, and it isn't Annie deciding to pretend to be an opera singer for a week."

Caroline jutted her head towards the security command centre, and both women entered the space behind the bridge. Caroline picked up the phone and asked to be put through to the stateroom attendant for Serena's room.

"What are you going to do?" Mara asked softly, not wanting to attract too much attention from the other people working in the room.

"See if she is in her room and then have her arrested," Caroline said. The call was connected, and Elvin introduced himself. "Oh, yes, Elvin, do you know if Serena Rubio is in her room?"

Elvin said he would go and check.

"She might be in trouble," Mara said.

"Then the brig would be the best place for her," Caroline pointed out, covering the mouthpiece in case Elvin was still by the phone.

"I know she hurt you—"

"She's an identity thief, Mara. This isn't anything personal; it's standard procedure." Caroline held the phone in an iron grip and stared at one of the screens.

She couldn't believe she had been taken in by this woman. She hadn't figured out what the play was yet;

perhaps she wanted money, or maybe it was to blackmail her to courier contraband aboard the ship for her boyfriend Diego, or maybe just for a laugh. She honestly couldn't fathom her reasoning.

She'd been played, but it had felt so real. And now it was crumbling down around Caroline quicker than she could cope with.

"Captain? Are we still departing?" Thomas asked, unaware of the disaster she was dealing with.

"Yes, carry on, Thomas," Caroline instructed.

She wasn't going to delay departure any longer, even if it would be easier to chuck Annie Peck off the ship in Napoli rather than keep her in the brig for the remainder of the trip. They were late, and they needed to get going.

"Captain West?" Elvin said on the line.

"Go ahead, Elvin."

"The room… it's been turned upside down. Miss Serena isn't there."

Caroline felt her blood run cold. "Thank you, Elvin. I'll take it from here."

She hung up the call and picked up the phone again. She connected to the switchboard and asked for the stateroom attendant for Diego Ortega's room. A few moments later she was connected.

"I need you to go and check if Mr Ortega is in the room. I just need to know if he is there, nothing more. Send some free Champagne on my compliments as an excuse," Caroline said.

The attendant agreed and said they would be back shortly.

Caroline held the phone and waited.

All around her, the bridge was coming to life as the intricate task of moving the enormous ship from its mooring began. From starting the process to the ship actually moving took around thirty minutes. Caroline was already mentally calculating how much extra fuel they would need to burn to catch up to the schedule. She'd have a lot of explaining to do in her next report.

Beside her Mara tapped away on her laptop, presumably doing further research. Caroline took a couple of breaths, trying to stay calm. She was too stressed to figure out what the scam was; she needed to relax a little. Nothing was making any sense, and she couldn't calm herself enough to try to piece together what she did know.

For the first time in her career aboard *Fortuna*, she wanted to get off the ship and go to *Serenity*. The idea of climbing into bed and tuning everything out sounded like utter bliss.

"Captain? There is no one in the room, but there has been a fight. The furniture has been turned over, a mirror is broken, and there is blood on the carpet," the attendant reported.

A RESPONSIBILITY FOR SAFETY

CAROLINE BRIEFED her head of security, Dan Lovell, on the situation and instructed him that she wanted a ship-wide search for both Diego Ortega and Serena Rubio. She also wanted a complete log of both of their movements for the past six hours.

She needed to piece together the puzzle and figure out what was happening. Her hurt and anger had to be pushed to one side so she could do her job. Getting the situation under control was her primary goal, figuring out what the situation actually was could wait.

She made her way to Diego's room. Hearing that there was blood present had shaken her. Anger tore through her at the thought of the sheer number of bold-faced lies Annie Peck had told her, but residual feelings lingered. The thought of her being injured caused Caroline's hands to shake as she marched through the hallways towards the stateroom.

Security officers were posted outside the door. One

stepped aside, and the other opened the door for Caroline to enter.

The door closed behind her, and the sound of it clicking shut swallowed Caroline's gasp. Dan looked up from the broken glass he was studying; it spread across a large swath of the floorspace.

Could all of that have come from just one mirror? she wondered.

"Hell of a tussle in here," Dan stated. He stood up and pointed to the chair which had been tossed onto the bed. "I think he used that to incapacitate her, there's blood on the leg. And then more blood in the glass here."

"No one saw anything?" Caroline asked in astonishment. The ship was nearly full, there were people everywhere. She refused to believe that no one saw or heard anything.

"No reports. We're searching the CCTV as quickly as we can. It happened when two of the big shows were on; they easily suck up three thousand people." Dan continued to look around the room. "He wasn't planning on staying long."

Caroline frowned, looking around the room for whatever had told Dan that.

"Didn't bring anything aboard with him," Dan explained, with a nod towards the wardrobe. "There's only hand luggage in here."

"We only have one more day, then we're back in Barcelona," Caroline said.

"True, but he brought nothing. No toiletries, for example. He purchased his ticket an hour before boarding. It all seems very last-minute."

"Everything about this is giving me a headache," Caroline confessed.

"At least it's not Marseille from last year," Dan pointed out.

"Don't remind me." Caroline walked around the room to see if she could find anything to unravel the mystery.

Cruise ships were often targeted by crime gangs who thought they could use the ships to transport drugs and other illegal cargo. The previous year they had discovered that a member of the hotel staff had been bribed into storing cocaine in one of the storerooms.

It had all been fixed in the end, but it had caused days of headaches and paperwork for everyone who had to clean up the mess caused.

"What do you make of this, Dan?" she asked, her own mind too cluttered to process it.

"I know men like Diego Ortega. They're arrogant bullies, and they don't show mercy. I think this woman's in a lot of trouble."

Caroline snapped her head around. "You don't think they are working together? That this was a heated argument over something that went wrong with their plan?"

Dan quickly shook his head. "Definitely not. Why would she take the risk to get on board *Fortuna* under an alias? On top of that, a famous alias? That's a huge gamble for someone to take. She could have been very easily found out, and if she was, then she would have been arrested and handed over to local authorities. And for what? What was the plan?"

"That's what I'm trying to figure out," Caroline said.

"Logically, the reason to take an identity like this

would be to leverage it on board, but my research tells me that she kept to herself. She wasn't soliciting money under the guise of a famous opera singer. She wasn't asking for favours." Dan folded his arms and leaned against the desk, sucking in a deep breath as he looked thoughtfully around the stateroom. "I don't see the reason for her doing it, which makes me think it was one thing and one thing only: desperation. Especially if she was in any way involved with the Ortegas."

Fear had been pricking at her insides for a while, and Caroline now realised she was holding it back with anger. Anger at Annie for fooling her. Deliberately fooling her, day after day. Even kissing her, dragging Caroline in with no regard for her feelings.

Now she realised she had to consider the very real possibility that Annie was somewhat innocent in whatever had gone on.

Dan's radio beeped. He answered it and held the device out so they could both hear the report.

"We have Diego Ortega in custody. He is refusing to answer our questions. He's denying any involvement in anything."

"Of course he is," Dan said privately to Caroline. "He thinks he's above the law."

"Not on my ship he isn't," Caroline said.

Dan spoke into the radio. "Put him in the brig. If he wants to say anything, then let him. Otherwise, let him stew. I want everyone looking for the female; she's presumed to be in a vulnerable state."

Caroline looked at the chair leg, a nasty splash of blood now dripping onto the white bedsheet below it. She was responsible for the safety and security of every single person aboard *Fortuna*, no matter her personal opinion of them.

She promised herself right there and then that she would do everything she could to find Annie and ensure her safety. Answers would come later. Not that she could think of a single scenario that would mend her broken heart and shattered trust.

A CLUE

Caroline paced the bridge. She'd radioed Thomas and told him to delay departure. She'd then made some private calls to contacts in the Royal Navy who she knew would love the opportunity to question Diego Ortega about his various businesses.

When Caroline worked for the service, the drug families were the bane of her existence, thoughtlessly flooding markets with drugs without a single care for what the end product did to people.

Caroline may not have worked for the navy anymore, but she still supported them wherever she could. Her own poor treatment from the higher-ups didn't mean she wouldn't assist in the overall mission for the service as a whole. And advising them that one of the big players in a large crime syndicate was soon to be arrested by the local police was a good way to help. They'd be able to take him in for questioning on any one of the outstanding charges they had against him, long before his network managed to bribe any local law official into letting him go without charge.

It meant a further delay to *Fortuna*, but it was worth it.

However, his refusal to say a word about Serena or Annie had infuriated Caroline further.

Dan was coordinating the security effort from the SCC and had all but kicked Caroline out when her constant questions and hovering became too much. She'd exited to the bridge, where she couldn't be asked to leave. A flurry of activity, and several officers leaving the area, caused Caroline to speculate that they had a lead. She didn't have to wonder long when Dan walked over to her.

"Diego took an all-access tour of the ship when he came aboard, a VIP thing," Dan explained.

Caroline closed her eyes and sighed. She'd always hated the tours. They were a terrible idea, and the VIP ones were the worse. Letting anyone view the entire ship's operation for a fee was a disaster waiting to happen. The VIP tours even allowed guests to pick and choose some areas to visit, within reason.

Diego didn't seem like the kind of man to have an interest in the engine room of a large ship, nor the kitchens behind the scenes of the main dining room. Just the thought that he had been in the crew areas set her on edge.

"He had a good look at deck two and deck one. And the boarding record shows that he checked in with a suitcase."

Caroline opened her eyes. "But there wasn't one in his room."

"Exactly, which means that it's somewhere on board. We're having trouble accessing the CCTV, it was one of the systems affected by the reboot, but I will bet my house that it will show Diego wheeling a suitcase out of his room at about the same time that Annie Peck went missing."

Caroline felt instantly sick. She put a hand out and steadied herself against the navigational deck. The image was too horrific for words.

"Do you," she lowered her voice, "think she's dead?"

Dan shrugged. "Impossible to say at this point. My instinct is to say no, there wasn't that much blood in the room. And no sign of a weapon. Besides, these mafia big shots like to play games. If he wanted her dead, he could have thrown her over the balcony in his room."

Caroline swallowed down the rising bile. She wasn't an innocent by any means; she'd seen terrible crime scenes and was no stranger to the sight of a dead body. But the thought of a woman she had seen a few hours ago being murdered shook her to the core.

"More likely he wants her to suffer," Dan continued. "And have a story to tell people. They are always trying to outdo each other in the most disgusting way to get rid of someone."

Caroline held up her hand to stop him from saying anything else. The last thing she needed on this terrible evening was to throw up all over the navigator's workspace.

Dan got the message. He straightened his spine and took on a more professional tone. "I have my men searching the lower decks."

"That will take hours," Caroline sighed.

"We don't have any better suggestions at the moment," Dan said apologetically. "I'm going to go and assist with the search personally; I'll keep you updated."

She dismissed him, and he turned and left the bridge. Caroline made eye contact with Thomas; he was vaguely aware of the issue and had fully taken control of departure from the port. He offered her a tight smile, one that said he was there if she needed him and that she could rely on him.

It meant more than he could ever know.

Mara had stayed on the bridge in one of the visitors' chairs and now walked over to stand beside Caroline.

"There must be something we can do. I feel utterly useless," she whispered.

"I know what you mean. But you know the lower decks: so many rooms, so many possibilities of where he could…" Caroline trailed off.

Was Annie dead? Had a murder taken place aboard *Fortuna*? It was a very real possibility. And a horrifying thought. Caroline took her responsibility for safety very seriously. Annie was probably the passenger whom she'd seen most of the entire trip.

She'd failed her miserably.

Caroline heard a crewman making a phone call, asking someone on the lower decks to close a door.

"The doors," Caroline said.

"What?" Mara asked.

Caroline entered the SCC. "The doors," she repeated. "We've had doors opening and closing on the lower decks today. Some of them might be a clue."

She approached one of the control screens, slinging

her arm across the back of the operator's chair. "Matt, can you isolate a list of door alarms we've had? I want to know which rooms were accessed between five and seven this evening, and then again between eight and ten."

Matt nodded. His hands flew across the keyboard.

"What are you thinking?" Mara asked.

"If Diego went on a VIP tour the moment he got on board, he must have been planning something. Why bother? It's not like he was bored and had nothing else to do. He was looking for something. I'm going to guess that he was looking for locations, especially for locations that weren't so secure. Maybe he tried a couple of doors when he was down there? See what he could open without a pass card? Maybe he even spoke to staff and figured out what he could convince them to open for him."

"Wherever he had luck, he'd return to later," Mara said. "After dinner, when he had Annie with him."

"It's just a guess," Caroline said. "We get these alerts all the time. Maintenance are famous for leaving doors open while they go and get a spanner."

"Here's a list of doors that were flagged in those hours." Matt pointed at the screen. "I'm going to guess that it wasn't these three; they aren't anywhere near the tour route."

"Which leaves us with two," Caroline said. "The incinerator and the dairy chiller."

She spun around and grabbed a radio from the rack.

Mara was right behind her. "Where are we going? Which one?"

"The chiller," Caroline said. "If it's the incinerator, we're already too late."

DEEP CHILL

Caroline hurried down the stairwell, thankful for the crew area. If she were trying to navigate the passenger area, she'd have no hope at all. She'd radioed ahead to Dan to tell him of her suspicions, and he was already dispatching officers to the two locations.

She could have stayed on the bridge and coordinated efforts from there, but that was never going to happen. She was a hands-on leader, and a passenger in danger was something she would always fight for.

Even if that passenger had consistently lied to her for days and broken her heart in the process. Whoever Annie Peck was, whatever reasons she had, Caroline had to push her feelings to one side.

She arrived on deck one, Mara a couple of flights of steps behind her, something Caroline would remind her of at a later time when staff physicals were underway.

"Matt, I'm on deck one, door 7B. Where am I going?"

Caroline knew *Fortuna* like the back of her hand, but the exact location of the dairy chiller wasn't ever going to be something she could locate without consulting a map. Or using a member of her bridge crew to guide her via the live CCTV feeds.

"Turn right, go for one hundred metres to the intersection, then left, and then it's the second door on the right," Matt replied.

Caroline sprinted. In the distance she could see one of the supplier managers, Clifford. He was looking at her in confusion, clearly having no idea what was going on.

"Clifford, dairy chiller?" she asked, out of breath.

"Which one?" he asked. "There are three."

Caroline would have screamed if she'd had the energy. Why did any ship need three dairy chillers? The excess of *Fortuna* staggered her sometimes.

"Matt, there are three dairy chillers, which one?"

There was a pause.

"I'll check, one second."

Clifford looked at the radio and then at Caroline. "Everything okay, Captain?"

"We believe a passenger has injured another passenger. There's a chance he brought her down here," Caroline explained.

"Shifty-looking tall guy?" Clifford asked. He nodded knowingly. "I knew that fella was trouble. He was on the tour." He waved his hand for Caroline to follow him and led her through a maze of short corridors. "He was asking all sorts of questions, questions a man with expensive shoes had no business asking."

They stopped outside a large metal door. Clifford entered a code on a keypad. It beeped in recognition and then he lifted the large handle and pushed the door to the side. Cold air seeped out immediately. Caroline would have shivered if adrenaline wasn't pulsing through her.

"Caroline?" Mara called from the distance.

"In here," she shouted back. She looked at Clifford. "Please go and get Doctor Perry, we might need her."

Clifford jogged back towards the main corridor while Caroline walked farther into the metal-walled industrial refrigerator. She passed pallets filled with boxes and plastic tubs of yogurt stacked to the ceiling.

Then she saw it. Nestled between two large pallets was a suitcase neatly parked up against the wall.

She hesitated only for a second, the fact that she may come across a dead body being pushed aside quickly. If that was the case, then she'd deal with it later.

Her fingers were already numb with the cold, and she fumbled for a moment to find the zip. She took a deep breath and pulled the zipper open around the extra-large, soft-sided suitcase. The lid fell open to the side and Annie tumbled out, gasping for breath as she did.

She's alive, she's alive, Caroline reassured herself.

She heard Clifford and Mara approaching and shouted for Mara to hurry.

Annie was deathly white. Dried blood caked the side of her face, and a gag prevented any sound from escaping other than the fast pants for air that echoed off the metal walls.

Caroline quickly loosened the gag, and it dropped to the floor. Annie knelt with her arms out in front of her, sobs coming in between deep breaths. Her hands were tightly bound with rope, and Caroline immediately set to untying them.

She was shivering uncontrollably. It started to dawn on Caroline that even though she was alive, there was a possibility that she wasn't going to come through the ordeal.

She felt Clifford appear behind her. He stripped off his work jacket and draped it around Annie's shoulders. Caroline released the rope around Annie's wrists; they didn't fall away as easily as the gag had done. The fastenings cut into Annie's skin, and Caroline removed the ropes as carefully as she could. Eventually, she managed to get Annie's hands released and dared to look up into her eyes.

"Caroline," Annie whispered. She started to lean forward; her arms outstretched to grab hold of her.

She lied to you, she's not who she says she is, Caroline reminded herself.

Caroline stood up and gestured for Mara to take over. She contacted Dan on her radio and advised that Annie Peck had been found. She requested further medical backup before looking at Clifford and jutting her head towards the exit.

The moment they were outside she rounded on him.

"How on earth does that happen? A suitcase in a chiller? This door is locked by a keypad code. I need a list of people who had access—"

"Captain West?"

Caroline stopped ranting and turned to see a young man behind her. He wore a wait-staff uniform and was staring at his feet.

"Yes?" she snapped.

"I opened the chiller for him. He… he had a VIP lanyard," the waiter explained.

Caroline felt her jaw drop open. "You let him put a suitcase in the chiller?"

"He said it contained imported cheese. Very expensive. He said he had permission."

Dan appeared with several security officers, all out of breath from having run the length of the ship, presumably from the incinerator. Caroline pointed to the chiller, and Dan went inside.

She looked at the waiter and slowly nodded. "Okay. It's not your fault; we need to have better procedures in place. And we need to reiterate the rules. A VIP lanyard does not give someone access to the whole of my ship." She turned to Clifford. "I want you to talk with your people about security. We'll be organising ship-wide training very shortly."

"What was in the suitcase?" the waiter asked hesitantly.

"A woman," Caroline said.

His eyes widened in shock.

"She's okay," Caroline reassured him.

Saying the words made it real in her own mind. She'd been operating on autopilot for so long that she hadn't given herself time to think.

She's okay, she reminded herself. *Mara will be able to heal her.*

Concern faded, and anger took its place. She could get answers now, but she wasn't sure she even wanted them.

She was on an emotional rollercoaster like she had never experienced before: one moment confused, the next hurt, the next terrified, and now… furious.

SHE'S A CRIMINAL

It was two in the morning when Caroline completed her final meeting. Reports were typed up, paperwork was filed, plans of action were in place, crew members were apprised of the situation, and head office had chewed her out.

She slumped in her chair.

It was, without question, her most stressful evening aboard *Fortuna*.

Questions would be asked for weeks and months to come. The rumours would go on far longer. If they were extremely lucky, the media wouldn't hear about any of it.

She leaned forward and wearily placed her hands on the conference room table and pushed herself to her feet. She couldn't delay it any longer; she had to go to the hospital and get a status report on their patient.

She felt emotionally wrung out but knew that sleep wouldn't come any time soon. She left the conference room and made her way down to deck two, taking the elevator this time as the majority of the passengers were tucked up in bed. The few who were awake were propping up the bars or losing everything in the casino.

The doors slid open, and Caroline walked sluggishly into the hospital. She'd had long days before, but this must have been a record. Not due to the length of time but simply the ups and downs of it all.

Was she really showing Serena Rubio around *Serenity* just a few hours ago?

She chuckled bitterly to herself. No, that never happened. She'd never even met Serena Rubio.

Seeing the light on, she walked into Mara's office, surprised to see her still on duty. "I thought you would have gone to bed," Caroline commented, taking a seat in front of her desk.

"I don't think I could sleep after all that," she said. "I've been researching."

"Oh yes?" Caroline wasn't sure she wanted to know but, considering that Mara's curiosity had basically saved Annie's life, she had no choice but to listen.

"Annie Peck, from Yorkshire, only child of Anita and Samuel Peck." Mara looked meaningfully at Caroline.

Caroline blinked. "Is that supposed to mean something to me?"

"Read a newspaper," Mara sighed.

"Too depressing," Caroline replied. "Who are they?"

"Who *were* they," Mara corrected. "They ran a large investment firm, very well-known couple. Did a lot of charity work, that kind of thing. They were swept away in floods, helping in a local village in Devon. You must have heard about that?"

Caroline frowned. It was ringing a faint bell, but she

couldn't put her finger on the exact details. Getting a copy of a newspaper hadn't been the easiest thing when she was in the service, so she'd eventually gotten out of the habit of being up to date with the news entirely.

Mara could plainly see her confusion. "It was that year we had all those floods in England. A small village in Devon was about to be hit by massive floodwaters when a river broke its banks. The Pecks had a holiday home there, and they were helping locals to get out. The water rose faster than expected, broke through a flood defence, and nine people were killed."

Caroline shivered at the thought. It was a terrible way to die. She remembered Annie's haunted look the night of the rough waters and wondered if there was a connection.

"But Annie survived?" Caroline asked.

"She was at the rescue centre, helping to prepare beds and meals for the people being evacuated," Mara said. "She vanished soon after they died, reports saying that she moved to Spain after that. Not to be crass…" She trailed off, seemingly uncertain whether or not to continue.

"Go on," Caroline encouraged.

"She must have inherited a huge amount of money. They were very rich and had no other children. Whatever this… thing… was, it can't have been about money."

"Maybe it was about transporting illegal goods aboard *Fortuna*. Or just the laugh of fooling me," Caroline suggested resentfully.

"So, you really think she'd go through all of this to fool you?" Mara asked. "Seems a little odd. She doesn't even know who you are."

"Maybe not. But why use Serena Rubio's name? How

does she have her ID?" Caroline countered, not having any answers but able to find plenty more questions.

"I spoke with Dan, and we contacted Serena Rubio's management—no easy task, I might add. They can't get hold of Serena at the moment but are going to get back to me once they manage to make contact. Keep in mind that it's late in Spain."

Mara leaned back in her chair and tossed her pen to the desk. She looked as tired as Caroline felt.

"How is she? Have you spoken to her?" Caroline asked.

Mara nodded. "She'll be fine. And, yes, I have spoken with her, at length."

"And?" Caroline pressed.

"And I think you need to speak to her for yourself," Mara replied. "I believe her, but I want you to talk to her."

"Is she well enough to go to the brig?" Caroline asked.

"Caroline!" Mara admonished.

"She's a criminal, Mara."

Mara folded her arms and pinned Caroline with a serious glare. "I'm not releasing her. She needs to be here."

"Oh, really?" Caroline argued.

"Really." Mara was clearly lying.

"You're impossible."

Mara shrugged. "Maybe I am. But she does honestly need to remain under supervision for a few more hours to be certain that her internal organs didn't suffer any permanent damage."

Caroline bit the inside of her cheek. She wanted to know more about what had happened and how serious

Annie's injuries were, but she also didn't want to ask. Didn't want to care.

"Go and talk to her," Mara ordered. "Try not to be too mean."

"Mean?!" Caroline balked. "Do I honestly need to remind you what she did?"

"Go and talk to her," Mara repeated. She sat up, pulled her laptop close, and started typing, signalling the end of the conversation.

EXPLAINING THINGS

ANNIE GENTLY LIFTED the edge of the gauze on her right wrist. She could see angry red marks and peeling skin. She assumed her left wrist looked the same. Both itched like hell.

The duty nurse had lowered the lights in her room, assuming that Annie would want to get some sleep. A few moments later, Annie had turned on the harsh reading light above her bed. She didn't want sleep to claim her. Nightmares and memories would surely come if it did.

Exhaustion and the pain medications were doing their combined best to take her away, and every now and then her eyelids started to feel unimaginably heavy.

A shadow emerged. She narrowed her eyes to locate the source.

At last, she thought once she identified it as Caroline standing in the doorway. She looked hurt and angry, exactly as Annie had expected.

Caroline stepped into the room, standing at the end of

her bed, hands clasped in front of her and gazing at Annie with a suspicious glare.

"Thank you," Annie whispered, her voice still weak from attempting to scream for help through the gag.

Caroline turned away; Annie imagined that her face wasn't exactly a pleasure to look at currently. Not that anyone had provided her with a mirror as she had requested. Soon, they had said. Tomorrow, they'd promised. It told her everything she needed to know.

"Just tell me... why?" Caroline asked. Rather than look at Annie, she walked over to the wall and studied a painting.

Annie had explained everything to Doctor Perry and had no idea what Caroline knew. She didn't care either. The opportunity to explain everything to Caroline was more than she thought she'd get.

She gently pushed herself into a higher seating position, careful not to put pressure on either of her wrists. She winced and struggled for a few moments before letting out a relieved sigh and leaning back into the soft pillows supporting her.

"My name is Annie Peck," she said. She swallowed quickly a few times to lubricate her throat. "I wanted to tell you. I know that's not an excuse, but I did try."

"Not hard enough. Why were you pretending to be Serena Rubio?" Caroline asked, her voice cold.

"Diego Ortega was my boyfriend, many years ago. We haven't been together for years, but I still lived with him. I stayed because, well, actually, I don't really know why I stayed," she admitted. "But a week ago I saw something. A crime. And I knew that just seeing it would mean the end of my life. So, I ran."

Caroline continued to look at the painting. Annie didn't know if she was listening properly or not.

"I didn't really have a plan. The Ortega clan are dangerous, they're criminals. Some might say mafia," Annie explained. "I was at Barcelona's train station about to get out of there, when this woman came into the bathroom where I was hiding out."

She started to giggle.

Caroline turned around and stared at her. "Is something funny?"

"It's just so ridiculous," she confessed. "Like, if you told me this, I wouldn't believe you. It's crazy, but it's true. This woman was the spitting image of me. We were both shocked, and she introduced herself as Serena Rubio. Which meant nothing to me."

Caroline took a small step closer. Her arms were firmly crossed, but at least she was now facing Annie.

"She thought God had brought us together." Annie laughed. She stopped quickly at the pain in her throat. "Ouch, right, no laughing."

She took a few slow breaths to calm herself before continuing. "Serena was booked on *Fortuna*, but she didn't want to go. Her manager booked it because she needed to rest her voice for her upcoming shows. But her boyfriend, whom her manager doesn't know about, was flying in from... Australia, I think?" Annie paused and thought about it. "Or was it America? I think it began with an A. It was a long way away."

"Is it relevant?" Caroline asked, exasperation clear.

"Oh, no, I suppose not." Annie shook her head softly. All of her planning and practiced speech had been forgotten. Not surprising when she'd nearly been murdered.

"He was flying in and she was devastated that she wouldn't see him. She came up with this crazy idea that I could be her. I'd told her that I was leaving town, leaving a bad relationship. She thought it was perfect: she'd go and see her boyfriend, her manager would think she was here, and I could hide out on the ship."

Annie reached for the cup of water on the table in front of her. Caroline stepped forward, picked up the cup, and placed it in Annie's outstretched hands. It was a simple gesture, but it warmed Annie's heart.

She took a sip of water and then rested the cup in her lap, grasping it tightly. "It was stupid, but I was running for my life and not thinking straight. And I suddenly realised that I had a twin walking around Barcelona, and if *I* couldn't tell us apart, then neither would Diego's people. I told her I'd agree, but she had to promise to get out of the city. Which she said she'd do. God, I hope she did."

There was a soft knock on the door; Mara stood in the doorway. "Everything okay in here?" she asked.

Annie nodded.

"Call me if you need anything," she said, casting a look towards Caroline before leaving again.

"I wasn't supposed to talk to anyone," Annie said. "I was supposed to sit in my room and never see anyone. Just order room service and stay in the room. But the day I checked in, someone recognised me... Serena... whatever. They made a big deal about it, and Graham Fucking Shelby overheard it. When he realised it was my first cruise, he wanted to give me some tips, or so I thought. He actually wanted to show off that he knew a celebrity."

Caroline perched on the edge of the plastic chair beside the bed. Annie was relieved that she was listening, but she knew she had a long way to go yet. Caroline hearing the story was not her believing it. And who knew if forgiveness was even possible.

"I had no idea he was sitting at the captain's table. If I knew I never would have gone. That first dinner I was terrified. I thought you'd see right through me."

"No, you had me fooled," Caroline said.

"I don't think I did," Annie argued.

Caroline opened her mouth to argue and then stopped herself. "There was something about you," she confessed.

"You knew something was wrong," Annie said. "And I so wanted to avoid you, but I couldn't. I just—"

Caroline held up her hand. "Let's not discuss that. So, you say you were running away from Diego Ortega. You had a convenient doppelgänger emerge. And then you were on *Fortuna*. All very implausible."

"It's the tr—"

"What happened next? What happened this evening?" Caroline asked.

Annie swallowed down her dejection at Caroline's obvious anger.

"I had no idea Diego was on board. I found out the moment he sat down next to me at dinner. And I panicked. I'd wanted to tell you everything earlier, and the day before—"

"What happened after I left the table?" Caroline asked,

repositioning the conversation to the facts and not the feelings.

"We had dinner," Annie said simply. It had been the most uncomfortable meal of her life. The food had been delicious, as always, but she had been in such a panic that her appetite had rolled over and died. "After, we went back to Diego's room. I… I'd hoped we'd go back to my room, and I could alert someone. Maybe Elvin would see something was wrong."

Elvin. Annie closed her eyes, realising that the sweet man was going to find out about her lies and probably be crushed by them. She'd probably never get a chance to apologise to him.

"And then?" Caroline asked.

Annie opened her eyes. "He hit me. A few times. Broke my nose, Doctor Perry told me. Then he was calm, told me he could fix things. Asked if I told anyone what I'd seen. I knew at that point that he was going to kill me. Diego doesn't leave loose ends lying around."

Annie paused. She'd seen fire in his eyes before he punched her the last time, the one that ultimately led to her falling on the floor and crawling away from him. Consciousness had been fleeting after that. Annie hadn't fought much, not wanting to be awake for what she knew was coming.

"And then?" Caroline pressed.

"I don't know, Caroline," Annie snapped. "I was beaten up, tied up, and shoved into a fucking suitcase. I nearly died in a freezer. I don't know what you want to hear!"

"I want to know what happened!" Caroline raised her voice in return.

"I told you!"

Mara rushed back into the room. "Okay, that's enough," she said firmly, directing her statement to Caroline. "She's a patient in my care, suffering from moderate hypothermia. If you want to shout at each other, you can do it when she's been discharged."

"She should be in the brig," Caroline said.

"Caroline," Mara warned.

"No," Annie said, "she's right. I should be in the brig." She put the water cup on the table and pushed the heated blankets away from her. It took several attempts, but eventually she tossed them to the floor. If Caroline wanted her in the brig, then that's where she would go.

She was sick of causing problems for Caroline. This was something she could do. Some small way she could help bring order and reason back to Caroline's life.

"Annie," Mara said. She crouched down to pick up the blankets.

"As long as Diego isn't in the brig with me," Annie said. She looked at Caroline. "Unless you want me dead?"

She slid out of the bed and wobbled, immediately falling back towards it when her legs failed her. Mara was on the other side of the bed, so Caroline stepped forward and took Annie in her arms, preventing her from collapsing to the floor.

"Of course I don't want you dead," she said.

"Careful," Mara instructed. "She has an IV."

Annie realised that her body was rapidly turning to

jelly and considered that maybe getting out of bed had been a bad idea.

"I'm sorry," she mumbled.

Her words came out a slurred mess, just as they had when she'd first arrived in the hospital wing. It was disconcerting that she was showing those symptoms again. She'd been feeling better, but she obviously wasn't. She started to wonder just how long her recovery would take.

Mara moved Caroline out of the way and helped Annie herself. "No need to apologise, you're still groggy. Let's get you back into bed, get the blankets back over you, and get you nicely heated up."

Once she was positioned back in bed, Annie could tell something was wrong. She looked around to find the source of the problem. Her eyes settled on her right wrist, the one where the rope had been tightly wound and cut deep into the skin. A red line was seeping through the gauze.

Mara followed her gaze. "I'll go and get some clean bandages."

Annie's head lolled on the pillow. Caroline was stood over her looking uncertain and a little anxious.

"I'm sorry," Annie repeated.

"Shh, we can talk when you feel better," Caroline said, the harshness leaving her tone.

"The last thing I wanted to do was hurt you," Annie said. "You won't believe me, but I really care for you, Caroline."

Caroline hushed her again. Annie wanted to say more, but exhaustion was slowly creeping in at the edges of her vision.

LIES, LIES, LIES

"I'm sorry," Caroline said when Mara returned to her office. She'd been dismissed from Annie's bedside the moment Mara returned with fresh bandages.

"Go to bed," Mara instructed. "Or just leave here and do whatever it is you're doing somewhere else."

"I needed to know what had happened," Caroline defended.

"Why are you here, Caroline? Why not send Dan? It's his job. It's not as if the captain needs to be here for this," Mara pointed out. She sat in her chair and pointed at Caroline. "Unless this isn't a work thing. Maybe this is a personal thing for you?"

"Mara," Caroline warned.

"Do you believe her?" Mara asked.

"I..." Caroline didn't know what she believed anymore.

"I do," Mara said. "I think she was frightened and planning to run away. She came across Serena Rubio in a piece of miraculous luck and fully intended to never come out of her cabin."

"But she did," Caroline argued. "And she dragged me into this."

"Or maybe she honestly fell for you?" Mara suggested.

Caroline laughed. "Are you so naïve, Mara?"

"Are you so pig-headed?"

Caroline put her hands on her hips. "She lied to me. Consistently. Every time we spent time together. Lies, lies, lies."

"Did she?" Mara asked.

Caroline reeled back. "Of course she did, have you not been paying attention?"

"I'm paying more attention than you are," Mara said. "I'm trying to get to the bottom of this, too, but I'm not blinkered by hurt feelings. So, tell me, did she lie to you? Did she tell you about all the amazing concerts she's performed?"

Caroline gritted her teeth.

"I'll take your palpable silence as a no. Did she talk about her family? Her parents? Her childhood? Her home?"

Caroline swallowed.

"How about the inside of a recording studio?" Mara forged on. "Did she talk about making an album, winning an award? Did she talk about the celebrities she's hung out with? Did she talk about Serena Rubio's work in any way?"

Caroline lowered her head, thinking back to the conversations they'd had. They'd avoided those conversations under the guise that she hadn't wanted to talk about herself, which resulted in never talking about her work or family life. Caroline had assumed she wanted time away from those things and was happy to keep to other topics.

It didn't mean that all of their conversations were shallow. Yes, they talked about books and their favourite meals, but they also talked about religion, women's rights, history, and more.

They'd talked for hours on end without once speaking about Serena's personal life.

"I'm guessing that she didn't talk about those things?" Mara asked. "And I'm going to assume that the reason for that was because she didn't want to lie to you. It would have been so easy for Annie to avoid you. You're busy, she's a passenger. You never need speak again. But she didn't take the easy way out, she kept spending time with you."

"But—" Caroline tried to argue.

"And seemingly without good reason. There's no in-depth scam here, Caroline. She wanted to spend time with you, she was in a tricky situation, but she did her best to keep her lies to a minimum. And I do believe she probably tried to tell you."

Caroline opened her mouth to argue but was instantly met with mental images of Annie saying she had to tell her something important.

"What you do with this information is ultimately up to you," Mara said, "but I honestly think that young woman fell for you, and I think she feels sick to her stomach for dragging you into this. And I know for a fact that she needs to rest, and so do you. You can come back and see her tomorrow at lunchtime, if you wish. But not before. And she will *not* be going to the brig."

Caroline opened and closed her mouth a couple of

times before realising she had nothing to say. She needed time to think about what had happened, to process what she knew, and to piece things together. She pinched the bridge of her nose. "I'm sorry, Mara."

"It's okay, I can't imagine how you must be feeling. Go and get some rest."

"I just… I don't know what to do."

"You decide if you can forgive her."

"But what if there is more to this?" Caroline asked. "What if there is something I'm not seeing?"

"You'll see it," Mara reassured. "You worked in security for years, there's not a scam you don't know about. But right now, you're tired and hurting. You can't think correctly; you need some rest and some time. Then you can come back and talk to her again and see what you think."

"There's so little time," Caroline said.

Mara looked at the clock on the wall. "Just over twenty-four hours. However, that doesn't have to be the end of it. If you want, you can always stay in touch with her after she's disembarked. Stop trying to wrap everything up in a neat little bow."

Caroline realised then that Mara was right. She'd been racing against the clock to find Annie, and now she felt the same about cracking the mystery as to her presence on the ship. But she didn't need to have all the answers when they arrived in Barcelona the next morning. It would be impossible for her to process her feelings and have an answer by then. And maybe that was okay.

"I'm lucky to have you as a friend," Caroline admitted.

"You are," Mara agreed, a smile dancing on her lips. "Now, go."

SHE'LL BE BACK

"What's this I hear about not wanting breakfast?" Mara asked. She breezed into Annie's room and checked the chart hanging on the end of the bed.

"No appetite," Annie replied.

It was the truth; she felt sick to her stomach and so unsettled that she knew she'd not be able to digest a single cornflake.

Mara tutted gently. "We need to get some food in you. You're on a cruise; it's legally binding that you put on at least one dress size."

Annie chuckled. "I'm not very good at following the rules."

Mara placed the clipboard back on the end of the bed. "I can tell."

"Am I going to be put in the brig?" Annie asked. There had been talk of releasing her from the hospital bay that afternoon, but she had no idea where she'd be taken. Nothing had been said, and she wondered if she was heading for prison. It was no less than she deserved.

"No." Mara shook her head.

"But, Caroline—"

"You're not going to the brig," Mara reassured her. "I need you to take a few bites of something, just so I know you've eaten. And then we can see about getting you back to your room."

Annie frowned. "My room? But I… I'm committing identity fraud."

"You did, but the cruise was paid for and I'm fairly convinced that what you've told me is true. Which would mean that *technically* the real Serena Rubio gifted you her trip. In a roundabout kind of way."

Annie thought there was a lot of grey area there but decided that she'd take it. Mara had been trying to help her all along, and Annie was growing to like and appreciate the woman.

"What happens to me next?" she asked.

"I can only answer questions about your treatment. The rest will ultimately be up to Captain West."

"I didn't mean to hurt her," Annie said, knowing that Mara and Caroline were friends. She didn't know if she'd get another chance to speak with Caroline, so this could have been her only chance of conveying that point. It was vital to Annie that Caroline knew that she'd never intended to cause her any pain.

"Caroline doesn't trust very well," Mara explained. "And when that trust is broken, well, it's hard to get it back."

Annie could understand that. Caroline had been let down badly by the Royal Navy, her career and her standing left in tatters. On top of that, her relationship had ended in infidelity. It wasn't a surprise that Caroline found it hard to trust.

Annie realised that she had almost certainly contributed to Caroline's trust issues tripling overnight.

"I thought so," she agreed. "I... I'll leave her alone. But if it does come out, like, when I'm gone. Please tell her that I never meant her any harm, and I... I really did like her."

Annie felt her cheeks heat up in a deep blush. It felt like high school, admitting to someone that you had a crush on their best friend.

"You should tell her that yourself," Mara said. "I have a feeling she'll be back."

"To arrest me and throw me in the brig?" Annie grinned.

"Depends on how well she slept." Mara winked.

A nurse knocked on the doorframe. "Doctor Perry? That call you were waiting for came in; I arranged a face-to-face conference in half an hour."

"Marvellous. Thanks, Sam." Mara looked at Annie. "How do you fancy speaking with Serena Rubio in thirty minutes?"

Annie bolted upright. "She's okay? You found her?"

"She's perfectly fine; her manager was a little confused to get my call but believed my story of your presence on *Fortuna* surprisingly quickly. I think Miss Rubio engages in this kind of nonsense quite often."

"Wouldn't surprise me," Annie said. "I'd love to talk to her."

Mara gestured for Annie to lift her wrist so she could check on the bandages. Annie obliged.

"Can you tell me where Diego is?" Annie asked.

She'd not asked about him at all since she'd been rescued, as if the mere mention of his name would summon him like the demon he was. But the question was racing around her head, needing to be soothed.

"Off the ship," Mara replied. "Caroline had him arrested."

Annie nodded slowly. "Okay," she said softly.

"You don't sound too pleased about that?"

"He'll get out," Annie said. "He always does. There's corruption everywhere, and he has a lot of money and knows a lot of secrets. He'll be back. Next time I probably won't be so lucky, but that's what you get for hanging out with the wrong people."

Mara covered up the bandage and remained silent. Annie couldn't blame her; there wasn't much that could be said. Annie had accepted her fate; Diego may not have killed her this time, but he'd no doubt be back.

She may have dodged an icy death, but things were far from over.

THE REAL SERENA RUBIO

SLEEP NEVER CAME, but an exhaustion-fuelled unconsciousness had. Caroline was glad for it; she felt slightly refreshed and nearly ready to take on another day. Just as long as that day promised to be nothing like the one that had proceeded it.

She prepared a mug of strong coffee in the kitchen in her stateroom, not willing or able to interact with other people just yet. She set up her laptop at the dining table, not wanting to sit in her office either. She needed to see out the window, to watch the small waves churning as they sailed by.

The water had always calmed her, the knowledge that nothing could compare to the almighty beauty and strength of the ocean. She firmly believed that if you looked at the water for long enough, you'd find a solution to any problem. Or be so soothed by the view that the issue felt less problematic.

She opened her laptop and accessed her emails. She sipped at her coffee while they loaded, arriving in large batches. There was nothing like an eventful day at sea to suddenly hear from everyone in the company.

She turned and looked out of the large window; one of the major benefits of her suite was the multiple windows. Her living area consisted of two windows, one by the seating area and one by the dining table. At the end of the room was a doorway onto a private balcony. Her bedroom also had a balcony, as did the second bedroom. It was the perfect suite for someone who loved a view. Not quite as perfect as *Serenity*, but it was a great second choice.

She could see the very edge of Corsica in the distance, which meant they were making up the time they had lost the previous evening. *Fortuna* always navigated its way in between the two large islands of Corsica and Sardinia on the way back to Barcelona. It made for great views and photo opportunities for the passengers on a day at sea with no stops.

Back in her email account she noted that Thomas had restructured and issued the crew schedule for the day. He'd marked Caroline down as 'admin' for the entire day, a trick they'd been using for years when either one of them wanted to avoid being roped into something by Dominic.

Usually it was just an hour here or there, but Thomas had fenced off the entire day for her. He even had himself attending dinner at the captain's table that night. Caroline was about to reply and put herself back on the roster when she paused.

Maybe it was a good idea to take the time. They arrived at Barcelona at five the next morning. If she returned to duty in the morning, then she could say goodbye to the passengers and effectively reset herself for the next sailing.

And the idea of taking a break wasn't too terrible, either.

Her inbox contained a message from Mara, too, and Caroline let out a long sigh. She sipped more of her coffee and took in the view again. Her thoughts and feelings were still in turmoil. She had no idea how she was supposed to process everything, and it still felt like a ticking clock was hanging over her head.

She opened the email. There was a brief and professional message explaining that a face-to-face meeting would be taking place between Mara, Dan, and Serena Rubio over a webcast—Caroline looked at her watch—in about twenty minutes time.

Caroline chewed her lip. The meeting would answer some lingering questions and probably present many more. She rubbed her forehead. There was no reason for her to be there, but like the invisible pull that had dragged her closer to Annie throughout the cruise, she knew she wouldn't be able to stay away.

Caroline arrived deliberately late. She watched from afar as Mara, Dan, and Annie filed into Mara's office. She took a couple of deep breaths and then walked into the office, stopping by the doorway so she could watch and listen, hopefully unnoticed.

Everyone took a seat, and Mara raised her laptop up

on some textbooks so everyone could see properly. A call came in and Mara answered.

"Hello, Miss Rubio," Mara said, "thank you for your time assisting us with this. My name is Mara Perry, this is Dan Lovell, and you hopefully know Annie?"

"Annie!" Serena cried. "You are hurt! What happened?"

Caroline wanted to laugh. Serena's speech pattern was nothing like Annie's. If she'd taken a second to listen to one interview, she would have rumbled Annie in seconds.

"I'm fine, just..." Annie replied.

"It was him? The relationship you were running from?" Serena asked.

"Yes. It's okay, though," Annie said. "I'm okay."

"I'm to blame, I should never have gotten you involved in my stupid plan. I was just so upset when we met. I wasn't thinking. And now you are in trouble, Annie, I'm so sorry."

"Miss Rubio," Dan spoke up, "I need you to confirm that you willingly provided Miss Peck with your ID and your personal belongings."

"Yes, of course I did," Serena declared as if Dan was asking the most ridiculous question she'd ever heard. "You think she stole them from under my nose? You think I'm too stupid to notice someone walking away with my handbag and my suitcase?"

"No, of course not, we're simply—"

"You are questioning this when Annie has been hurt?" Serena continued. "Isn't it your job to keep her safe? Her beautiful face is cut, her nose is... broken? How? How does this happen aboard your ship?"

"Details of the incident aren't avail—"

"You are useless," Serena dismissed Dan and turned her attention back to Annie. "Oh, Annie, I am so sorry that this happened to you. I should never have encouraged you to do this. I should have left you to take your train. This is my fault."

"No," Annie denied. "This is my fault. I made a lot of mistakes, committing identity fraud was one of them, but it was a mistake I made myself."

"If it wasn't for me, you wouldn't have been hurt…"

Caroline stepped forward. "Miss Rubio, I'm Captain Caroline West. If anyone is to blame for what happened to Miss Peck, it's me. Safety is my number-one responsibility, and this incident is unforgivable. Believe me, investigations are underway, and I'll not rest until the gaps in security have been tightly sealed. As I'm sure you're aware, identity fraud is a criminal offence. In this situation, you have also committed a crime by encouraging and allowing Miss Peck to knowingly defraud the company. I'm willing to let it go on this occasion, but I would request that you not do anything like this in the future."

Serena grinned and inclined her head, aware that she had been politely told off. "Of course, Captain."

Caroline was under no illusion that Serena would change her ways. She seemed like the sort who enjoyed getting her way and never played by the rules. A celebrity, through and through. This was who she had expected that first night at dinner; instead she'd gotten Annie.

Annie, who was shyly looking at her through her messy curls, her hair pushed to the side to accommodate the gauze and bandages that covered the wound on her head and the cuts to her face.

Caroline tore her gaze away from Annie. Dan was talking to Serena, getting more details from her for his paperwork. Caroline turned and left the room; she had nothing else she needed to say or hear. She'd almost made it to the door when a passenger exited one of the rooms.

"Captain! Oh, do you have a minute?"

Caroline tried to smile and look pleased to see the woman. "Of course, how can I help?"

"My son, Jamie, got hurt on the water slide." The woman held up her hand. "His fault, he was being silly. Boys being boys and all that. He's feeling a little sorry for himself, but I know he'd love to meet you. He's so very interested in sailing."

"I'd love to meet him," Caroline said.

She entered the room dedicated to children, the colourful characters painted on the walls giving the room a light feel. An elderly woman, maybe the grandmother, sat in a chair beside the bed holding Jamie's hand. Jamie was dressed in pyjamas covered with a cartoon character she couldn't identify. His arm was in a sling and his front lip was bloodied; she wouldn't be surprised if a tooth or two was missing.

His eyes widened as he saw her. "Captain," he whispered in awe.

"I hear that we have a sick patient," Caroline said. She stood to loose attention by the side of the bed. "How are you, Jamie?"

"I broke my arm," he said, one tooth definitely missing. Caroline pictured the water slide being closed and a poor staff member crawling through it in the search for a tiny enamel pearl.

"So I see. I broke my arm once, taught me to be more careful on waterslides," she said.

Jamie smiled, not knowing whether she was joking or not.

"How old are you, Jamie?"

"Ten."

"Ten? You must be a member of the Pirate Club?"

"Yes, I went every single day," he replied with a smile that would have been bigger if he could move his mouth without it hurting.

"He loves the kids' clubs," the probable grandmother said.

"When I grow up, I'm going to work on a ship like this," Jamie announced, his shyness waning.

Caroline wanted to tell him about her last twenty-four hours and ask if he wanted to have a stab at being a fireman.

"Ah, after my job?" she asked instead.

His eyes widened in horror at potentially offending her.

"No problem," she reassured him. "I hope to be retired by the time you're qualified."

"Do you think I could be a captain?" Jamie asked.

"If you study hard in school, and then work hard, absolutely. We need more good captains. I'm sure you'll make a fine addition."

"See, James?" the mother said. "You can do it. You just need to focus more in school."

Jamie looked disappointed at the prospect of having to work for his dream.

"There's a lot of maths involved in sailing," Caroline said.

"Really?" Jamie blinked in surprise.

"Really. Calculating weather patterns, tidal paths, wave swells. A lot of maths."

Caroline could almost see the idea of being a captain vanish from Jamie's eyes in that moment.

"I'm really bad with numbers," he confessed.

Caroline pulled up a chair. "Can I tell you a secret, Jamie?"

He nodded.

"I was very bad with numbers; I'd even say I was a little frightened of them. But one day I decided that if other people could be good at maths, then maybe I could be okay at it. I made a decision that I wouldn't be scared of numbers anymore. So, I tried really hard, and I spoke to my maths teacher about getting more homework to help me be better. After a while, I started to understand it. The numbers that hadn't made sense before started to be clearer. Once I applied myself and made an effort, it became easier. Like training to play football or playing a video game, you get better when you try harder."

Jamie sucked up the motivational speech like a sponge. His eyes were bright, and his head bobbed in understanding. "I can do that," he agreed. "I'm going to ask for more maths homework when I get back to school."

"Excellent, you'll be a captain in no time."

"Did you always want to be a captain?" Jamie asked.

Caroline thought about the question for a moment.

"I always wanted to be at sea," she replied, "and I wanted to do something worthwhile. I used to be in the Royal Navy, I commanded ships that did a lot of good work."

"And now you're here, keeping us safe," Jamie said. "Like you said at the muster drill, safety is the number-one priority."

He looked up at her as if she were some kind of hero. Caroline gave him her best attempt at a smile. She didn't feel like she'd met the brief of her number-one priority lately.

She hadn't kept Annie safe. Leaving at dinner was probably the worst thing she could have done, and she agonised over what might have happened if she'd stayed. Would Annie have discreetly told her she was in trouble? Would Caroline have figured it out for herself?

Things could have been very different if Caroline hadn't allowed her hurt feelings to drive her actions, and yet, she was still allowing her feelings to determine her movements. She was actively avoiding Annie.

She stood up. "It is. So, no more fighting with our waterslide?" she said good-naturedly.

Jamie grinned. "Aye, aye, Captain."

Caroline made a mental note to speak to Dominic about getting some gifts sent to Jamie's cabin. He seemed like a nice kid, if a little enthusiastic.

She said goodbye to the family and stepped outside the room. She stood in the hallway for a couple of moments, gathering her courage. When she felt like she couldn't stand there any longer, she walked towards Annie's room.

She stood in the doorway, about to knock, but was distracted by Annie looking at herself in the mirror.

"Wow, what a mess," Annie mused to her own reflection.

"It will heal," Caroline reassured her.

Annie turned and looked at her, uncertainty clear in her eyes.

Caroline stepped into the room. "I'm sorry to barge in."

"No, please, barge away," Annie said. "I'm being discharged, they're sick of me here."

Caroline smiled. "I'm sure that's not the case."

Annie turned away. She picked up a comb and attempted to brush it through her hair. She really did look like she had been through the wars. Caroline didn't want to stare openly but knew that averting her eyes wasn't the answer either.

She hated that everything was so difficult now, nothing like the carefree afternoon on the hills above La Spezia or their evening enjoying all of the facilities on the ship.

"I was wondering if we could talk?" she asked.

"Sure," Annie said casually.

"I mean, talk properly."

Annie paused her movement and turned to regard Caroline curiously. "I'd like that."

"Maybe we could have dinner in your stateroom this evening? Clear the air?" Caroline didn't know what she was doing, had no idea what she wanted to say, or what result she was hoping for. All she knew was that the animosity she held towards Annie had to be dispersed somehow, and she needed more answers.

Annie nodded. "Yeah, that… that would be nice."

"Six o'clock?" Caroline suggested. It would give Annie enough time to get to her room and clean up if she desired. It also gave Caroline a little more time to think about what she wanted to say.

"Sure, six sounds good."

"Wonderful, I should go," Caroline said. She had nowhere to be, but being there any longer would become increasingly uncomfortable.

"Okay," Annie said. "I'll see you soon."

Caroline nodded and stepped out of the room. In the corridor she saw Mara, looking at her with a knowing grin.

Caroline walked past her. "Not a word," she warned.

EXHAUSTION

Mara accompanied Annie back to her stateroom. She'd explained that someone, presumably Diego, had broken in and turned it over, but the staff had put everything back and repaired the lock.

Annie guessed that Diego had attempted to find her in her room prior to dinner. Luckily Annie had gotten ready early and sat up on the pool deck to get some fresh air. She'd been preparing herself to tell Caroline everything. All of that seemed so far away now.

"Here we are," Mara said.

Annie was so grateful that Mara had decided to help her to her room. It meant that no one stopped them to try to fish for what had happened or why she looked like she'd been in a boxing ring.

Mara opened the door and gestured for Annie to step inside. She did so, looking around the room to see if anything was out of place. It all seemed in order, but she still felt a little dazed, so it was impossible to tell.

Mara placed a paper bag of pain medication on the

desk. "I'm going to send Arjun to see you this evening to change your bandages. I've left a note in the bag of what we did; you can pass it along to your doctor."

"Thank you for everything." Annie smothered a yawn behind her hand. "Sorry."

"It's okay, I'd be exhausted if I were you. Get some rest, and if you need anything, just press the medical cross button on your phone." Mara patted her arm softly. "It was nice meeting you, Annie. Despite all of this."

"Thank you, I'm sorry about everything."

Mara smiled warmly. "I'll see myself out. Take care of yourself."

Mara left, and Annie sat on the sofa. She stared at the carpet. She couldn't even begin to process what would happen next. Serena had offered Annie her apartment in Madrid to recuperate, even offering to have a car meet her at the port in Barcelona.

She'd said she'd think about it. It appeared she was now friends with a crazy opera singer whom she resembled and who believed every stroke of luck to be a sign from God. And that wasn't even the weirdest thing that had happened to her that week.

She wanted to sleep but couldn't seriously entertain the idea with so much spinning around in her mind. She felt more lost and confused than ever. On top of that, Caroline wanted to talk. To clear the air, whatever that meant.

Her hands shook, and she clasped them tightly. Was it going to be round two? Or would Caroline turn up with a waiver form for her to sign to absolve Dream of all responsibility?

Annie didn't know what to expect or what she would say.

Annie jolted awake. She sat up on the sofa, blinked, and looked around the room. She wondered what had dragged her from her sleep. She heard a knock on the door and jumped to her feet, realising that it hadn't been the first.

She looked through the peephole and saw Caroline, frowning.

"Shit," Annie whispered.

She'd fallen asleep on the sofa rather than trying to shower and change like she had intended. Now Caroline was here, and Annie was as unprepared as ever.

She opened the door, not wanting to leave her waiting any longer. "I'm sorry," she said. "I look a state. I fell asleep instead of cleaning up. I'm so sorry."

Caroline hesitated in the hallway. "I could come back later?"

"No, please, come in." Annie stood to one side. She wasn't going to let any chance of seeing Caroline slip through her fingers.

Caroline stepped inside. She looked nervous, which Annie took as a good sign; it meant she wasn't there to start a fight. Annie closed the door, and they stood in silence for a moment.

"Oh, I should order food. Sorry, I literally just woke up." Annie jumped into action, heading for the phone.

Caroline held up her hand. "Are you sure you want to do this now? I can come back."

"No, it's fine. I just need to wake up a little."

Caroline looked her up and down. "Okay, I'll call for food. You go and freshen up in the bathroom if you like. It will take fifteen minutes to get here anyway."

"Are you sure you don't mind?" It sounded like heaven. Annie could wash her face and brush her teeth and feel slightly more human.

"Absolutely. Any special requests? Mara tells me you haven't eaten much."

Annie grinned. "She's such a traitor."

"She is," Caroline agreed readily. "How about some of the Key lime pie you demolished so readily the first night?"

"I didn't demolish it," Annie argued. "But yes, that sounds lovely."

Caroline smiled, and Annie felt a weight lift from her shoulders. She'd worried that the conversation would be awkward and stilted, but Caroline was doing her best to make sure that wasn't the case.

"Okay, I'll make the call. Take your time."

Annie grabbed a change of clothes from the wardrobe and headed into the bathroom. Inside the small room, she initiated battle stations. She had fifteen minutes to make herself look like she hadn't been dragged through a hedge backwards. One glance at her reflection in the mirror told her that would be a very tall ask.

EXPLANATIONS OVER DINNER

Caroline called the stateroom attendant and placed an order for a selection of finger foods, some sandwiches, some meats, grilled vegetables, breads, and some cakes. It surprised her how easy it was to order for Annie, instinct taking over.

She crossed over to the balcony and looked out at the view. They'd long ago passed by Corsica, and now there was nothing but sea for as far as the eye could see. In the distance she saw a tanker; she watched it slowly crossing the horizon.

She didn't know what she expected from this talk with Annie. She'd spent the last few hours making lists of what she knew, what she thought she knew, and what she wanted to know. It was like piecing together an enormous murder mystery.

She shuddered. It very nearly had been.

Annie's bruised face had haunted her the evening before. She felt responsible even though she logically knew she wasn't.

She must have stood there for a while because suddenly there was a knock on the door and room service had arrived. She opened the door and recognised Annie's stateroom attendant, Elvin.

"Hello, Captain West," he greeted, an enormous smile on his face.

"Hello, Elvin. Please come in."

He pushed the trolley into the room. "Inside or on the balcony?"

"Inside," Caroline decided, not wanting anyone to eavesdrop on their conversation from the balcony.

He pushed the brake on the trolley and lifted two flaps, turning the trolley into a table. He positioned the desk chair on one side and pulled a foldable chair out of the trolley to put on the other side.

The bathroom door opened, and Annie stepped out. She saw Elvin and looked timidly down at her feet.

"Miss Annie," Elvin greeted. He crossed over to her and softly hugged her. "I'm so happy to see you are okay."

Annie pulled him deeper into a hug. "I'm so sorry I lied to you, Elvin."

"Miss Serena, Miss Annie, it doesn't matter. You are you," he said simply. He stepped back. "Call me if you need anything else."

He said goodbye to the two of them and left the room. Caroline gestured for Annie to take the desk chair, reasoning that it would be far more comfortable.

Annie had changed and now wore a simple white T-shirt and jeans. She wore some light make-up and had done something with her hair—dry shampoo, Caroline assumed. She looked much better than she had when she'd arrived.

Caroline's gaze was drawn to the obvious signs of injury: bruises on her arms, bandages around both wrists, angry purple marks across her nose, and the cut that started on her forehead and vanished into her hair.

"It looks worse than it is," Annie said, not looking up but obviously knowing that she was being analysed.

"I think you're trying to make me feel better about it," Caroline noted as she sat down.

Annie didn't reply. Instead she set about pouring herself some water and offering to do the same for Caroline. They each served themselves a small plate of food and took a few sips of water.

The silence was deafening.

"Was any of it real?" Caroline suddenly asked. It hadn't been the calm interrogation she'd expected.

Annie's eyes flickered up to meet her. "Yes," she said softly. "For me, *all* of it was real."

A sarcastic quip found its way to Caroline's lips, but she swallowed it down. She took a sip of water instead. "I want to know about you," she said. "I feel like I'm sitting opposite a stranger. You know so much about me, and I don't feel I know that much about you."

"I'll tell you anything you want to know," Annie said.

"Start at the beginning," Caroline suggested.

Of course, she'd researched Annie Peck; she'd ravenously consumed every scrap of evidence she could find about her. But she needed to hear it from the woman she knew as Serena, to try to make sense of it all by hearing it directly.

"Okay, well, firstly, I'm thirty-one," Annie said. "My name is Annie, which you know. I was born in Yorkshire, but I lost that accent really fast because my parents moved around a lot. I went to school in Cheshire, and then in Southampton, and then in Chelmsford. So I didn't have many friends because I was never in one place long enough."

Annie finished her first glass of water and poured a second one. "No siblings. One aunt, my father's sister. My parents died when I was twenty-five. Then I went off the rails a bit, met Diego in Spain—"

"Wait, wait," Caroline said gently.

Annie had glossed over the death of her parents in one second flat. She might not have wanted to talk about it, but Caroline wanted to hear more about that part of Annie's life. As painful as it must have been, it was also a catalyst for what came next.

She was piecing together this stranger, and the death of her parents was obviously an enormous part of who she was. She recalled Annie chastising her about her assumptions over age; she'd said that people were defined by their experiences. She'd said something about people losing everything at a young age and having to rebuild their entire world.

Caroline had suspected there was a story behind that statement then, but she'd had no idea it would lead to where it did.

"What happened to your parents?" she asked.

"You know," Annie said, plucking a bread roll from the basket.

"Not from you," Caroline argued.

Annie cut the roll in half. "They drowned. Well, maybe. They might have been hit by falling debris." She placed the knife on the side plate with a thud. "It wasn't clear."

It was the first time Caroline had seen Annie emotional; it radiated from her.

"I'm so sorry," Caroline said.

Annie shrugged. "Not a lot that can be done. They were good people, but they died. What do they say? 'Only the good die young?' Or so we tell ourselves to cope with the unexpected loss of good, young people."

Caroline felt taken aback by the passion in Annie's voice. The emotion may have been borne from heartache, but it was real and fierce. Caroline had felt the same when her father had passed away in service, and she completely understood and agreed with Annie's feelings on the matter.

Annie focused intently on buttering the bread. Caroline suspected it was to avoid eye contact through fear it would encourage tears.

"I fell apart, felt kind of rudderless," she confessed. "A friend was going to Spain for a holiday, and I said I'd go with her. We went to Barcelona, and the second night we were in a bar and Diego walked in. And he was so charming, just everything about him. He was carefree and fun and so intense."

Caroline shifted uncomfortably in her chair. Hearing Annie talk about Diego was never going to be easy.

"We started seeing each other. He kind of… dealt with everything, you know? Like I didn't have to think about things anymore, which was a relief at that time in my life.

He was safe and secure, treated me like a queen. The holiday came to an end, and he convinced me to stay. I didn't have anything to go home to, so my friend went back but I didn't."

Annie took a sip of water. "We were in a relationship for… a year? Probably less. I realised what he was pretty quickly." She chuckled. "At first, I thought I'd save him. Typical woman bullshit, thinking I could stop him being a terrible person and we'd be happy forever. Then I realised that wouldn't happen and that I wasn't in love with him and that he'd never really loved me. There would always be someone new. So, that was that. We drifted apart."

"But you stayed?" Caroline asked.

Annie sighed, looking ashamed with herself. "Yes. At first, I just didn't want to go home. Later, he kept me close, a part of his entourage, I suppose. I realised that I knew quite a bit about Diego's business dealings and the people in the organisation, and he was keeping me close because of that. But I didn't care because it was an easy life."

"Partying?" Caroline guessed.

"At first, but that bored me pretty quickly. I was never very good at a party. Soon, I started to do my own thing. I helped out charities; I've got a degree in marketing, so I helped with social media and email marketing. That kind of thing. In the evenings… no, you'll laugh…"

"Try me."

Annie took a deep breath. "I joined a book club."

Caroline smiled. "A book club?"

"Yep." Annie leaned on her hand. "A book club. I kind of missed English and I have a terrible ear for language, so

I was getting nowhere learning Spanish. Diego's other girls were Spanish, so I thought I'd join an English-speaking book club. Mainly expats, all old, except for me."

"You don't speak Spanish?" Caroline queried.

Annie snorted a laugh. "No."

"You lived there for *five* years," Caroline stated, shocked that someone wouldn't pick up the local language in all that time.

"I would have loved to speak Spanish; I went to so many different teachers, but I just couldn't pick it up. I don't know, I just couldn't hear it properly, and so I couldn't repeat it."

Annie took a bite of food. Caroline did the same. The air between them was clearing, but Caroline wasn't ready to forgive and forget yet. She was still angry, even if that anger was being shoved into a tiny box at the back of her mind thanks to Annie's endearing company.

"So, book club?" Caroline asked.

"Yes. It was great, I spent a lot of time there."

"So, you enjoy reading?"

Annie's eyes sparkled. "Love it. My mum used to recommend books to me all the time; she'd read about two to three books a week. When she died, I suddenly lost that. There was no one to talk about books with, no one to recommend the next book to pick up. So I stopped. Took me a long time to get back into it. And it was lonely, reading a book and then just closing it and putting it back on the shelf."

"Sounds like a book club was a good thing for you," Caroline said.

"It was. I even got most of them online so we could

talk when the book club wasn't meeting. Aggie, she's eighty-three, was blown away when she discovered Twitter. Now you can't stop her, she's always tweeting and hashtagging things."

Caroline could tell that Annie was stalling. She didn't mind; she knew it wasn't easy to condense your life story into a few short statements. Especially when you'd made mistakes, or something life-destroying had happened.

"You'll have to teach me. I've almost mastered Facebook," Caroline said.

"Twitter's good, different crowd." Annie took a bite of a sandwich.

"Have you always been interested in men?" Caroline fished.

"I've always known I'm bisexual," Annie answered. "I've been in relationships with both men and women. I've always connected more with women, though. Maybe I'm seventy percent into women, thirty percent into men. I saw Diego kill someone."

Caroline's breath caught. She'd thought as much, but hearing the confirmation out of the blue, after a discussion of Annie's sexual preferences, was still a shock.

"So, I ran. Because I knew he'd never believe me if I told him I wouldn't say anything. And, to be honest, I didn't believe me either. What I saw… I couldn't unsee that. And I couldn't not do anything about it." She rubbed at her eyes, exhaustion obvious in her. "I ran. No plan, no idea of where to go or what to do."

"And then you bumped into Serena Rubio," Caroline said.

Annie chuckled. "Yeah."

Caroline smiled. "And you thought, 'I know, I can fake being an opera singer'?"

She said it good-naturedly, and Annie grinned wider. "Yeah, of course! Who wouldn't have thought that was an amazing idea?"

"Everyone." Caroline picked up a mini cupcake and put it on her plate.

"True," Annie allowed, the grin growing into a smile. "Well, as I said, I was in a panic and had no plan."

"I understand," Caroline said.

"Do you?" Annie asked.

Caroline met her eyes. "I think I do, yes."

As far-fetched and ridiculous as it was, the evidence was pointing towards it all being true. And now, sitting across from Annie, Caroline couldn't detect any deception in her. In fact, she could sense relief, palpable relief at finally being able to say what she had been trying to tell Caroline for the last couple of days.

"I meant everything that happened between us," Annie said. "I never wanted to lie to you. In fact, I tried to tell you."

"I know you did," Caroline confessed. After reflecting on their time together, she'd realised that Annie had been trying to tell her something.

Annie let out a relieved sigh. "That night when I didn't go to dinner and you met me on the pool deck, I was so close to telling you. But there were people everywhere. And…" She put her head in her hands.

"What?" Caroline asked.

Annie looked up. "I wanted to tell you that I had real feelings for you, and then explain everything. Tell you who

I really was. But I only managed to get the first part out. And then you said you felt the same, and I felt so guilty."

Caroline looked down at her plate. Embarrassment shot through her. She wasn't someone to put her feelings out there, doing so when the other person was… what? Lying to her? Trying to say something else? It was mortifying, something she'd rather forget all about.

"I meant everything I said," Annie said. "Everything I felt was real. I couldn't stay away. It would have been far easier for me to ignore you and stay away, but I couldn't. I kept thinking about you. I still do. If I could roll back time and meet you as me, I would."

"I—" Caroline started.

"Actually," Annie interrupted, "no, that's a lie. I wouldn't."

Caroline felt her eyebrows raise in surprise. "You wouldn't?"

"I wouldn't go back and meet you as me. The only reason I met you was because Graham thought I was famous. If I'd boarded *Fortuna* as Annie Peck, I'd never have met you. If I had the choice between being Serena and having the chance to meet you but having to lie to you, or being myself and never meeting you, I'd choose the lie."

"This is a very strange apology," Caroline pointed out.

"You wanted honesty; this is honesty. Meeting you, being able to spend time with you, has been one of the best experiences of my life. And it's selfish, but I wouldn't want to give that up."

Caroline felt the heat rising on her cheeks. She wasn't used to this kind of attention.

"But I damaged your trust," Annie continued, "and I'm not going to repair that trust quickly. I think it's going to take a lot of time and work, but I'd like to try. If you'll let me."

Caroline didn't know what she wanted. Everything had happened so quickly. She'd fallen in love at a breakneck speed and then had it snatched from her just as quickly. Now she didn't know how she felt or what she wanted to happen. She felt fragile and raw.

"What are you suggesting?" she asked.

"Whatever you're comfortable with," Annie said. "I'll give you my number, my email address. If you want to contact me, on your terms, in your own time, I'd like that. Maybe we can talk some more, get to know each other again."

"I..." Caroline sat up a little straighter. "I don't know. You hurt me a great deal."

"I know," Annie said. "And I don't think I deserve another chance, but if you were to grant me one then I'd be the luckiest person. But I don't think for one moment that now is the right time to discuss it. I know I hurt you, and I know you'll need time to heal from that and to get over everything that happened. If you can even get over it."

Caroline looked down at her plate. Annie was reading her mind, sensing her uncertainty and her internal struggles. "I wish I could give you an answer," she said.

"I don't want one now," Annie reassured her. "You're not ready to. All I ask is that I can leave you my contact details, and if one day you are ready, you'll get in touch. Even if it's just to have another friend."

Caroline nodded, her gaze still set on the *Fortuna* dishware. Annie was right. She wasn't ready. And she didn't know when she would be. Feelings and relationships had always been hard for her, harder since her last breakup.

She licked her lips and looked up. She needed to steer the conversation back to work matters. Answers regarding their relationship may have eluded her, but she had other answers that might help Annie.

"I'll think about it," she said. "In the meantime, we need to talk about something else."

PUTTING THINGS RIGHT

Annie knew not to push Caroline any further. She couldn't imagine the turmoil of emotions that must have been swirling around inside of her. It was time to lay her cards on the table and walk away, letting Caroline decide the next moves.

"Go ahead," Annie said. She took a forkful of Key lime pie.

"I spoke to some ex-colleagues. I presume it won't come to any surprise to you that Diego Ortega is heavily involved in the drugs trade," Caroline said.

Annie's heart fell. Of course she knew. Her inaction over the years was a constant source of discomfort for her. She tried to tell herself that she wasn't personally committing the crimes and therefore she needn't get involved, but of course, that was ridiculous.

"I was never involved," she said.

"I didn't say you were—"

"I'm so ashamed that I never did anything. I honestly think I was living in a haze for the first couple of years,"

Annie explained. She didn't want Caroline to be disappointed in her, but she couldn't see any other way to go forward. "It's no excuse, I just ignored things. It doesn't explain things, it doesn't excuse them, but I honestly just put it to the back of my mind. By the time I realised what I was involved in, I knew it was too late to get out."

She pushed the pie to one side, having lost her appetite.

"Once I decided to stay, I paid my own way. I lived in an apartment building that Diego owned, but I paid my own rent. I paid for everything myself, kind of telling myself that made it all okay. I wasn't personally gaining from his… business, but I look back and I want to shake some sense into myself. I really just seemed to get stuck there, knowing I had to leave, but not seeing a way to be able to."

"I can understand that," Caroline admitted.

"Really?" Annie blinked.

"Really," Caroline confirmed. "I've worked with many of these situations, people in the wider circle not having a clue that people they knew were involved in these crimes. Or knowing but not knowing what to do. It's a very difficult situation to extract yourself from."

"Exactly," Annie said. "I mean, it's no excuse. I could have gotten out if I really wanted, I could have spoken up. But I didn't. I moved myself to the very edge of Diego's life, still one toe in even if the majority of my life was out. Luckily, he knew not to try to involve me in anything. He asked once, but never again after that."

"He's in custody," Caroline explained. "There's an international task force looking to break up the entire organisation. Arrests have been made, bank accounts frozen, they have a number of people willing to speak out on the record."

Caroline refilled Annie's water glass for her.

"In fact, I suspect that his blatant display on *Fortuna* was a result of him knowing that things were soon about to come to a head. To do what he did to you, he must have known the net was closing in and that it was all going to be over soon."

Annie felt her throat go dry. She'd always thought Diego and the Ortegas were above the law, that there was no one that they didn't have in their pocket.

"This has actually happened?" she asked. "The arrests, I mean?"

"Yes, over eighty arrests took place this morning," Caroline said. "An ex-colleague of mine is one of the leads on the task force. They have plenty of people willing to give statements. But the more there are, the harsher the sentence that will be handed down."

Annie felt her eyes widen. Caroline was asking her to be an informant.

"You don't have to say anything," Caroline said, "but if you do, it would help."

Annie stood up and ran a hand through her hair. She'd resigned herself to a life of constantly looking over her shoulder, expecting Diego or one of his men to eventually find her. If it was true, if the whole organisation was in tatters, then there was a chance she'd be safe. She knew Diego had much bigger problems than her; she could think of at least fifteen people in the inner circle who would sing like canaries if it meant saving themselves.

Diego was charming, but he wasn't smart when it came to picking his associates.

Having the chance to make amends for her years of inaction was a gift. If her words added just one week to anyone's sentence, it would be worth the risk.

"I'll do it," Annie said.

Caroline looked surprised. "Oh."

"I can't use grief as an excuse for five years of inaction. I lived in that circle, I knew what was happening. If my testimony can help, then I'll do it."

"I'll put you in touch with my colleague," Caroline said.

"Thank you."

Caroline stood up, placing her linen napkin on the table. "I should go, let you rest."

Annie knew not to push. Caroline needed time. She lowered her head and stood to one side, allowing Caroline room to leave.

Caroline walked around the table and paused in front of Annie. Annie slowly raised her eyes.

"You said you'd give me your email address," Caroline said.

"Oh, yes, of course." Annie crossed over to the desk and quickly jotted down her email address, phone number, and Twitter handle. She tore the piece of paper off the pad and handed it to Caroline.

Caroline took it. "I *will* be in touch," she said. "When I'm ready."

Annie smiled. "That's all I ask."

"It was a pleasure to meet you, Annie," Caroline said.

"Likewise, Captain West." Annie held out her hand.

Caroline chuckled and shook her hand. "Take care of yourself."

"You, too." Annie watched as Caroline left the room, wondering if she'd ever see her again. She didn't think she deserved to, but if for some miraculous reason she got a second chance, she'd treasure it.

TIME HEALS ALL WOUNDS

Annie kicked off her sandals and closed the front door to her new apartment. She carried the shopping bag into the kitchen and put it down on the countertop. She looked up at the air-conditioning unit and sighed.

"Really? Today?"

It had heated up throughout June and now Spain was in the grip of a heatwave. Her new apartment in Alicante was okay, but in the two weeks she had been there, things had slowly begun to break.

In the first week, one of the wardrobe handles in the bedroom fell off, soon after the satellite signal went hazy, then the hot water decided to only work in the evening. Now the air-conditioning unit in the kitchen seemed to have given up.

"I suppose this is what happens when you decide to rent a place in ten seconds," Annie mumbled to herself as she put the groceries in the fridge. She wondered when that would also fail her.

It wasn't like she didn't have the money to go and rent

a new place, she just didn't want to go through the upheaval of moving again. When she'd disembarked *Fortuna*, she'd quickly made arrangements to travel south. By the afternoon she was in a city she had occasionally visited; by the evening she had found an apartment to rent.

A few days later, she sent some muscular removal men to her old place in Barcelona and asked them to bring back her things.

Despite all of that, it still didn't feel like a home.

Her phone beeped, and she pulled it out from her back pocket and looked at the screen. Her breath caught in her throat. It was an email, from Caroline.

She hadn't expected to ever hear from her again. It had been more than three weeks since she'd last seen her. At first, she had waited by the phone and constantly refreshed her email app. Gradually she realised that Caroline wasn't going to contact her.

She sat at the breakfast bar, sucked in a big breath, and opened the email.

Annie,

I hope you are doing well? I'm sorry it has been so long. I was in Marseille today and passed our ice cream stand and thought of you.

Best,
Caroline

Annie smiled. A typical apology from Caroline and a

vague mention of their first almost-date. Caroline was reaching out, testing the waters to see if she was still wanted. Annie's heart soared at the thought. She quickly typed back a response, wanting to show that she was keen to reconnect with the speed of her reply.

Caroline,
I'm good, missing Elvin. Do you know, I've had to make my own bed every day since I got off *Fortuna*? Scandalous.
I found an apartment in Alicante. I hate it, but it isn't Barcelona, so it has that going for it.
Annie

She read and reread her reply. It was light, playful, and hopefully nothing that would pressure Caroline. In an ideal world, Annie would get down on her knees and beg for forgiveness. Annie would throw herself on Caroline's mercy and ask for her to consider allowing her back into her life.

But that wasn't fair. Caroline needed time and space. Annie knew that, and she'd respect that. Caroline had reached out; now Annie needed to keep things casual between them.

She hit the send button and waited. After a few minutes she realised the kitchen was sweltering and moved into the bedroom. She lay on the bed, still staring at the screen and hitting the refresh button.

After ten minutes, she opened a game application she'd been playing and started to collect magic and potions. A few minutes into the game, she received a notification of another email from Caroline. She swiped it open immediately.

Annie,

I don't believe for a second you make your bed every day. I bet you are one of those people who leave it unmade.

I'm sorry you hate your apartment in Alicante. Any local book clubs?

I'll advise Elvin that you miss him. But I have to wonder if you miss anyone else?

Best,
Caroline

Annie giggled with joy. Was that flirting? She didn't know, but she thought it was. She loved that she was communicating with Caroline again but hated that she couldn't see her face. Caroline's light blush and nervous gaze were always a giveaway.

She bit her lip, debating whether to flirt back or to keep things light. She started to compose a reply.

Caroline,
I always make my bed, it makes it more luxurious to slide into it of an evening.
No book clubs, there is a bowling club which my neighbour wants me to go to.

And, as a matter of fact, I do miss someone else. I was fortunate enough to dine with the captain a couple of nights on my cruise. So, of course, I'm missing Graham Shelby.
Annie

She read, reread, and then read once more before hitting send. She wondered if she'd get a reply soon or if Caroline would be called away and she'd have to wait. She went back into her inbox and read the two messages Caroline had sent her.

She read them over and over, trying to picture where Caroline was when she wrote them, what she was wearing, what she was thinking.

She waited and waited, and when forty minutes had passed, she decided that Caroline had other matters to attend to. She locked her phone, hoping she'd get a reply later.

THE START OF SOMETHING

Caroline pulled her tie off and tossed it onto her desk. Then she snatched it up, folded it neatly, and put it in the box in her desk drawer. She'd lost enough ties in her career to know that an effort made now meant less stress later.

She turned on her computer and watched a few new emails trickle in. There was nothing too urgent, so she could finally return to the one Annie had sent her two days ago. She felt guilty about the long delay but hoped that Annie would understand.

She opened the email and reread the teasing note. She decided not to touch on the comment about sliding into bed; that was too dangerous. And she didn't have much to say about book clubs or bowling.

She chewed at the inside of her cheek, wondering what to say. She'd never been good at these kinds of things. Talking face to face was difficult enough, but with this form of communication she had hours or even days to consider what to say. Which made it harder. The potential to overthink things was amazing.

Annie had a signature at the bottom of her email which included a link to her Twitter account. Caroline clicked the link and browsed through Annie's profile. Annie had posted about her new apartment, her lack of air conditioning in the hottest room, and several new books she was reading.

Other users were replying to Annie, and Caroline read the comments with interest. One woman in particular seemed to be all over Annie's profile, posting comments and animated gifs of people hugging. Caroline looked at her profile. She was young, blonde, and irritating as hell. The rainbow icon beside her name, Mindy, suggested she was also gay.

Two could play at that game. Caroline quickly created her own Twitter account. She did the bare minimum and started to look around the platform. It didn't make much sense, but it seemed to be important to Annie.

She opened the email from Annie and hit reply.

Annie,

Would you like me to pass your email address onto Graham? Seeing as you miss him so much?

By the way, I started a Twitter account. It appears to mainly be pictures of cats. I'm not complaining.

Best,
Caroline

It wasn't her best work, but it would do. If she

agonised any more about what to write, she'd leave it another two days. She hit send, closed the email, closed Twitter, and tried to get on with some work.

It was only five minutes later when another email came in from Annie. Caroline didn't know if young people just replied quickly because they were always online, or if this was a sign that Annie was particularly keen.

She hoped it was the latter.

Caroline,
I'll survive without Graham. If I'm honest, I have someone else on my mind. Someone I hurt and want to make it up to, if that's even possible.
Twitter is a lot of cats. Follow me so I can send you the best cats.
Annie

Caroline opened Twitter again, quickly found Annie's profile, and clicked the follow button. She returned to Annie's email to reply but swiftly realised she didn't know what to say. She knew Annie was sorry, and she knew she missed Annie terribly. She had forgiven her, but she still didn't know if that meant there was a future for them.

Was there a point in continuing things when there was so much standing in their way? Annie had a new apartment in Alicante, which was a five-hour drive from Barcelona. She'd checked. And then there was Caroline's job, the fact that she'd be in the Caribbean in a few months. Not to mention the age thing, which still bothered her.

She closed down the email. She was tired; she'd try to

reply the next day. Maybe she'd be able to think of something to say by then.

REACHING OUT

ANNIE WAITED NERVOUSLY. She'd done it, she'd asked to see Caroline again. Emails were fine, but she wanted to actually speak to Caroline face to face. She looked back at the email she had received three days ago, the one which had lifted her mood after a terrible day.

Annie,

I think it might be possible to make it up to someone you hurt, if you're serious about such things.

I followed you on Twitter.

Best,
Caroline

After spending the day giving statements to investigators regarding everything she knew about Diego and his various businesses, it had been the best salve for her soul.

Caroline was admitting that things could be fixed. Or at least that she could be forgiven. Annie had been too tired to reply, knowing that anything she typed while so exhausted would no doubt be impulsive and over the top.

She'd left it until that morning to reply.

Caroline,
I've never been more serious about anything in my life. I don't want to rush you, but I'd love to see you again. Any thoughts? I'm enjoying emailing you, but an email every 2-4 days is hardly enough. I'm crazy about you, I want to see you. Please?
Your Twitter account is a disgrace, you follow eight people.
Annie

She didn't know when she'd get a reply. Caroline was busy. Sometimes she heard back within a few minutes, sometimes within a few days. Maybe this would be the message she wouldn't get a reply to at all.

She got up and made some coffee, peeking at her phone every few moments as she did. Then she opened her post and did some filing. Then she took the laundry out of the machine. It was as she was about to start preparing lunch that she heard the notification.

She swiped so fast, she nearly knocked the phone out of her hand.

Annie,

I'm in Barcelona every Sunday. It's changeover day so I

can't devote much time to a meeting, but I can certainly clear an hour or so for you?

I took your advice and unfollowed CNN News. I have BBC, so why do I need two news accounts? Seven seems much more manageable.

**Best,
Caroline**

Annie shouted with joy and danced around her ridiculously warm kitchen. Then she stopped and quickly checked the train times between the two cities for that Sunday.

She had a date with Caroline West.

A CHANGE OF SCHEDULE

"That's terrible," Caroline finally managed to say, once the shock had dissipated. "He's always seemed so healthy."

Mara nodded. "Heart attacks are unpredictable. Anyway, I thought I'd give you a heads-up as this will obviously mean that head office will ask you if you want to extend your contract."

Caroline sipped her tea and stared straight out of the window of her stateroom, out at the sea. She couldn't believe that David, her co-master, had been taken ill. It was all so sudden. She'd been preparing to end her contract in two weeks and spend some time in Napoli; now she wasn't sure what she'd do.

On top of that, she was still on cloud nine from having seen Annie that morning. They'd only been able to share less than an hour together before Caroline was called away. She'd felt guilty, considering the amount of time Annie must have spent travelling to get to Barcelona, but Annie hadn't seemed concerned. In fact, she'd seemed very happy to see Caroline.

The warring emotions of joy at seeing Annie and sadness at hearing about David were quite overwhelming for her.

"Is everything all right?" Mara asked, obviously detecting Caroline's unsettled mood.

"Yes, I..." Caroline hadn't planned to tell anyone, but this was her best friend, and she could probably do with the advice. "I saw Annie this morning."

"I know," Mara said casually.

"You... know?" Caroline blinked.

"Yes, I follow her on Twitter. She was on the train to Barcelona, so I assumed she was coming here. How did it go?"

"You don't follow *me* on Twitter," Caroline complained.

"You follow seven people, and I see you every day. What could I possibly learn from your Twitter account?" Mara sipped her own tea. "How did it go?"

Caroline put her mug down on the table and huffed. Mara seemed to know everything before she did. "Surely you saw that on Twitter?" she asked.

"So mature." Mara chuckled. "Just tell me, what happened?"

Caroline smiled. "It was... good. Awkward at first, but within a few minutes we cleared the air. Everything went back to normal. Unfortunately, I couldn't give her that much time. It's changeover day, so everything was crazy as usual. But... I enjoyed seeing her."

"Tell her," Mara instructed.

Caroline could feel the blush on her cheeks. "I'm not sure—"

"You obviously like her. You really liked her before, you seem to have worked through everything and forgiven her for the whole Serena business, now you need to go for it."

"Go for it?" Caroline blinked. She wasn't sure she liked the sound of that. It sounded frightening and like things could go wrong. Like she could get hurt. Again.

"Get your phone out and tell her you had a nice day, or that you want to see her again," Mara said. "Go on, I'll wait."

"I can't ask her to come here again. It's a five-hour train journey," Caroline argued.

"Tell her you enjoyed seeing her again and let her make the decision on whether or not she wants to travel. Don't not give her the opportunity."

Caroline thought about it for a moment.

"Come on, do it now," Mara urged.

Caroline sighed. There was no way Mara would let it go. She got her phone out of her pocket, connected to the ship's Wi-Fi, and composed a short message.

Annie,

Thank you for coming to see me today, I'm sorry I couldn't spare more time.

I find myself missing you already.

Caroline

She hit send before Mara could demand to approve it

and probably make changes. She knew it was short and sweet, but she didn't know what else to say. The idea of putting herself out there to be shot down was too painful.

"Done," she said.

"Good," Mara replied. "Will you take the extra contract now that David will be out of action?"

Caroline shrugged. "I'm not sure. I'd been looking forward to spending time in Napoli."

"If you stay on board, you'll be more likely to see Annie again," Mara commented. She made eye contact with Caroline.

Her phone beeped, and she looked at the screen. Annie had replied already. She opened the message.

Caroline,
Forty-eight minutes was better than zero minutes. Can I come and see you again next Sunday? I know I promised to give you space and not to push. If you feel I'm pushing then just say. I'm happy to just email.
Annie

"You're smiling," Mara said.

"She wants to come up again next Sunday," Caroline explained. She sighed and lowered the phone. "I don't… I… How is this supposed to work, Mara? We email forever? Catch half an hour here and there? It can't work."

"Talk to her. Tell her how you feel, see how she feels. If it's supposed to work, then you'll both find a way."

"That's not an answer, that's inspirational mumbo jumbo."

"Fine, then tell her how you feel and arrange to see her

more frequently. Ask her to come aboard *Fortuna* for a sailing. We're all allowed to bring our friends and family on board," Mara reminded her. "Thomas' girlfriend has been on board for five weeks. She lives in the whirlpool. I'm amazed she doesn't look like a wrinkled hundred-year-old."

"She'd have to say here." Caroline gestured to her stateroom.

"I know, scandalous, isn't it?" Mara winked.

"I can't invite her to effectively live with me for a week!" Caroline said. "It's too much too soon."

Stepping up from maybe an hour a week to a full week with someone as her guest was a big leap. Caroline didn't know how she felt about that. And had no idea how Annie would feel about it.

"Rumour has it that if you don't renew your contract they will ask Per Johannsson," Mara said, suddenly changing the subject.

"Per?" Caroline's eyes widened. "That bumbling idiot?"

"Bumbling idiots often find themselves available at a moment's notice."

"They can't seriously be considering putting him in charge of *Fortuna*?" Caroline couldn't believe it. Per was old and careless. He was without a doubt the most useless captain in the company.

"They need a backup plan in case you can't renew your contract. It will be a long stint on board for you, though, if you do renew."

"I'll renew," Caroline promised. "I'm not leaving *Fortuna* in Per's hands. It will be at the bottom of the Tyrrhenian Sea within a week."

"Well, that's that. You can arrange to see Annie in Barcelona whenever she has time to visit. That won't be too much too soon. Just an hour or so, once a week, if she can."

"And then what?" Caroline asked.

"Whatever you both decide. Caroline, remember, you don't need all of the answers now. Don't push away happiness because you can't see a path ahead. Maybe Annie will surprise you by supplying the answers."

"She's certainly surprised me so far," Caroline agreed. "I don't know what she sees in me."

Mara chuckled. "The uniform?"

"Must be."

"You're quite a catch," Mara said.

Caroline laughed. "I'm really not."

"You are. Successful, competent, funny. The uniform. I'm running out of things. Clearly, Annie sees something. And you like her."

"I do," Caroline agreed.

"Have you forgiven her?"

"I don't want to," Caroline admitted, "but I think I have. No, I know I have."

Mara raised her mug. "To new beginnings."

Caroline picked up her mug and leaned forward to tap it against Mara's.

"To new beginnings."

A GAMBLE

Annie sat on the wall and waited, hoping that her plan had worked. Hoping that the rest of her plan would work. Hoping that she hadn't gone too far.

It was a pretty big decision, especially as she'd made it without consulting anyone. Well, just one person. She just had to cross her fingers that it had been the right choice.

A familiar Vespa pulled off the main road and made its way down the small, cobbled path towards the castle.

Well, I'm about to find out if this was a stupid idea, Annie thought to herself.

The bike slowed. The driver stared at her, confusion obvious even through the visor.

Annie hopped down from the wall and tried to cover her nerves with a big smile.

Caroline stopped the bike, snapped up the visor. "Annie?"

"Hey." Annie waved. "Surprise!"

Caroline got off the bike and pulled off the helmet. She looked adorably confused. "Have I been set up?"

"Yes, I asked Mara to make sure you visited today," Annie admitted. She'd been in a conversation back and forth with Mara for the last three weeks, explaining her impulsive plan. Mara had been generally supportive and helped to get Caroline off of *Fortuna* and over to Megaride at the right time.

Annie stepped forward and held out her arms. Relief washed over her when Caroline stepped into the hug and returned it.

"I missed you so much," Annie whispered into her hair.

"It's been less than a week," Caroline said.

"And I missed you so much," Annie repeated.

"I've missed you, too," Caroline sighed happily. "What are you doing here?"

"That's a long story," Annie said.

Caroline pulled back and looked at her suspiciously. "What's going on?"

"Let's sit down and have some lunch," Annie suggested. "I'll explain everything."

Caroline parked up her bike and put the helmet on the handlebar. They walked across the courtyard, Annie snaking her hand into Caroline's as they did.

Caroline squeezed her hand, and Annie walked beside her, enjoying being so close.

"Oh, at last!" Hazel said as she saw the two arrive.

Annie had already spoken to Hazel at length. First to explain what had happened and beg forgiveness for her deception, and later to get her opinion on her plan. An excited twinkle in her eyes and a small clap of the hands had told her that Hazel was on board, though she couldn't tell Annie what she thought Caroline's reaction would be.

"You knew about this?" Caroline asked, smiling.

"I know everything," Hazel said. "Now, sit down. I'll get you some lunch."

They sat down, Annie guiding her to the table where they'd sat before.

"You look well," Caroline commented. Her hand drifted up to the scar forming on Annie's forehead. "That's healing nicely."

"It will fade," Annie said. "I'll always look like I've been in a bar brawl, but that will just made me look badass."

Caroline hummed, not agreeing or disagreeing. She'd confessed recently that she felt extreme guilt at walking away over dinner and leaving Annie with Diego. Annie had told her that it wasn't Caroline's fault but knew that it would take a while to fully convince her.

"It's good to see you," Caroline said. "A surprise, but a nice one. What are you doing in Napoli?"

Annie bit her lip.

"What's wrong?" Caroline asked.

"I've done something you might not like," Annie admitted in a soft voice.

Caroline laughed. "That's not a great opening to a conversation, Annie."

Hazel returned with a tray of drinks and a bread basket. "Have you told her yet?"

"She's about to," Caroline said.

"I'll leave you to it, then." Hazel hotfooted it away.

"So, she knows," Caroline assumed. "And Mara must

know because that's obviously why she suddenly needed me to get some guidebooks from my apartment that I assume she *doesn't* need. Am I the last person to know?"

She didn't look angry. More bemused.

Doing what she had done and turning up out of the blue was a risk, but once the idea had entered Annie's head, she couldn't let it go.

She reached into her handbag and pulled out a set of keys and placed them on the table.

"Keys?" Caroline asked.

"The keys to my apartment," Annie explained.

She paused, suddenly wondering if she'd made a terrible mistake.

"I've moved." She licked her dry lips. "To Naples. Napoli," she quickly corrected.

Caroline's eyes widened. "You… you moved here?"

Annie nodded quickly. "I'm not pressuring you. I just… I liked it here. My mum has family in Italy, and I thought I'd look them up. Not seen them since I was three, but I can't have changed much, still adorable. Badass scar, but cute as a button," she rambled.

Caroline continued to stare at her in silence.

"I… I just thought that as things are, I'm interrupting you on the busiest day of the cruise. And you feel guilty when you have to cancel, or you have to cut things short. It's been four weeks of travelling to and from Barcelona from Alicante, and I had this idea on the train back that it doesn't have to be like that. I know Napoli is a quieter day for you, and if I'm here, and you want to, we could see each other for a few hours. Maybe an afternoon in Napoli rather than one hour in Barcelona."

Annie leaned forward at picked at the label on the drink in front of her. "I want to get to know you more, and let you get to know me. And I know we want to take things slowly, we both agreed that everything moved way too fast on *Fortuna*. I thought it would be a nice surprise. But now I think it might have been a mistake."

Caroline put her hand over Annie's arm. "Not a mistake at all."

Annie looked up. Caroline had finally moved on from stunned silence and was now beaming.

Annie let out a relieved sigh. "Sorry I didn't say anything beforehand, I just wanted it to be a surprise. And I'm not just moving here for you, well, you're a big reason behind it. But I don't want you to feel pressured—"

"Maybe sometimes I need a little push," Caroline said. "I still can't believe how lucky I am to—"

She retracted her hands, the walls going up again. Caroline sat up a little straighter.

"Annie, where do you see this going? Honestly?"

It was the first time Caroline had actually brought up the subject of the future. Annie had patiently waited, knowing that it would rear its head at some point. She knew it played on Caroline's mind and had put a lot of thought into it for when she was finally ready to bring up the topic. She was ready to convince Caroline that she was serious.

"I don't want to be with anyone else," Annie said.

Caroline shook her head and looked away; a laugh bubbled up and escaped her lips. "I'm much older than you, I work twenty-four seven for twelve weeks at a time, longer right now. I don't have a set schedule, I can't guarantee you any of my time. When I'm not on *Fortuna*, I want to be at sea. It's a lonely life."

"I don't care about the age gap between us. If you do, then tell me now," Annie demanded.

"I... I worry for you. When you're fifty—"

"You'll still be you. I know what I'm getting myself into, Caroline. And if you die in thirty years and leave me behind, then I'll get a really cute black veil and I'll wear it every day and be thankful that I got thirty years with you."

Caroline opened her mouth, a rebuttal clearly on her lips.

"Maybe I'll get sick, and I'll die in six months," Annie said. "Do you want to end this now, in case that happens? In case *I* die first?"

"Of course not," Caroline argued.

"As for your schedule," Annie moved on, "I don't care that you can't guarantee time with me. I get that you have a career, and I'm happy to accommodate that. I have never been upset when you have been called away or when you can't spend time with me because I get it. I know you think you have to keep apologising, but you don't."

Annie reached out and took Caroline's hand in hers. "My parents were both really busy people. We didn't always get to spend that much time with each other, but we enjoyed the time we did. I'm used to a life of obligations; it makes you enjoy the time in between even more."

Caroline twisted her hands, threading her fingers in between Annie's.

"I can be your girl in port, or even your girl at sea when you're ready," Annie said. "If you just want to spend an afternoon with me once a week here, then that's fine. If you want me to come aboard *Fortuna* with you, then that's fine, too."

"If you came aboard *Fortuna*, you'd be under a microscope. The captain being a woman is a novelty. The captain's girlfriend being aboard…" Caroline blew out a breath. "You'd never have a moment's peace."

"I'd be with you," Annie said. "And I've been a celebrity on a cruise ship, piece of cake. And cake, I get that Key lime pie whenever I like."

Caroline chuckled.

"Caroline, you seek out problems. You have a list of reasons why we can't be, but guess what? I have a list of reasons why we can be. You stack them up, I'll knock them down."

"You're here now, but when I go to the Caribbean for five months at the end of October, what then?" Caroline asked.

"If you want me to be with you, I'll come aboard *Fortuna*. If you're not ready for that, then I have literally always wanted to see… where do you go?"

"Miami, Key West, Mexico—"

"Yes, those places!" Annie declared. "Always wanted to see them. I'll be your girl in port, over there."

"And when I'm not on *Fortuna*?" Caroline asked. She nodded her head back, towards the marina behind them. "When I want to be on *Serenity*?"

"You have room for me, don't you?" Annie asked.

Caroline smiled. "You want to be cooped up on there?"

"With you? Of course." Annie lifted Caroline's hand and brought it to her lips, pressing a soft kiss to the slightly weathered skin. "I want to spend more time with you. Caroline, I'm serious about you. About us. I want to be the captain's girlfriend, if you'll let me."

Caroline stared at her, a small smile on her lips. "You have an answer for everything, don't you?"

"Yes." Annie nodded.

Caroline leaned in close and pressed a kiss to Annie's lips. "I love you, Annie."

Annie grabbed Caroline's face and pulled her in for a bigger kiss. Chaste, sweet kisses were all well and good, but a declaration of love required so much more.

"N'aw!" She heard Hazel say from behind them. "Look at that, Matteo. So sweet!"

EPILOGUE

CAROLINE OPENED her eyes and stretched out her limbs. It took a few moments for her understand where she was. She let out a contented sigh as she realised she was aboard *Serenity*.

She loved *Fortuna*, but she enjoyed the time she wasn't at the beck and call of the ship, and all aboard, even more.

She turned over in bed and stared lovingly at the shapely back of Annie Peck. It was a sight she was growing quite used to. It had been a year since they'd first met. They'd spent a summer getting to know each other in Napoli, followed by a week-long sailing around the Mediterranean.

After that, the afternoons in Napoli and the emails they shared just weren't enough. Caroline had dug deep and found the courage to ask Annie to join her more permanently on *Fortuna*.

They sailed to Miami together, promising that if the fourteen-night trip didn't work out, then Annie would fly back to Napoli once they arrived. She'd visit sparingly rather than force them to stay together for the entire tour of the Caribbean.

Three days in, though, Caroline couldn't imagine being without Annie ever again. They never discussed Annie getting off the ship; it was an unspoken agreement that she'd stay indefinitely.

They toured the Caribbean on *Fortuna* when Caroline was on duty and rented boats to sail around the Gulf of Mexico when she was off. It was perfection. Caroline had never felt so happy, nor had she realised how miserable she had been before. Her insomnia vanished, ironically, overnight.

Word had quickly got out that Captain West had a partner, thanks mainly to Dream deciding to publicise the hell out of the fact. Annie had taken it all in her stride and now spent as much time entertaining the passengers as Caroline. They were the golden couple of the Dream Cruise Company, passengers even ignoring Caroline to have a conversation with Annie instead.

She couldn't blame them.

Caroline rolled closer to her, pressing her naked body close to Annie's. She lifted her head and whispered in Annie's ear, "Good morning, good morning, good morning."

Annie giggled sleepily.

"This morning we're in Marseille. The weather is…" She looked towards the window, seeing the shadow of raindrops against the blind. "Raining."

"You promised," Annie said, still half asleep.

"The shore excursion for today will be ice cream, a few months late, but who's counting?"

Annie turned onto her back, wrapping an arm behind Caroline's head and pulling her down for a kiss. Caroline settled her body on top of Annie, wondering if she could distract her from the ice cream idea and convince her to spend a lazy day in bed instead.

Annie pulled away from the kiss. "Ice cream," she growled.

"Fine, fine, ice cream," Caroline agreed. "Ice cream in the rain."

"What do you think umbrellas were invented for?" Annie got out of bed and walked over to the wardrobe to get some clothes.

Caroline watched her get dressed, still not believing how lucky she was, but willing to push the whispering doubts to one side and enjoy the moment. She planned to enjoy every moment, from here on out.

PATREON

I adore publishing. There's a wonderful thrill that comes from crafting a manuscript and then releasing it to the world. Especially when you are writing woman loving woman characters. I'm blessed to receive messages from readers all over the world who are thrilled to discover characters and scenarios that resemble their lives.

Books are entertaining escapism, but they are also reinforcement that we are not alone in our struggles. I'm passionate about writing books that people can identify with. Books that are accessible to all and show that love—and acceptance—can be found no matter who you are.

I've been lucky enough to have published books that have been best-sellers and even some award-winners. While I'm still quite a new author, I have plans to write many, many more novels. However, writing, editing, and marketing books take up a lot of time… and writing full-time is a treadmill-like existence, especially in a very small niche market like mine.

Don't get me wrong, I feel very grateful and lucky to

be able to live the life I do. But being a full-time author in a small market means never being able to stop and work on developing my writing style, it means rarely having the time or budget to properly market my books, it means immediately picking up the next project the moment the previous has finished.

This is why I have set up a Patreon account. With Patreon, you can donate a small amount each month to enable me to hop off of my treadmill for a while in order to reach my goals. Goals such as exploring better marketing options, developing my writing craft, and investigating writing articles and screenplays.

My Patreon page is a place for exclusive first looks at new works, insight into upcoming projects, Q&A sessions, as well as special gifts and dedications. I'm also pleased to give all of my Patreon subscribers access to **exclusive short stories** which have been written just for patrons. There are tiers to suit all budgets.

My readers are some of the kindest and most supportive people I have met, and I appreciate every book borrow or purchase. With the added support of Patreon, I hope to be able to develop my writing career in order to become a better author as well as level up my marketing strategy to help my books to reach a wider audience.

https://www.patreon.com/aeradley

REVIEWS

I sincerely hope you enjoyed reading this book.

If you did, I would greatly appreciate a short review on your favourite book website.

Reviews are crucial for any author, and even just a line or two can make a huge difference.

ABOUT THE AUTHOR

Amanda Radley had no desire to be a writer but accidentally became an award-winning, bestselling author.

She gave up a marketing career in order to make stuff up for a living instead. She claims the similarities are startling.

She describes herself as a Wife. Traveller. Tea Drinker. Biscuit Eater. Animal Lover. Master Pragmatist. Procrastinator. Theme Park Fan.

Connect with Amanda
www.amandaradley.com

ALSO BY AMANDA RADLEY

FITTING IN

2020 Amazon Kindle Storyteller Finalist

Starting a new job is hard. Especially if you're the boss's daughter

Heather Bailey has been in charge of Silver Arches, the prestigious London shopping centre, for several years. Financial turmoil brings a new investor to secure the future and Heather finds herself playing office politics with the notoriously difficult entrepreneur Leo Flynn. Walking a fine line between standing her ground and being willing to accept change, Heather has her work cut out for her.

When Leo demands that his daughter is found a job at Silver Arches; things become even harder.

Scarlett Flynn has never fit in. Not in the army, not in her father's firm, not even in her own family. So starting work at Silver Arches won't be any different, will it?

A heartwarming exploration of the art of fitting in.

ALSO BY AMANDA RADLEY

GOING UP

A ruthless executive. A destitute woman. Both on the way up.

Selina Hale is on her way to the top. She's been working towards a boardroom position on the thirteenth floor for her entire career. And no one is going to get in her way. Not her clueless boss, her soon to be ex-wife, and most certainly not the homeless person who has moved into the car park at work.

Kate Morgan fell through the cracks in a broken support system and found herself destitute. Determined and strong-willed, she's not about to accept help from a mean business woman who can't even remember the names of her own nephews.

As their lives continue to intertwine, they have no choice but to work together and follow each other on their journey up.

ALSO BY AMANDA RADLEY

SECOND CHANCES

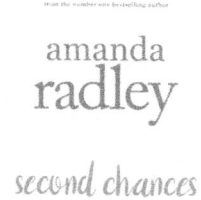

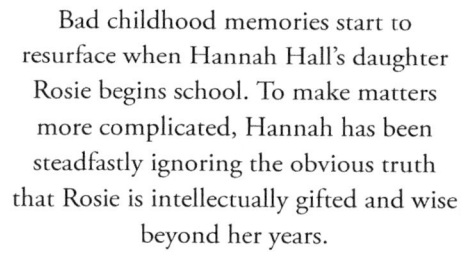

Bad childhood memories start to resurface when Hannah Hall's daughter Rosie begins school. To make matters more complicated, Hannah has been steadfastly ignoring the obvious truth that Rosie is intellectually gifted and wise beyond her years.

In the crumbling old school she meets Rosie's new teacher Alice Spencer who has moved from the city to teach in the small coastal town of Fairlight.

Alice immediately sees Rosie's potential and embarks on developing an educational curriculum to suit Rosie's needs, to Hannah's dismay.

Teacher and mother clash over what's best for young Rosie.

Will they be able to compromise? Will Hannah finally open up to someone about her own damaged upbringing?

And will they be able to ignore the sparks that fly whenever they are in the same room?

Copyright © 2019 Amanda Radley

All rights reserved. No part of this book may be reproduced in any form on by an electronic or mechanical means, including information storage and retrieval systems, without permission in writing from the publisher, except by a reviewer who may quote brief passages in a review.

This is a work of fiction. Names, characters, places, and incidents either are the product of the author's imagination or are used fictitiously. Any resemblance to actual persons, living or dead, events, or locales is entirely coincidental.

Printed in Dunstable, United Kingdom